Goalie Oriented

Minnesota Fury #1

Emma Kathleen

Contents

Dedication

To Jacob Tierney, whose amazing show inspired this book, even though he will never read it.

And to the loons who are sitting at the cottage with me as we patiently wait for season 2. I hope this book helps make the wait more bearable.

CW List

Substance abuse

Medical trauma

Addictive tendencies

Alcohol use

Driving while under the influence

Death by drunk driver

Homophobia

Use of homophobic slurs on page

Family Issues

Gaslighting

Emotional Manipulation

Body Weight Mentions (including Weight Gain),

Coming Out

Injury, Blood (Including imbibing blood)

Underage Drinking (Referenced)

Vomit, Child Verbal Abuse (Past and Referenced)

Financial Abuse by Parent

Gambling (Referenced)

Parental Abandonment (Past)

Broken Bones

Pain Medication

Concussion

Childhood Illness

Parental Abandonment

Discussion about Heart Transplant

Teen Pregnancy (Past)

Abortion (Attempted in Past)

Mental Health Hospitalization (Past)

Therapy

Suicide (Mentioned)

Feminization (author's note)

This is an open-door romance that shows explicit sex scenes between consenting adults.

Author's Note

Like I included in the content warning, there is feminization kink portrayed in this book. One male main character refers to the other male main character's asshole as their pussy. He also calls him "Baby Girl" a few times. If you think that may be at all triggering, please take care of your own mental health first. That's the most important.

Chapter 8

Chapter 20

Chapter 22

Chapter 33

Chapter 35

Feminization does not occur in all the sex scenes, but is scattered throughout them haphazardly, so please use your best judgement if you think it might be triggering

Playlist

These are just the songs I listened to on repeat while writing this book. I've begun associating these songs with Goalie Oriented. Aside from the two that we'll never associate with anything other than Heated Rivalry, maybe you will associate them too. Check out the Playlist I made on Spotify

Talk – Hozier

Take Me Back To Eden – Sleep Token

My Moon My Man – Feist

Stupid In Love – Max, Huh Yunjin

Work Song – Hozier

Holocene – Bon Iver

Mixtape: On Track – Stray Kids

Granite – Sleep Token

Like Real People Do – Hozier

Beggin For Thread – BANKS

DOMINO – Stray Kids

I'll Believe In Anything – Wolf Parade

Good Girl – SLOWBURN

Self Control – Frank Ocean

Easy – Stray Kids

The Summoning – Sleep Token

Liability – Lorde

I Wanna Be Yours – Arctic Monkeys

exile – Taylor Swift, Bon Iver

Almost (Sweet Music) – Hozier

Victory Song – Stray Kids

Motion Sickness – Phoebe Bridgers

Play With Fire – Sam Tinnesz, Yacht Money

Red Lights (Bang Chan, Hyunjin) – Stray Kids

King For A Day – Pierce the Veil, Kellin Quinn

Hollow – Stray Kids

Untouched – The Veronicas

Movement – Hozier

Abstract (Psychopomp) – Hozier

Gooey – Glass Animals

Electric Love – BORNS

I Am YOU – Stray Kids

Do I Wanna Know? – Arctic Monkeys

Would That I – Hozier

Angel of Small Death and the Codeine Scene – Hozier

Earned It – The Weeknd

My Pace -Stray Kids

Seven – Jung Kook, Latto

Home is You – John Wiilde, Rosie Darling

Chapter 1

Beau

Darlene creaks and groans as I pull into my designated parking space at the arena. I can't help but commiserate with her antics. I glare up at the multimillion-dollar hunk of metal that pulled me away from the only home I've ever known.

But I'm here now. New town, same old me, and a hockey team just on the brink of missing out on the playoffs year after year.

The Minnesota Fury.

Minnesota's PHL (Professional Hockey League) team, ranked number seventeen in the league and my new home away from home.

Traded.

I really can't believe Dallas traded me for a left winger with half my skill and a draft pick. Is that all I was worth to them? I pause as the thought consumes me, my body wracking with an ache from being forgotten.

I let loose a sigh and stare up at the arena, the glaring midday sun reflecting off the metal structure and making the view excruciating, my glare turning into a pained squint. If that doesn't say exactly how this year is going to go, I don't know what will.

I've only been in town a few days, less than a week, rotting away at the hotel my new team has me set up in. I'm tired of working out in that tiny gym, and the nerves surrounding meeting my team aren't really going away. So I'm bucking up and braving meeting my team.

I hop out of Darlene, and she creaks as my weight lifts from the front seat. I can't help but be a little offended. I stuck to my diet plan over the summer, a lot more than I usually do.

Okay, okay, that's not saying much because I usually don't stick to it in the summer at all, but I definitely didn't put on that much weight. Besides, I'll need the extra layer up here to stay warm once winter hits.

Sub-zero temperatures? Sleet and snow and ice, oh my.

I grew up in Texas, in a town just west of Dallas, actually. I grew up in that heat where a twenty-degree winter is wild and snow is a temporary thing even in the dead of February. Where cowboys are real and not just movie stars in hats and boots. Where there are honest-to-god tumbleweeds rolling across the highways.

Here in Minnesota, the only thing rolling across highways is some wild potholes. I had to swerve to avoid them.

I run my hand down my chest, nervous energy rolling off me in waves. It's no fun going through a breakup at the same time as a major move in my career, even if the split was amicable. It does something to your self-esteem when someone says they don't want you anymore.

It sucks.

But does it really have to suck so much?

I'm two hundred and twenty-five pounds of muscle, and I'm not humble enough to pretend I don't know how good I look. This doesn't have to be so bad. I'm in a new city, surrounded by tons of new people. I no longer have the weight of my dead-end relationship holding me back. And most importantly, I can finally act on the side of me I had to keep so under wraps in Dallas.

I smile to myself at the thought, my skin blooming with goosebumps as a gust of wind blows over my exposed arms.

Being bisexual in the PHL hasn't been the easiest, especially when my agent always has some wild, albeit valid, excuse for me to stay in the closet.

First, he kept piling on that, because I was in a relationship with Bianca, there was really no reason for me to come out. Why should I be the first out queer guy in hockey when I'm in a hetero-facing relationship? Now that we've broken up, I thought he'd loosen the reins a little, but he's now worried that if I come out so soon after the breakup, Bianca will face backlash for "turning me gay." Insert biggest eyeroll ever right here. Nine years of hiding such a huge part of myself, and for what? So my agent could sleep better at night?

A shiver runs up my spine, and I sigh. The air is crisp and sharp.

I'm really not ashamed of my sexuality, of being bisexual. It doesn't change anything about me. It doesn't change how skilled I am on the ice. It doesn't change the plays I've perfected and honed into my own personal arsenal. It doesn't change that I'm an all-star player who has won several gold and silver medals in both the Winter Olympics and the World Cup.

So why should it matter to the rest of the world?

I am still one of the best wingers in the entire league, if the stats are to be believed, and the only thing that might affect that is being on this absolute stinker of a team.

I sigh, reach into Darlene's bed, and pull out my hockey bag. The air is crisp, already cold. Yeah, Dallas can get a little chilly, but it's barely September and already in the high sixties. I was obviously well aware when I moved here that Minnesota would be a major change for me in many ways, weather being a big one, but I guess I didn't realize how quickly that drop would happen. I wrap my arms around my middle, trying to rub some warmth back into myself.

Training camp is still a week away, so nothing is formal yet, but I figure it's as good a time as any to start getting back into my routine.

The team that bought me needs to see that their purchase was a good one.

And maybe I'm a little curious about my teammates. Maybe I'm a little nervous to see what they'll think of me.

Obviously, I know them. I've been playing against them for years now. But I also know we've got to start bonding if we're going to make it to the playoffs this year. I've spent the last nine years coming so close to the Cup, last year being the absolute closest, getting knocked out before the finals. I want that Cup, and I'm not going to let this trade take that away from me.

I walk across the parking lot with my bag slung over my shoulders and think about what I'm walking into.

The gym is packed. Clearly, the other team members had a similar idea to my own. Maybe this will be an easy click after all. Maybe I can make this work.

"There he is." Paxton "Matty" Matthews walks up to me as I push open the training room doors. He has this confident swagger in his step as he makes his way through the room. His voice is loud and commanding. When he speaks, everyone stops what they're doing to watch him approach me.

I can tell why he's the captain. There's this air about him that exudes "respect me", and you kind of just do.

He extends his hand to me, and I grasp it, taking the opportunity to check out my linemate.

So to speak.

He's drenched in sweat, wearing a cutout T-shirt and showing off his body in the kind of gray sweats that cling to every salacious curve.

His black hair is short on the sides but a little longer on top, sticking to his head in a weird way because of the sweat. He's a good-looking guy.

Paxton's grip is firm and warm, sweaty from his vigorous workout. He pulls me into a kind of side hug, swinging his arm around me and giving a little squeeze. I'm not opposed to the touch, but I am surprised by the immediate closeness. Most hockey guys are worried about too much touchy-feeliness and coming off as gay. Maybe the rampant homophobia doesn't reach this far north.

He begins pointing out everyone else in the gym, introducing me to a ton of people all at once, and obviously sharing their hockey nicknames.

We then happen upon a super familiar face.

Brennan Von and I were on rival teams in juniors. Our history isn't one of sunshine and friendship. We had a pretty intense rivalry as kids, which is reflected in how he greets me. I hold out my hand to him, but all he gives me is a stiff nod, not even removing his headphones. Paxton gives him a quirk of his head and a raised brow. I wave it off, not wanting to air the bad history in front of everyone. We're not going to be besties right away, so it's nothing to worry about right now, right?

But the thing is, I guess we're going to be linemates. He's right wing, and I'm left. We have to build a better relationship if we're going to work together. We have to be able to communicate well on the ice, and that's just not going to happen if he's closed off to me off the ice.

I'll invite him out for drinks or something.

We move over to the more open area of the gym, and my eyes zone in on the player box jumping off in the corner, away from the rest of the team. He's got to be clearing thirty-six inches with each jump. His light blond hair is drenched in sweat, and his skin is glistening. The shorts he's wearing are riding up his thighs, and that delicious hockey butt is threatening to make an appearance.

My eyes widen, following the flex and stretch of his muscles as he gets into position to jump again. My curiosity is piqued.

I give my head a little shake, pulling myself out of the horny head fog. A hand claps my shoulder.

"Hey, Haller!" Paxton calls, reaching out to tap his muscled shoulder.

He turns from his workout, pulling out an earbud, and I almost gasp.

He's so beautiful.

His eyes are a vibrant seafoam green, with so much depth I could drown. I want to lose myself staring into those eyes, want to swim in them.

His skin is flushed from the exercise, and I salivate, wanting to lick every drop of sweat.

Those lips.

I want to write a damn song about those lips. Plump and smooth and a delicious pink. I bet they taste incredible.

I have to get this reaction under control. I can't be attracted to him. I have my rule.

I don't hook up with teammates. That's a rule I set for myself when I was drafted. It wasn't always a rule, but there's a good reason behind it.

I used to hook up with one of my teammates in juniors. Let's just say it did not end well.

Sometimes I wonder what happened to him, why he never actually outed me if he was so angry at me for ending things. I've thought about looking him up but have always decided against it.

The rule has never come up before now because I always had Bianca. We were together for almost ten years. I knew the trade would potentially put a strain on our relationship, but she was the smart one and rightfully called it quits. She was just promoted at her job, and neither of us is built mentally for long distance.

So now I'm single for the first time in a long time, and the rule is set firmly in place.

The real problem is that hockey guys are exactly my type.

I school my features and let my focus fall back to just meeting my teammates.

He holds out his hand like a proper gentleman, and it makes me feel a little giddy.

"Milo," he says, looking me right in the eyes with intention. But then those eyes drop, and I swear he's looking at my lips.

Interesting...

Nope, no, not interesting. I'm not thinking about him like that.

"Beau Bennett," I respond, reaching out to grab his hand and giving it a little squeeze.

"Uh-oh!" a heavily accented voice calls out. Someone, Jagger maybe, plops a sweaty hand down on my shoulder. He has a wide, toothy grin, simply beaming at me. "Beau Bennett, yes?" There's a glint of gleeful mischief in his eyes.

"Yeah." I smile back at him. "My old teammates called me..."

"No, no, no!" His head shake is animated, and he still has the biggest smile plastered on his face. "That will not do!" His accent makes his speech come out a tiny bit slower as he finds the correct words. He's utterly charming.

"Jagger..." Paxton warns, but the Swedish giant waves him off confidently.

"BB," he says with an affirming nod, his arms crossing as if he's daring me to defy him. This guy is built like a tank, so I'm not going to argue with him.

"Baby?" I ask, a brow raised. I'm not entirely opposed, but I'm not sure I heard him right.

"Nej." He shakes his head, blond locks flinging sweat. "BB. Two B." I nod, understanding him a little better. It's a silly nickname, but I have no opposition.

I look around the gym and see other heads nodding in affirmation. I guess I'm BB now.

Whatever, I didn't like "Benny" anyway.

Pretty Milo is watching the interaction with a slightly cocked head, taking in everything with what looks like careful consideration. He catches me watching him and gives me a little nod. I return the nod with a lopsided smile. It seems to startle him, and he takes a small step back. His eyes widen, and he's definitely staring at my mouth now.

Very interesting.

"So"—Paxton pulls me back from my little eye exchange with Milo— "have you found an apartment yet?"

I give my head a shake. "No, I'm still at the hotel."

The hotel that the team puts new players in is pretty nice. I just feel so cramped in the small space. I've been looking at apartments and houses, but nothing really feels like home to me.

"I'm tired of the hotel life," I complain, getting some nods of agreement. Most of the guys would have stayed somewhere similar when they started up here. "It's quite the drive from the rink too. Why couldn't they have picked something closer?"

"You can come stay with me."

I turn to see who spoke, surprised to see it's Milo. His voice is quiet, a little shy. It suits him.

I'm surprised by his offer. Something about him strikes me as a loner. Working out in the back corner by himself, not interacting with the other guys. Matty is clearly surprised as well, only affirming my observation. Milo is obviously not the kind of guy to just offer up his space. But he shakes off the shock, turning to give a friendly pat on Milo's back.

"I live close to the rink," he says, pretty eyes wide, as if he doesn't believe what he's offering. "I have a few extra rooms."

"Team player, Haller, team player. Way to step up."

I can't tell if that's a blush creeping up Milo's cheeks or if he's still flushed from his workout. I take a step toward him, and I can smell the deep notes of citrus mixed with his sweat. He's watching me just as closely as I'm watching him.

There's something about this guy that I just want to understand. Something in those steady breaths and nervous eyes. Those eyes that keep getting caught on my lips. I desperately want to explore that, even though I know I shouldn't.

I can't.

My smile is genuine as I cross my arms over my chest. "Alright, roomie," I say with all the ease I don't feel, fully aware I'm about to walk into a fire with my eyes wide open.

walk into a fire with my eyes wide open

Chapter 2

Milo

*W*hy did I say that?

Why, why, why?

My brain is running about a million miles a minute as I try to piece together whatever the fuck I was thinking. I turn back to my box and start jumping again, only to immediately trip over myself. I stumble, falling to the floor in a bit of a heap, more embarrassed than hurt.

I feel the blush blooming across my face and down my neck.

"Fuck, Haller, you good?" Brennan rushes over to help steady me. My face is flaming hot. I blow out a bit of a stuttered breath and look around the room quickly. I find myself relieved to see that Beau seems to have missed it.

That sends me spiraling back to my little freak-out, because *why on earth would I invite him to come live with me?*

He's hot.

Like, painfully hot.

Like, so hot I apparently lose all the filters between my brain and my mouth.

Because that is the only explanation I can think of as to why I offered my spare bedroom to the most attractive man I have ever seen.

He's tall, has to be nearly six foot three, and the man is rugged. Deliciously rugged. He's giving all kinds of "sexy lumberjack" vibes. His hair is a dark chocolate color and curly. I can't see it all because his tank top is incredibly fitted, but I'd bet anything he's got hair on his chest and everything. I can just picture running my hands down his broad chest and...

Oh shit.

I adjust uncomfortably as my cock begins to plump up.

Thank goodness Brennan has already started walking away.

Back to my mind spinning out.

It's more than that, more than just sexual attraction. It feels like he saw me. Like he saw through the mask I wear to hide my very being.

I've never been *seen* like that.

I shove my palm down against my now aching cock as I turn back toward the box. Thankfully, the training room doesn't have mirrors everywhere, like most gyms, so I can discreetly palm myself to try and ease the discomfort. I definitely don't want to feel seen in this moment.

I feel so dumb for inviting a straight guy to come into my home when I clearly am developing a big, fat crush on him. It's basically just signing myself up for heartache and constant hard-ons. Hard-ons that I won't even be able to properly hide because he'll be in my home.

The doors to the gym open, and I turn to look, my headphones still in my hand. Mia, one of our athletic trainers, walks into the room, and I watch as Beau eyes her.

I've always had a thing for straight boys, it seems.

I think back to the boarding school I attended from sixth to twelfth grade. It was right at the peak of my sixth-grade year that I realized I might be gay, in the middle of changing into my goalie gear for the first district game of the season. I had never really cared about girls, which I never questioned, but that day in the locker room, I turned to my closest friend to ask him a question and was met with his half-naked body. I remember noticing how well hockey was treating his body and, to my utter horror, how much I liked it.

I didn't know what to do with these feelings of attraction, but my parents had always taught us to hide our extreme emotions, so I tucked it away.

But I kept noticing how attracted I was to some of my friends. I kept noticing their bodies and how my body would react to them. It got to be so bad that I would change in a bathroom stall before every game, and my friends chalked it up to the goalie being weird.

I don't even know this guy. He just walked in here looking like a rugged Henry Cavill, and I immediately folded for him.

"Haller, where's your head at?"

I look up, and Paxton is staring at me, a little tilt to his head. He looks kind of like a puppy when he does that. Like a husky, maybe.

"Thinking about dogs," I say, because I am. I'm not going to tell him I'm picturing *him* as a dog. That would be ridiculous.

I must have been staring off mindlessly for some time now.

"Oh, do you have a dog?" Beau walks over. Well, more like he saunters over. There is this swagger, and confidence, in his step that is just seeping from every pore in his body. It's intriguing and terrifying.

His tank top is clinging to his body like a second skin, and I'm carefully trying not to notice it.

"No, I think I'm more of a cat person." I really don't know. We never had pets growing up, so I'm not entirely sure what I'd like. I just know a dog would be a chore of a roommate, especially with our hectic game schedule. They need constant love and affection, and sometimes I just want to be left alone. Sometimes I want to hide in my room with a book and disappear for a few hours. I really don't have anything against dogs; I just can't imagine owning one, not on my own anyway.

"Ah, I can see that." He nods as if he immediately knows me. Beau has a nice voice. It's all deep and velvety, and it feels like being wrapped up in a warm embrace. I feel like I could melt for him. Like I could just become a puddle at his feet.

I look down at my feet then, suddenly very overwhelmed by his presence. This feels like the middle school locker rooms all over again. I'm raw and vulnerable and exposed, and I hate it.

Our parents always instilled in us that letting people see behind the mask would only end in hurt. I've always tried to keep that mask up. But it feels like Beau might know how to take that mask apart, piece by tiny piece.

I peek back up at him, and he's watching me with a careful smile on his face. It's soft. I take a deep breath before looking at him a little more closely. He has a small scar next to his left eye, a thin sliver of raised skin. I want to ask him about it.

I kind of want to know him. There's this air of mystery and intrigue surrounding him that pulls at my curiosity.

"Do you want my number?" he asks, holding out his hand for my phone. I cock my head. Is he that bold? "You know"—he raises an eyebrow and smiles a wicked smile—"so you can text me your address?"

Oh.

Duh.

That feels so obvious now that he's said it. Of course, if we're going to live together, even if it's just for a week or so, he would need my number.

He reaches out, and I hand over my phone. He looks up at me with a raised brow and a small smile before scrolling to my contacts to enter his number. He sends himself a quick text and hands it back.

I look down at my phone.

Beau.

I look back up at him. Middle school me would have been jumping up and down at scoring such a hottie's number. A real-life main character straight out of one of my romance novels.

Well, little did that version of me know that we're still stuck firmly in the closet at the ripe age of twenty-three, with absolutely no end date in sight.

I'm pulling into my driveway when my phone starts ringing. My mom is calling.

I let out a long-suffering groan, inhaling the car's leather interior scent before picking up.

My parents are … great. Really, they're fine. They just worry way too much. They worry about hockey, they worry about me living alone, and ever since I came out to them in high school, they worry about me being found out. Their concern is sincere, or at least, I'm pretty sure it is.

When I sat them down and told them I was gay, my mother started crying. Like, full-blown sobs. Sniffling and snot-nosed, with tissues everywhere. She and my father assured me they were not at all disappointed that I was gay, just scared of the hardships I would face being in the closet. Somehow, them telling me they weren't disappointed completely unprompted made me feel the exact opposite. They stressed and stressed and stressed that if I were to follow my dream of being a goalie in the PHL, I would never be able to come out.

There isn't anyone out as anything other than straight in the hockey world. Not a player, not a coach, not even an equipment manager. Okay, maybe that's a little bit dramatic. I don't know every team's equipment manager situation. And I'm not naive enough to think I'm the only gay man playing hockey professionally. I can't even imagine how many could possibly be on my own team.

But I don't want to be the first. My parents and my agent keep shoving the fear down my throat. That I'll be the first and immediately be kicked from my spot as starting goalie. That I could potentially be kicked from the team. I'm so firmly in the closet that I've set up camp there and have fully resigned myself to spending the rest of my career here.

I hate it, though. It's cramped and lonely in the closet. It's kept me from getting close to my teammates. It's kept me from meeting anyone, even as just a friend, let alone a lover.

Maybe if someone else came out. Maybe then I could be brave. Maybe then I could come out and have a relationship. Maybe then I could fall in love. But as it stands right now, I'm stuck between a rock and a hard place. And that hard place is my...

"Honey?" My mother's voice comes through tinny over my car's speakers. Shit. My mother.

"Yeah, Mom." I try to relay urgency in my voice. I want this to be as quick a call as I can manage. Mostly, I just want to be inside, under my own shower. But it's hard to think about that while I'm talking to my mom.

I'm still hesitant to shower beyond a quick rinse with the other guys. The fear of accidentally popping a boner with twenty-plus other men naked and sudsed up is incredibly real and kind of ruling my life. It's not even that I would be looking at them. I keep my eyes firmly planted on the wall. It's just that the stupid thing is so sensitive. I'm sure the other guys just chalk it up to the weird goalie being weird. It's how I've explained away pretty much everything I do and don't do.

"Honey, it's been weeks since we last spoke," she whines.

"We spoke two days ago," I say.

"Now that can't be right. Are you sure?" Her voice is condescending, and it makes me cringe.

I'm sure.

"What's up, Mom?" I try to keep my annoyance out of my voice. I know she really means well. I know she's trying to make me feel better. I just can't help but resent her a little bit.

She loves me, but...

She doesn't care that I'm gay, but...

But, but, but.

She doesn't realize how big that "but" feels.

"What? Can't a mother just want to catch up with her son?" I can practically hear the pout in her voice. "I worry about you, you know. I just like making sure my baby boy is okay."

"Well, I'm fine. I promise." I sigh before remembering the extent of my day. Do I tell her about Beau? Do I tell her about the new, potentially dangerous position I've put myself in? At least that's how she'll see it.

No, I don't need the added stress of her anxiety piled onto my own.

"Have you gotten out your winter clothes yet?" she asks. It's only September, so that answer is a big fat *no*. I tell her as much, and she launches into a speech about preparedness, one I've actually heard dozens of times.

I hear warbled grumbling on the line. "Your dad says hi." She interrupts her own lecture to interject. I'm sure he does. Dad took my queerness the hardest in my family.

He gives me the same spiels that my mom does.

More buts.

Mom has tried explaining it as "he just wants a son he can relate to," as if we aren't both hockey players, even if he never made it pro. I can't imagine what it is exactly he wanted to relate to. I've always been exceptionally private, so it's not as if I'd be sharing all the gory details of hookups, even if it was with women.

I decide I'm not going to tell my mom about Beau. She would just go into a tirade about why it's a bad idea. And I'm already perfectly aware of exactly how bad this is going to go.

I am clearly incredibly attracted to Beau, a fact that will not be made better by my mother's lectures.

While she continues her lecture, I look down at my phone, resigning myself to at least a few minutes of her tirade.

There's a new text waiting for me.

From Beau.

Beau: Hey Milo, are you ready for me?

Am I?

My cock perks up, and I groan.

I'm so fucked.

Chapter 3

Beau

"So, this is it."

Milo, it turns out, is a timid little mouse when he's at home. He somehow makes his big, six-one frame seem so small. It's a skill unlike anything I've seen before. I wish I knew *why* he was making himself small. He should be uplifted and made to feel exactly as large as those big, expressive eyes.

I turn to look down the street, noting the trees with swings hanging from their branches and bicycles littering the yards.

I think I feel something for this guy. At first, I thought maybe it was just pure lust, but he intrigues me more than that. Something about him calls to me. I just haven't figured out what.

I roll up to his home with two suitcases and a duffel bag in the bed of my truck. I wasn't really attached to any of the things in the apartment I shared with Bianca in Dallas, so I let her keep most of it. The rest of my stuff is in a storage unit back in Texas. It's not like I need a La-Z-Boy while I couch surf.

I didn't miss the confused look Milo gave Darlene when I pulled up. She's still giving exaggerated groans when I hop out, but I choose to ignore her complaints.

"You know our contracts are worth millions of dollars, right?" He eyes her sideways, but I give her the loving pat she deserves. Darlene was the first thing I ever bought for myself way back in high school, before I made it big. She's been my protector for over a decade. I'm not giving up on her just because she's a little older.

"I don't need anything flashy," I say with a bright smile, making my grin all toothy and sincere. "I've had her since I was eighteen," I explain. "She's kept me safe all these years, and I don't want to turn my back on her."

My phone rings, and I pull it from my pocket, looking at the caller ID. A sense of dread fills my stomach like tiny bees, flipping and fluttering about when I see who it is.

Dad.

Nope, I don't have the energy for him right now. Not while I'm trying to move into my new normal.

I silence it and slip it back into my pocket. Looking up, Milo is staring at my pocket, a question on his face.

"You're just ... ignoring it?" he asks. There's concern on his face. "Don't you get in trouble?" He looks up and meets my eyes. The worry seems genuine.

I can't help myself.

I double over and laugh and laugh and laugh.

Standing up, I wipe a tear from my eye, the laughter dying on my tongue. But he looks confused.

"Oh, are you really serious?" I'm shocked, my jaw dropping a little at this grown man who looks genuinely concerned that I, another grown man, might get in trouble with my dad for not answering his call. "Dude, I'm twenty-seven. He's just calling for a handout." I shrug. "Do you really still get in trouble with your parents?" I raise a brow in question, genuinely curious.

He looks perplexed, staring at me for a moment before continuing slowly.

"My mom freaks out if I don't answer," he explains carefully. I can tell he's holding back, but we just met a day ago, so I don't push it. "She'll keep calling until I do answer." He pauses for a moment, feet shuffling. "She just worries, that's all."

I'm not entirely sure what to say to that. This man is a multimillionaire and one of the top goalies in the league at only twenty-three years old. I did a little googling, so sue me. And he's still scared to upset his parents. I guess I can understand that to an extent. It's not like I don't still give in to my dad. You sometimes just feel like you owe your parents for raising you and keeping you alive, but when is enough, enough?

I'm lucky in the sense that my parents don't give a fuck about me, so it's a lot easier to blow them off now that I've accepted it. My dad just calls every few weeks to ask for money, and my mom... I don't know where my mom is. And I don't care to know.

My history with my mom is not one I like getting into without a stiff drink.

"You're a grown man, Milo." I suddenly feel serious. "You have an entire life you're living that shouldn't revolve around what your parents think." I shrug, tipping my head down, because maybe I went too far. "Sorry, it's not my business."

I give my shoulders a little shake, trying to dislodge the uncomfortable conversation from my brain. I shove the thought of my mom into a mental box and lock it tight. Right now, I need to focus on the gentle man standing in front of me.

"So, give me the tour." I try to smile, but I know it's shaky at best and a grimace at worst. I hate thinking about my mom.

He reaches out and snatches my suitcases from me, spinning on his heel and wheeling them back to his house. What a fucking gentleman.

It looks nothing like how a professional athlete's house is *supposed* to look. Bianca was in charge of decorating our apartment in Dallas, and she knew *exactly* how it should look according to some made-up rules in her head. All sleek edges and neutral tones. Milo's home is different. It's smaller, very soft around the edges, and instantly warm. It's the kind of house that feels like it exhales as soon as you step inside.

The entryway is a narrow nook, with hooks crowded by jackets and a little wooden bench with scuffed legs. There's a woven basket underneath, filled with mismatched scarves and gloves. I get the sense that he keeps extras around just in case someone else might need them.

I stop as soon as I walk into the living room. It is an absolute cottagecore fantasy. The couch is deep and over-stuffed, draped in knitted blankets, with a warm yellow lamplight on the side table. He has a whole damn fireplace, framed by stone, with a few logs stacked and ready to light.

And the books. Books everywhere. Books on the mantel. Books on the coffee table. Books spilling off shelves.

"Wow." I'm kind of speechless. This house is the polar opposite of the house I shared with Bianca, but in all the best ways.

The penthouse we had in Dallas was sterile. Everything was constantly clean, and there was no personality. It looked like it was transplanted directly from a magazine. I distinctly remember her constantly flitting around the apartment any time there was the slightest mess, the smallest sliver of proof it was lived in.

But this...

This is a home.

The air even smells different, like new paperback books and citrus, instead of the floral scent heavily laden with notes of bleach that Bianca insisted on.

"I'm sorry it's a mess." He gestures around at nothing. This is the absolute cleanest mess I've ever seen in my life. Everything looks like it's exactly where it's supposed to be.

I shake my head and smile.

"Come on, show me the rest." I leave my suitcases at the entry to the living room and follow him further into the house.

He walks us into the kitchen, and my jaw clenches. This is exactly the kind of kitchen I've always wanted. It's cozy and a little cluttered in a comforting way. Open shelves show off chipped ceramic mugs he clearly didn't buy as a set. There's an actual kettle on the stove, a bowl of apples on the counter, and a window framed by linen curtains over the sink. A small round table sits in the corner, the kind that really forces two people to sit close.

"Cozy," I comment, nodding at the table and picturing breakfast there. Picturing breakfast there with him. And maybe he's shirtless.

Fuck, and now I'm getting turned on.

I turn and palm my cock, flexing my calves to try to will it down.

"What else, Milo? Let's see the bedrooms." I start walking down the narrow hallway. The wall is covered in art, photographs of landscapes and birds and wildlife. "Did you take these?" I ask, my finger running along the frame of a particularly beautiful picture of some kind of flower.

"Yeah," he says, coming up behind me. He has my suitcases trailing behind him. "Those are my hydrangeas; we passed them coming in." He nods a little in confirmation. There's the tiniest bit of a smile at the corner of his lips. As if maybe he's proud of himself.

I hope he's proud of himself. I'm by no means an art connoisseur, but there's something about these photos that screams talent to me. Maybe I'm wrong, but I don't think I am.

We walk further down the hall, passing by what is obviously Milo's room. It's all warm wood, a messy stack of books on the nightstand, and a chest at the foot of the bed. It looks like a genuine antique, not something you buy just to make the place look antique. Just the little glimpse I get makes me want to snoop and see what other fun treasures I might find.

"This is you." He holds open the door, gesturing inside.

The bed is made, but the sheets don't quite match. The window looks out at the small backyard garden with raised beds full of what look like very dead plants.

It makes me smile to think of him out in the backyard on his hands and knees. Maybe he has a sunhat on. Maybe he's wearing cute little gardening gloves.

Fuck, I like the picture of that.

I try to discreetly readjust myself while Milo sets my suitcases by the bed.

"I'll let you get settled," he says, backing out of the room slowly, watching me. His eyes catch on mine, and I smile at him. He blushes, and it's the prettiest sight. I like the way his freckles stand out as the pink floods his cheeks.

I get to work putting my clothes away and settling in. The house is quiet for some time as I work.

When I'm almost done, I hear Frank Ocean crooning in the living room. I venture out of the bedroom and see Milo curled up on the couch, a book in his hand. I don't want to disturb him, so I try to sneak out, but I step in just the right spot for a loud, ominous creak of the floorboards.

Milo shoots up from where he's sitting, the book flying to his chest. He's breathing hard, but he spots me and laughs.

"I forgot you were here for a minute. Fuck, you've been so quiet." His laughter turns into a chuckle. He grabs a bookmark and sets down the book.

"Whatcha reading?" I ask, walking over and plopping down on the couch near his feet. Fuck, this couch is comfy. I let out a deep groan as I get myself comfortable. He doesn't answer, so I look up and smile at what I see.

Those cheeks are *flushed*, a bright, pretty pink blooming down his neck, and I bet spreading across his peachy chest. His pale blond hair looks almost yellow in the lamplight.

"What, are you reading something smutty?" I ask, waggling my brows at him. He barks out a laugh.

"How do you know that word?" he asks, still laughing.

"That's not denial. What are you reading?" I try to peek at the cover.

"It's a romance," he says, grabbing the book and hugging it against his chest. I smile at him.

"I think you're reading a naughty book." I nod at the book in his hands. "Hey, I'm all for reading your porn instead of watching it." I shrug. "C'mon, tell me." I lean forward, turning my body toward him and reaching for his book.

He sighs a very dramatic, long-suffering sigh, and hands it over to me. My smile grows as I'm careful not to just snatch it from him. Reading the back cover, I see it's a fantasy romance between former friends.

Two men.

Very interesting.

He's clearly still closeted, whatever his orientation is, so why is he showing me this? Why is he trusting me, someone he just met? Why is he letting me get this glimpse of the real him?

Regardless of what his secret really is, regardless of what closet he's hiding behind, I don't plan on betraying his trust. I'm going to prove to him he's not making a mistake by trusting me.

I look back at Milo already buried back in his book. I feel something settle in my chest, something I don't quite have a name for.

Chapter 4

Milo

I settle myself onto the couch, letting it swallow me as I pick up a book from the side table and begin reading. I have a hard time focusing, though, as thoughts of Beau begin to filter through my mind.

He's been here a week, integrating into my life. He got all his stuff from the hotel that first day, and I told him he could move the rest of his things from his storage unit in Texas, but he declined, saying it was mostly furniture that wouldn't really fit in here anyway.

Boarding school and away games are the only times I've had roommates in the past, and I've always hated every second of it. I like my space. I like my routine. I like not having to hide my boners when they pop up seemingly out of nowhere, because they always show up at the most inconvenient times.

But I don't seem to hate having him here.

I haven't seen him look at apartments, and honestly, I haven't pushed him to. I kind of like having him in my home. I like how he takes up space, how he's entirely himself.

I don't think he's straight, not anymore, but I also haven't been brave enough to ask him. I've caught him watching me, caught his reaction to me simply existing. I don't know. I think he might be interested in me. Just the way his eyes follow me as I move through the house makes me think that maybe I'm onto something.

What would I even do if it turns out he's interested in me?

We haven't spent a ton of time actually together, and I think today I'm going to change that. It's been a long day. Training camp is well underway, and I don't know about Beau, but I'm exhausted. I want to just relax, spend the night in, maybe enjoy each other's company. Or at least find out if we can.

Aside from that first night when Beau interrupted my reading, we haven't been in the same place in the house for more than maybe five minutes. I haven't actually even seen him in the kitchen. He's mostly kept to himself.

I know the feeling, the need to be in a new place by yourself and just let yourself be. Let yourself feel. Not only is he new to my home, but he's new to this state. He moved away from the only home he's ever known.

I did a little googling the other day. He was born and raised in Texas, in a small town in West Texas. Sweetwater, I think, is what it's called. Small, compared to the giant megacity, Dallas, where he's lived for the past almost ten years.

And he was in a relationship for those ten years. He actually might still be in it. The internet seems to think he still is. That's one of the things I want to get to know.

My stomach does an unhappy little flip at the thought of him still belonging to someone else. Because I have been watching him. Day after day, catching snippets of him simply existing. Of him playing video games and getting so focused he has to blip his tongue out to help himself concentrate. Of him humming some country song in the morning when he drinks his coffee on the back porch. And of him singing along with the radio, very off-key but without a care in the world.

Because the way he's been watching me, the way those eyes have followed me when we are in the same room ... Those eyes are full of hunger. It looks like a hunger that doesn't really match the "happily taken" headline I skimmed, and that contradiction sits uneasily in my gut. If he's trying to be discreet, he's failing miserably.

Although, to be fair, I'm pretty sure I've been looking at him with the same intensity.

My cheeks heat thinking about it. Thinking about watching him.

Fuck, at the rink, after a long day of skating and conditioning, he has managed to catch me off guard every single day. I'll be sitting at my stall, slowly pulling off my uniform, and he'll walk up to me, a towel slung low around his waist, dark curls dripping.

He never comes over for very long, just enough to catch my attention and leave me wanting more of him.

Just yesterday, he asked if we could start carpooling to the rink together. I guess his truck is getting up there in age, and I don't blame him for maybe occasionally wanting a ride in a more durable vehicle. Though you'd be hard-pressed to find me in that truck, so I imagine carpooling will mostly be me driving.

Then I was picturing the tension between us in that tiny space. Thinking about those heavy looks. He'll give me one glance and have me leaping from my seat into his lap.

The grandfather clock in the hallway chimes ten. I'm letting my thoughts get away from me this early weekend morning when I hear the front door open.

Beau, dressed only in a pair of basketball shorts and a loose tank top, walks into the living room. His skin is glistening with sweat, dark curls stuck to his head. His cheeks and chest are flushed an overheated red. He turns a little, pulling out a headphone, and I swear I see something shining on his chest. He must be wearing a chain or something.

"Hey, roomie." He smiles broadly at me, all teeth and crinkled eyes. I like his smile quite a bit, so I match it.

"Hey yourself," I say back, knowing I want more of him than these little snippets but not entirely sure what I'm going to get.

I look down at the coffee table, covered in books and candles and... Oh!

"Hey, Beau," I call out right as he starts walking away.

"Yeah?" He quirks a brow, still breathing heavily. His chest rises and falls with each staggered breath. He must have run hard to still be so winded.

"I know this is out of left field," I start, leaning forward to snatch the deck off the table, "but would you be interested in playing cards later?" I can feel my own cheeks flushing, warm and pink. This is stupid. He's not going to...

"I'd love to." He smiles at me, warm and sweet. I feel my smile growing, beaming at him. "I just need to go shower first, and I'm all yours."

If only.

He comes out of the bathroom in a pair of breathtaking gray sweatpants. They hang loosely off his body, the faintest outline of his, ahem, package on full display. I can feel the blush start at my cheeks and bloom down into my chest. I quickly look down to where I'm shuffling the deck, hiding the flush from him. I roll my eyes internally. Could I be any more of a cliché?

When I look back up, though, he's smiling slyly like he caught me with my hand in the metaphorical cookie jar. I guess in this case, my hands are my eyes and his crotch is the cookie jar.

He flops down next to me on the couch, letting loose a lengthy sigh. His curls are still dripping, making the collar of the T-shirt he's wearing soaking wet.

"You're not going to be able to do that come winter," I say, pointing to his wet head of hair. "You'll freeze to death two steps out the door."

He laughs, shaking his head and letting the water droplets fly. I cover my face, trying to protect myself from the onslaught of wet he unleashes on me. I find myself laughing too.

"Thanks for the warning, Frosty. I'll be sure to keep that in mind in January." He rolls his eyes, but he still has a smile on his face.

"Try November." I laugh a little harder. What a Texas boy. "We actually get winter when it's supposed to start, and not for one month out of the year." I smile a teasing smile, and he meets it.

"So," he says after a beat of us just smiling at each other, "what card game do you want to play?" I'm shuffling the deck, and he's watching me, watching my hands move cutting the deck, holding the cards at the ready, and letting them mix. "I'll be honest, we weren't a games family. My parents were not the biggest on spending time together when I was growing up."

A pang of sympathy, sharp and sudden, hits my chest. My fingers, busy shuffling the deck, still for a second.

"Oh? My parents kind of made us when I was a kid," I muse, thinking about my own family and the loud, uncomfortable game nights we would have. They always ended with my mother throwing down her cards and leaving in a huff. I want to pull at the thread he left bare about his family but don't want to pry. I want to know him, sure, but I want to know what he's willing to show me. I don't want to poke around where I don't belong.

"Yeah, my parents just didn't really like each other all that much." He nods slowly, and I don't breathe. What more will he tell me?

After a moment of quiet, I decide to gently encourage him on.

"They stayed together for you?"

He barks out a laugh, shaking his head.

"No, no," he says, still biting back his laughter. "More like they stayed together for their own selfish reasons." He holds up one finger. "My mom stayed to keep appearances up." Then he puts up a second finger. "And my dad was too drunk to be able to notice that they were unhappy. That we all were unhappy."

He leans back, throwing his arms behind his head and letting himself get comfortable. His eyes close as he sinks into the couch. I wait a moment, unsure what to say. I don't think there's anything I can say.

"Go Fish?" I ask.

"What?" he asks, one eye popping open.

"The game? We can play Go Fish." He smiles at me.

"Yeah, we can play that one."

It turns out that two hockey players playing cards is not the best idea. We're a highly competitive group of guys, and even if it's just the two of us, Beau has almost flipped the coffee table at least three times.

"I asked you for twos three turns ago!" he seethes at me.

"I didn't have twos then; I just drew them!" I retort. "You have to hand them over." I lay my palm flat for him to place the cards on, which he does, begrudgingly.

"I still think you're cheating," he grumbles at me, holding his cards tightly in his hands while I lay down my pile of twos.

"I promise I'm not." And I'm not, but I'm sure my promise doesn't mean all that much to a guy I just met a week ago.

But he nods and keeps playing.

"Do you have any fives?" he asks.

"Go fish." I smile, and he glares at me, but picks up his card. His face lights up.

"Oh, I got a five. I get to go again!" He smiles widely before his face pinches, and he sticks his tongue out at me. He would be so awful at poker. The thought makes me smile too.

He bites his lip as he decides what to ask for next, and the look is just so sexy. I watch as that full bottom lip is worried between his teeth and think about biting it myself. I must be staring at it for quite some time, because when I look up, he's watching me.

That bitten lip turns up into a smile, and I feel myself flush, so obviously caught. But he doesn't say anything, simply continues to play.

"Any jacks?" he asks, and I hand him three.

Chapter 5

Beau

Training camp has been absolutely brutal. Coach Waldor is heavily determined that the first line is able to read each other inside and out. I haven't run this many passing drills since I was in high school.

I may be exhausted at the rink, but what's been especially trying has been my home life.

My interest in Milo has grown more and more every day. And I'm not certain, but I think he feels the same way. I've caught him watching me, looking at me when he shouldn't.

He watches me on the ice the most, but that's more as if he's trying to learn how to read me than trying to undress me with his mind. Even when his gaze is more appreciative than studied, I don't ever feel objectified by him.

The only time I don't like the way he looks at me is when I'm driving us to the rink.

He looks at me like we're about to die.

I'm not that bad of a driver.

A point I'm trying to make as we head back to the parking garage where Darlene is waiting for us. Milo stops in front of her and makes a face, nodding at the several dents she's sporting.

Yeah, maybe I had a rocky start when I first got her all those years ago. I wasn't exactly the most skilled driver. What eighteen-year-old is?

"I'm not trying to say you're the worst driver. I know plenty of people who are worse than you." I wait for him to name someone, but he just tosses his bag in the bed and hops in the passenger side. I shake my head and follow suit, pulling myself into the driver's side.

"You act like I'm going to drive us off the road, or something," I grumble.

"I just don't want to know what else 'or something' could be," he says, sticking his tongue out at me.

I have the strongest urge to suck that tongue into my mouth, but I shake it off.

We've been living together for about two weeks now, and he hasn't made a move on me yet. He probably isn't interested. Maybe he's just keeping me around to look at.

Or maybe I misread his looking at me. Maybe he was just spacing out?

I start the drive home, pulling out of the parking spot and out of the garage. There's a ton of construction on our route, caution cones everywhere, and Darlene is not happy about the wild, uneven road we're driving on.

I'm swerving every which way to avoid the potholes and the bumps, but Milo gasps, drawing my attention to him. I glance over at him and miss the pothole at the last second, hitting it with a *thunk* and a *pop*.

Suddenly, she's driving unevenly, wobbling and shaking.

"Fuck," I groan. "We blew a tire." I pull into a parking lot off to the side of the road. I look over at him and have to laugh. Milo's eyes are wide, and he's gripping the "oh shit" handle like he's expecting to be yanked from his seat.

He scowls at me.

"Don't laugh," he says indignantly, releasing the death grip he has on the handle. "That scared me!" He huffs and pouts, sticking out his bottom lip.

I have the strongest urge to bite it, but I contain myself.

Hopping out of the cab, I go to inspect the damage. It's the front driver's side tire that's blown, and holy hell has it blown. The rim is threadbare, no tire left to inspect. I pull the kit out from beneath the seat and walk around to the back to lower the spare. Milo has hopped out of the passenger side and is leaning on the bed, watching me.

This is honestly going to put such a damper on my week. It's Friday. I should be planning a night out. I had been toying with the idea of asking Milo to check out one of the clubs in town with me this weekend. I feel like this is just a big sign that I shouldn't.

I get to work jacking up the truck and taking off the frame of the old tire. The sun is high in the sky, and while it's not hot, it's definitely not cold yet. I am sweating up a storm.

I pull off the shirt I'm wearing, leaving only the under-shirt on, and use the discarded shirt to mop up the sweat on my brow.

As I pull the shirt away, I notice him watching me. Milo is standing at the end of the bed, leaning against Darlene, and he's watching me intently. His eyes are full of hunger.

I feel a drop of sweat roll down my temple and see his eyes track the movement. I try to keep my reaction in check, but a victorious, giddy thrill shoots through me.

He is checking me out. He is looking at me with interest. Maybe I should test the waters some. Maybe I dip my toe in before I take a dive.

I run my fingers through my curls and catch his eye. I nod at his crotch, where he's now sporting a very obvious chub. He instantly flushes and walks behind the truck, hiding from me.

Fuck, maybe I went too strong. I need to ease him into it. Ease him into being comfortable sporting a hard-on in my presence. I certainly wouldn't be opposed to it.

I make quick work of the spare tire, cranking the last of the bolts back into place and chucking the bits of the old tire into the bed.

I climb back into the truck, where Milo is waiting for me with his bright red cheeks. He is staring directly into his lap and is adamantly not speaking, so I follow his lead.

The rest of the drive home is quiet, tense.

I can tell that Milo isn't really interested in talking, probably embarrassed that I caught his arousal. Who wants to be caught with a crush, especially when neither of us has even come out to each other?

Should I tell him I'm bi, just to make him feel better?

I should tell someone, right?

I want to. I want to tell anyone so desperately. But the last call I had with Grady, he said no. But he can't stop me from coming out to my teammate.

A sudden thought occurs to me: what if Milo thinks I'm coming on to him by telling him? I still have my rule for a reason. Regardless of how attractive I find him, I'm not going to sleep with him. And if he has a crush, dangling hope in front of his face and tearing it away ... That would hurt him. It's what happened before, even if I didn't mean for it to. I won't make that mistake again.

What sucks about that is that, deep down, I really am interested. If we weren't teammates, I would have come out to him right away. I would have told him about my own crush and acted on it.

Assuming he was also interested.

All of this tension between us is exhausting. I want desperately to just let loose.

We get home, and I immediately beeline for the bathroom. The silence in the house feels heavy. I'm dirty and grimy and want nothing more than to stand under the warm spray and get lost in thought. A shower first, and then I'll come up with something.

The shower helps me clear my mind. I feel incredible surrounded by the heat, surrounded by the wet warmth. I know what I need tonight. I just hope he's on board with it.

"We should go out tonight."

I call this out to him as I walk from the bedroom to the living room. He looks up from where he's sitting and reading. He's squinting down at the novel in his hands as if he should be wearing glasses.

"Go out?" He cocks that brow. I want to lick it.

"You know, go out? Like, we can go to that club downtown." I want to dance. More specifically, I want to dance with this man's hot hockey butt rubbing against my crotch. "We're not going to have time in a few weeks to do much of anything beyond eating, sleeping, and hockey, so we might as well have some fun while we can." I wink at him mischievously, a sly smile curling my lips. "Please. We've stayed in the past two weeks. We've been good. We can afford to be a little bad."

He smiles, kind of shyly, and god, it's adorable. "Yeah, sure," he says, giving a little shrug, trying to be casual. "Why not? Let's go." His hands run down the front of his shirt, kind of smoothing it out. As if maybe he's a little nervous about what a night out could entail. And maybe I'm a little nervous too.

I don't sleep with teammates. I don't sleep with teammates. I don't sleep with teammates.

I keep repeating it to myself as I get dressed in the room. Maybe if I repeat it enough, it'll actually stick.

Bianca always hated going clubbing with me. She said the way I dressed was embarrassing. I used to go to raves when I was younger, and I like dressing... a certain way when I go dancing. But Bianca isn't here to tell me what to do anymore. She isn't here to complain about what I wear. She isn't here to put me down for being a bit more out there.

So I pull out the mesh crop top and slide it over my head. My black jean shorts hang loosely around my hips. I turn and admire myself in the mirror. It's giving very elder emo.

I sit on the edge of my very comfy bed and slide on a pair of high-tops.

I walk out to the living room to see Milo all dressed up.

And god, does he look great.

His ass is being hugged in all the best ways by his jeans slung low on his hips. The crisp black button-down is stretched across delicious muscles. Fuck, he's stunning. I'm overwhelmed with the desire to lick him.

No, bad Beau.

He turns around while fixing his sleeve and pauses. His jaw tenses, and his hands fall to his sides, fists clenching and unclenching.

Shit, does he hate this? Am I going to embarrass him too? All the eye rolls from Bianca and being told constantly that I'm *too much* by my mom come flooding back.

"I can..." I'm about to offer to go change when he interrupts me.

"You look great," he says on an exhale, and I pause, looking down at what I'm wearing.

I feel great.

I give him my most sincere smile, batting my lashes a little for dramatics. He laughs, and the sound shoots straight
to my cock.

"Thanks, man." I give him a once-over again, just admiring the fit of his clothes. "You do too."

He blushes so damn hard, the flush rushing up his neck
and blooming across his nose. It makes me notice a light
smattering of freckles on his face. How beautiful to have
been kissed so fervently by the sun.

I smile at him.

"Let's go."

Chapter 6

Milo

The car ride is just as tense as the ride in Darlene was earlier. I'm so obvious with my crush on him it's honestly painful. And who knows if he's even gay? What if all the times I thought I saw him watching me, I was just seeing what I wanted to see?

Maybe he's bringing me here so I see him dancing with a bunch of women and just get the fucking hint. I wish he would just be straightforward. That he would just tell me that he's not interested. Sometimes I just need it spelled out for me.

My grip tightens as we pull to a stop just a few lights away from the club. My breathing is shallow, harsh, as I maintain a white-knuckle grip on the steering wheel. Beau is sitting next to me in my very sensible BMW X5. So much better for driving through the snow than his ... Darlene.

I can barely think of his poor choice of vehicle, because he is sitting next to me, and he is dressed in the sluttiest little crop top I've ever seen.

I would feel stupid for my reaction, but I mean, come on.

His sleeves are long, the mesh gripping his biceps perfectly. It stretches across his chest, hanging off his pecs like it just can't bear to let go.

Fuck.

Fuck, fuck, FUCK.

Fuck.

I grip the steering wheel harder, knuckles blanching, as we pull up to a light, and I try to discreetly appreciate his body.

I was right when I first met him in the gym; he does, in fact, have a nice, hairy chest. All I want to do is cling to those dark curls and bury my face in the softness. I want to lose myself entirely to the beauty that is his body, to his defined pecs, to his soft abs.

But more than that.

His.

Happy.

Trail.

I want to trace the dark trail of curls that leads suggestively from his belly button to his shorts.

It turns out that I find hair on men incredibly attractive.

It also turns out that I enjoy a man who's not blatantly ripped. Because Beau, he's all muscle, but he has, like, a thin layer of fat over it. Like a cushion.

I want to just squeeze him. I want to grip his obliques and dig my fingers into his flesh, just so I can enjoy the give.

My fist flies up to my mouth at the very thought, and I bite down a little to keep from groaning.

He hooked his phone up to my car's sound system and is kind of in his own world right now, thank all that is holy. So I'm able to have this little freak-out completely uninterrupted.

He just radiates this confidence that illuminates his star-dom. It makes me want to gravitate toward him. Like the sun, he shines.

Downtown Minneapolis is busy on a Friday night. We drive past Vibrant and pull into an open spot right on the street. The air is crisp and cold when we get out of the car. Beau has such a swagger in his step as we walk to the club together. The bouncer takes one look at us, and a big smile spreads across his face.

"Milo Hall?" he asks, and I smile sheepishly. I nod a little, and he lets us both in.

I realize how different we look walking into this club but can't find it in me to care. Beau looked so nervous earlier when he came out of his room, dressed like an emo kid at a rave. I couldn't tell exactly why he looked so nervous; I just know that I hated seeing him so on edge.

We walk into the club together, and my senses are immediately assaulted by a barrage of smells and sounds as we step onto the floor. The music is too loud for me to even think straight, but the way it moves within my body feels different. It feels unnatural. The bass is rattling my ribs like it's trying to shake something loose. I clench my teeth to try and keep them from being shaken directly from my head.

All around us, there's shouting. Or maybe it's laughter? Maybe singing? I can't really tell one sound from another, only that there's a lot of it. Beau faces me and says something, and all I can do is smile at him in return. He laughs, and I know that he knows I don't have a single clue what was just said.

Lights flash through a string of colors: blue, then red, then nothing at all, just bodies moving and gyrating through the dark. Every time the lights flash, I catch pieces of people—a grin, a shoulder, a flash of eyes.

Then the lights catch on Beau. They catch on something on his chest that I can't quite make out, something flashy. A necklace, maybe?

Wait...

Is that...?

He adjusts the mesh of his top, and I can finally make them out.

Oh fuck.

Fuckity fuck, fuck, *fuck*.

His *nipples* are pierced.

Pierced.

He's watching me, so I can't freak out properly. I want to throw my head back in exasperation. I definitely want to take them in my mouth and give a little tug, just to see what sounds he'd make.

Fuck, I've been reading too many romances.

He smiles at me, and I do my best to smile back, but I know it looks constipated.

I need a distraction. Any distraction. Something unsexy. Something boring.

He leans in much too close, and I hold my breath. I can feel his nipple piercings rub against my arm. This is neither unsexy nor boring.

"Let's get a drink." His voice tickles my skin, and I feel goosebumps cover my whole body. A shiver runs up my spine, then back down. Thank god I'm more dressed than he is. My nipples are rock hard, and all I want is to rub them against his body.

We walk over to the bar, my feet sticking to the floor due to spilled drinks and what looks suspiciously like vomit.

We wait in line, and Beau is just swaying to the music. A smile breaks out across my face. He has absolutely no rhythm, but he clearly doesn't care. I mean, don't get me wrong, I have no rhythm. I have two entire left feet. But the difference is that I kind of care too much about what people think of me.

Despite this, I do some little head bops as we wait for our turn. He just puts me in such a good mood.

The bartender, a very attractive man with a name tag that reads Miguel, smiles and leans suggestively across the bar. "What'll it be, guys?"

Oh, I don't really drink. I didn't exactly think about that coming up when Beau invited me out tonight.

"Got any kind of mocktail for this guy?" Beau slaps a hand down on my shoulder, a winning smile on his face. He sees me looking at him and *winks*.

I raise a brow at him, a little confused as to how he knows I don't drink. He leans in close again, and I let out a tiny shudder. Fuck, I like having his breath against my skin.

"You're driving, man. No drinks for you."

Oh.

Duh.

He orders himself a shot and a drink. Miguel obliges with a smile. I wonder if he recognizes us.

Throwing back his shot, Beau grabs my hand and pulls me toward the dance floor. The music pulses, lyrics bleeding into noise, bass rattling my bones. There is no standing still. Someone is always touching me, brushing past me.

The room is so hot. Hot in a way that feels alive, as if it's breathing with us. The smell is pungent, assaulting my nose. It smells like spilled liquor and perfume that's started to sweat off.

While Beau and I bump and grind to the music, looking as awkward as two fully grown men dancing alone at a club can look, I watch him.

Fuck, he looks so free.

I'm deep in my head.

But then there's this guy. This guy dressed like a total slut, dancing across from me. He's just losing himself to the music. Swaying his hips and bouncing around on the balls of his feet, he makes me think maybe I can buck up and handle this night. Like maybe I could actually try to enjoy myself.

Despite how absolutely overwhelming the environment we're in is.

And just when the sounds and smells are becoming a bit too much, I feel a presence join our group. I open my eyes, not remembering closing them.

A man—a giant, really—has stepped between us, snaking his hand into my back pocket and pulling me flush against his body. He's huge, maybe six-five or six-six. I'm not the biggest man on our team, but my six-one frame is nothing to sneeze at. I don't hate the touch, but it's not the one I really want.

I look up at the stranger. His jaw is soft, but with strength defining it.

Holy shit, my parents are going to flip if this gets out.

"Hey, man," Beau says, giving the ginger giant a warning glare. "You kind of just stole my date." My eyes bug out of my head.

The man throws up his hands in defeat but still manages a winning smile.

"My bad." He chances a glance at me, giving me a wink, and I blanch. "From where I was standing, it looked like he was dancing alone."

He walks away, and I watch his retreating form. Once he's out of earshot, maybe half a foot away, I reach out and yank Beau in close, pressing my lips to his ear.

"Beau?"

"Yeah?" He's still bopping along to the music.

"Are we at a gay club?"

"It's technically a gay-*friendly* club."

I groan, rubbing my fists into my eyes, utterly exhausted. It's coming to me now. I think I've heard some of our teammates mention this club, not always kindly.

"Do you have any idea what people would say if we were seen here? If we were caught here? Together?" I gesticulate wildly between us.

He steps back, his face falling. Literally all the sunshine that had been beaming from his smile dims, his frown taking over his whole face. His eyes droop a little, and his cheeks puff. He looks so dejected, and I immediately want to take everything back.

"Am I embarrassing you?" he asks, voice so low I can barely hear him over the music.

The words hit my face like a physical blow. I watch the light leave his eyes, and my stomach drops.

I'm not sure exactly what it was about what I said, but I know immediately that I've done something very, very wrong.

He wraps his arms around himself protectively, as if he wants to make himself small.

I reach out my hand, looking to comfort him, and he kind of flinches away. What was it he asked? Was he embarrassing me?

"Oh, Beau," I start. He keeps his arms wrapped around himself like a shield. I hate this. "No, Beau, you're not embarrassing me." I sigh. "I embarrassed myself. I'm not... I mean, I'm..." I look around, suddenly remembering we are, in fact, in the middle of a very crowded club.

I want nothing more than to take him into my arms and comfort him, but this isn't the place.

This isn't the place, and he doesn't seem to want touch.

"Let's get out of here, okay?" I try again.

He looks up from the ground, head tilting, eyes almost comically large. How can such a big man look so small right now?

I take a deep inhale, taking in his scent.

Sweat and cedarwood.

"One more dance?" he asks, voice near silent in the cacophony of sound.

"One more." I nod and reach out my hand to him. He nods and takes it, his eyes lighting up significantly.

I pull him to me, and we dance.

Chapter 7

Beau

Our bodies are slotted together, bumping and grinding to the music. My thigh between his, and his hard cock grinding against it. Lust floods his eyes, his pupils blown wide, and his hands rub all over my body.

This music, this dance floor, him. It's all too perfect.

I know I'm sweating, but seeing the little droplets run down his temple... The urge to lick every drop hits me like a fucking freight train. It is taking every ounce of strength I have to keep my tongue to myself. His jaw is so sharp I could cut myself, but I want to risk it for a taste.

My hand is on his hip, and the other wraps around his neck, holding our gazes tight. His one hand snakes up my side, the other finding purchase where I hold his hip, sliding further until it grabs my ass. I lean into his touch.

We just move together, holding each other close. Grinding on each other.

Fuck, I could come like this.

We're both breathing heavily, kind of just holding each other, sweat dripping and mingling where our bodies are joined.

Both of our cocks are still very much hard, each heavy inhale and exhale rubbing them more fervently.

I pull off him, carefully unwinding our legs and holding him at a distance.

His cheeks are flushed, either from exertion or from embarrassment, the blush climbing up his neck and standing out stark against the black button-down he's wearing.

Fuck, I didn't say anything earlier, but he looks suave as hell.

Our eyes meet, and I wink at him. I don't know why I do it, just a force of habit, maybe? But it spooks the hell out of him. As if he's suddenly remembered where he is. The poor guy jumps about a foot in the air and scrambles back away from me.

"You want another drink?" he asks, even though my drink was long since abandoned. "I'll go grab you one." He starts to shove his way back through the crowd. I let out a chuckle and follow behind him. No, I want to be sober for this conversation. Because the hard cock he was rubbing against me warrants a sober conversation.

I grab his shoulder just as he shoves his way up to the bar. He really is about to buy me another drink, the sweetheart, when I interrupt him.

He looks at me, pupils blown, and I know. We can't do this here. Not with all these eyes.

What's-his-name, Miguel maybe, looks bummed as hell when I grab Milo's pinched shoulders and turn him toward the exit. I don't know if it's from the loss of business or the loss of the hot piece of ass I have in my hand, but I send him a warning glance.

"Let's just get out of here," I purr.

Fuck, I want to call him baby so bad.

For someone so stone-cold sober, he stumbles a lot as we make our way outside. The bouncer gives us another friendly nod, watching Milo with an easy smile on his face.

I try not to openly stare, but it's hard not to watch him out of the corner of my eye. Milo's grip on the steering wheel is white-knuckled, and he's sitting ramrod straight. I've never seen such anxiety. I wonder, what does he think is going to happen?

When we finally pull into the driveway at home, I'm buzzing to figure this guy out.

I think it's kind of obvious that he falls somewhere on the queer scale, but I'm not sure which side he tips toward.

We get home, and I can tell Milo is trying to shake off his anxiety. Like, physically shake it off of himself as we walk through the front door.

We stumble through the front door, a little drunk on the tension. The car ride was almost painfully quiet, both of us clearly lost in thought.

Maybe he's shaking off the anxiety, or maybe he's psyching himself up for something. He walks across the living room and flips on the lamp, the light casting the room in a golden glow.

When I finally plop down on the couch, I feel almost too tired to undo my laces. I'm nowhere even close to drunk, but the thought of getting ready for bed feels far away.

Milo walks over, plopping down next to me. The cushioned couch swallows our exhaustion right up.

"What a fucking night," I say, throwing my head back and letting out a loud exhale that almost sounds like a whoop.

Milo mirrors me, throwing his own head back and letting out a little laugh.

"Everything you dreamed it would be?" He's teasing me, but I look over at him and smile.

"Almost."

Because, right now, the only thing that could possibly make this night better is him on my lap. Him straddling my legs, with that thick tongue down my throat. His gorgeous ass grinding against my hard dick and just begging for it to be inside him.

Fuck.

Fuck, fuck, fuck.

I need to calm down.

I can be an adult here.

"So," he starts, eyes suddenly downcast. He's looking anywhere but at me. "I think it's pretty obvious that I'm … that I'm also … or … well …"

"Yeah." I decide to put him out of his misery. Because he's right; it is pretty obvious. I think it's even more obvious that I am too. Or … that I'm…

I'm not ashamed of myself. But I'm embarrassed of how obvious I've been in my attraction to him.

"I'm gay," he says finally, while I struggle with my own internal bullshit. I smile at him.

"I'm bi."

"I figured." He smiles back at me. "That's what made this easier, I guess." He closes his eyes. "Knowing we have the same secret."

We both just sit there, lounging on the world's most comfortable couch with the world's most uncomfortable confessions hanging between us. We watch each other for what feels like hours but has to be only a minute or so.

I don't know why, but I feel like there's something about him that's inexperienced. As if he doesn't quite know how to handle his queerness. Does he not...? I don't even know how to ask this, but I feel like I have to know.

"I downloaded Grindr the second Bianca and I broke up." I laugh a little, thinking back to that awkward first hookup in Dallas. It was weird and uncomfortable being with a guy for the very first time. It's the only time I've done anything like that. It was awkward and fast and not at all what I'd hoped for. Milo deserves better than that.

When I look over at him, he looks confused.

"I know you know what Grindr is."

He nods in affirmation. "I know what it is. I just don't understand." His eyebrow cocks in utter confusion. "I don't understand how you can risk using a dating app like that. What if you're found out?"

"It's pretty easy to stay anonymous." I sigh. "Guys are either in a similar situation, or they're just good people." If anyone is going to be understanding about being in the closet, it's other queer people.

Well, he's not a Grindr guy. Okay, good to know.

So how does he...? What does he...?

"So how do you handle it?" is what I finally settle on, because that seems like a safe-enough question.

"How do I handle what?"

Okay, maybe too safe of a question.

"How do you handle dating, fucking? You're not out, obviously."

"I, um ... I ..." The flush starts at his chest and blooms up his neck and across those freckled cheeks.

Oh.

Oh.

"You do get to hook up, right?" I know it's not my business, but the blush spreading across his cheeks just made it feel like my business.

The shake of his head is so small and so shy, my heart leaps in my chest. Does that mean what I think it means?

"Milo," I ask tentatively, because I'm about to ask the most personal question ever and I'm not quite sure I deserve the answer. "Milo, are you...?" Okay, maybe I'm about to half-ass asking the most personal question ever.

His face is beet red, so I know he knows what I'm asking. The only question is: will he actually answer it?

"Milo...?" I start again, when he interrupts me.

"I've never had sex," he blurts out, immediately staring down at his big hands. Hands that I've had very inappropriate thoughts about. I mean, a virgin's hands have no right being that veiny.

I'm kind of stuck. I'm not the *most* emotionally mature person I know, but I'm definitely not the most emotionally *immature* person I know. That has to count for something.

"Do you want to...?"

"Oh my god, yes." He closes his eyes and lets out a long-suffering sigh. "I'm going absolutely wild." His hands clench and unclench, those veins popping out as he flexes and relaxes.

So Milo is a virgin, okay. I was going to suggest dating apps but maybe not so much. I can just picture him opening it for the first time and immediately being assaulted with a dick pic. Or meeting up with someone and having the worst, most awkward sex of his life.

He can't lose his virginity that way; he just can't.

He should be taken care of that very first time. He should be cherished. He should be cared for and made to feel good. His first time should be all about him, and he is just not going to get that on an app.

He could really only get that from someone who understands what he is going through. Someone who has been where he is and knows the struggle.

The same thought spins out in my head over and over. Do I suggest it? Do I really go there when I barely know him? When I've only been here maybe two weeks.

"I just never wanted to sleep with someone random, you know?" Milo kind of squawks, nervousness taking over his voice entirely. "I don't like that I will not know what to expect. I don't like that it could be bad. That I could ... that I could mess it up."

Oh, sweet baby.

Okay.

Okay, maybe I should suggest it.

"I get it," I say, my hands coming together to clutch in front of my body. They sit on my lap and do a great job of hiding my excited cock. He knows what I am about to suggest, and he is very enthusiastic about it. "The first time is kind of scary." I close my eyes and nod a little, getting really into my pensive conversation. I need him to know I am only suggesting this because I care. "It's important to do it with someone who understands you. Someone you trust will take care of you."

He turns his head and cocks a brow. Maybe I'm being too subtle?

"Yeah, you really just want someone who can hold your hand through the experience. Who you know will do their best to make that first time, magical for you." I look at him with wide eyes and an innocent smile. Or at least, what I hope is an innocent smile.

He cocks a brow.

"What do you mean?"

Chapter 8

Milo

"So what are you suggesting?" I try to keep my voice steady, even. I think I know *exactly* what he's suggesting. In fact, I'm sure I know. I just need to hear it from him. I need to see those lips form the words, need to hear it off his tongue.

"I think you know…"

"I know." I sigh. "Please just tell me, in your own words, what it is that you want."

He opens his mouth, and I can practically hear the snarky comment forming. "I'm serious, Beau."

That shuts him up.

"I don't know, Milo," he starts, suddenly acting much too shy for someone who just suggested we sleep together. "I just think your first time should be with someone who makes it special for you. I think you deserve to have someone take their time with you, to really make sure you enjoy yourself. The dating apps are great if you're just looking for a quick hookup. But I feel like that isn't you."

"We've known each other for, like, two weeks." I let out a hollow chuckle.

"Are you saying you really want a random hookup as your first time?" he asks me, his brow rising nearly to his hairline.

Okay, he's got me there. But sleeping with my teammate? Yeah, he's attractive. Incredibly attractive. He's exactly my type, or what I always imagined my type to be. But that would make things messy. Am I actually considering this?

I say as much, and he lets out a rough chuckle.

"I have my own rule about sleeping with teammates. I get it. But I'm a big boy. I can separate sex and feelings just fine if you can."

That's the thing, though. I don't know if I can. I've never had to before.

"Look," Beau says, grabbing my hand and giving it a small squeeze, "I'm not going to pressure you if you really don't want to. Just know the offer stands."

He stands and starts to walk away, but I reach out and grab his wrist, pulling him back toward me. Fear of the unknown suddenly seems smaller than fear of never knowing him. His brows lift as he looks back at me.

"If we do this," I start, refusing to meet his eyes, "we should have rules, right? So we don't cross any lines?"

His eyes soften, and he smiles.

"Yeah, man, we can have rules."

"I want to be…" I start, then shame hits me like a wave. God, how do I ask this? "I want … you know?" Why couldn't I just say it? It's a simple request and definitely something that should be established before we do any-thing.

"You want me to fuck you?" His smile is almost a smirk, confidence rolling off him as he looks at me. I give a small nod. Maybe he knows me better than I thought. "You're not nervous about…?" He pauses, and his face flushes hard.

"No, I have a thing." Both his brows shoot up, and we sit in this weird, agreeable silence while I wait for him to pick up what I'm hinting at. This time, though, he stays quiet, nodding at me as if to encourage the confession. My face burns. "You know, a … dildo." I whisper it like it's a dirty word. I bought it when I was eighteen, and I shouldn't be ashamed of what I like.

He stands stiff for a moment before abruptly turn-ing and heading toward the bedrooms, with a surprising amount of determination.

"Where are you going?" I call after him as I scramble to my feet. He marches straight into my room, pushing open the door.

"I need to see it," he says. "I need to know how big it is. I need to know what color it is." I skid to a stop just outside the doorway, watching in horror as he reaches into my bedside table and pulls out my eight-inch sparkly purple dildo. He grips it in one hand and looks up at me slowly. Holding the dildo, affectionately named Heath, he stares at me.

I open my mouth to explain, but all that comes out is a mortified whisper: "I thought it was pretty." I blush furiously. He starts walking toward me. Stalking more accurately. His eyes are focused and, god, it looks like he wants to devour me. We haven't even gotten to talk about any other rules. "We should talk more, right? More rules?" I ask.

"Is that what you want?" he asks, eyes hungry.

I watch him for a moment before shaking my head. I meet his gaze, feeling suddenly powerful, and dare him to take me.

He grabs my arms and pulls me to him, capturing my mouth in a searing kiss.

Well, fuck.

His lips slant against mine, hungrily seeking heat, his tongue toying with the seam of my lips. I moan, granting him entrance.

His tongue explores my mouth fervently, battling mine for dominance as our kiss intensifies. He pulls at my buttons, trying desperately to undo them with shaking hands. Mine aren't doing any better as I fumble with his belt.

Finally, he pulls away from our kiss, staring me directly in the eyes, and says, "I'll buy you a new one," before ripping my shirt open. Buttons fly everywhere.

He licks down the column of my neck, and I let out the most embarrassing whimper. But fuck, it feels incredible. He licks and nips across my shoulder before biting down and sucking.

When he pulls back, he leans close to my ear. "Fuck, sweetheart, I want to mark you up."

I whine.

He turns us quickly, backing me up until my legs hit the bed and I fall back. His fingers make quick work of my pants, popping open the button while he leans in and tongues my nipple.

I let out a heated hiss as he bites down and gives it a little tug with his teeth. Fuck, it feels so good.

He yanks my pants down, pulling them and my loafers clean off, and I'm bare before him. I wait for embarrassment to make me shy, but the way he looks at my naked body... the way his eyes drink in my hard cock... Fuck, I feel so sexy.

I mentally prepare myself to flip over so he can prep me, but he absolutely stuns me with his next move. His hands grip the back of my thighs and he pushes them up to my ears. I'm entirely exposed to him, my hole bared for his viewing pleasure.

"Wha— what are you do— Oh!" I lose my voice in a moan mixed with some other embarrassing sound as he crouches down and licks a firm line from the back of my balls to my asshole.

Fuck, I was not expecting that.

His tongue continues to lick and prod at my hole, and I mewl and whimper.

"Baby, you taste so amazing." He groans, and the vibration against my tender ass has me leaking all over my stomach. His eyes catch mine and gesture haughtily toward the mess I'm making of myself.

Well, the mess *he's* making of me.

I'm getting dangerously close to the edge as he continues his tongued assault on my ass. Fuck, if this is just how good his tongue feels, what will his fingers do to me? His dick?

"Fuck, fuck, fuck, c'mere." I grip his hair and pull him back up my body, dragging his mouth to mine. "Give me a second. If you so much as breathe on my ass, I'm going to explode." He chuckles against my lips and continues his assault on the northern front.

I'm practically purring as he moves back down to my neck, biting and sucking. My knees are still by my ears, and I still feel entirely exposed. But it's a good feeling, I think. I just don't know how to explain it.

Like, I'm warm all over, my chest feels loose, and there's a little flurry of butterflies in my belly.

"I'm going to grab the lube and a condom," he says, finally pulling away from my body long enough to look into my eyes, his pupils absolutely blown with lust. "Hold your thighs exactly like they are. Don't move an inch." I obey with shocking ease, my hands gripping my thighs and holding the stretch.

He pours a generous amount of lube on his fingers and begins to circle my hole, the muscle already pliant from his relentless tongue. He pushes in slowly, and I bear down, trying to relax as my hole is breached for the first time by something other than my own fingers and dildo.

Fuck, this is hot. This is so sexy. Why have I waited so long to let someone else do this for me?

It's when he meets my eyes that I remember.

"That's it, baby. Open up for me. Good boy."

I never realized how much I needed this. How much I needed him inside me. How much I needed him to be the first.

He was so right when he suggested my first time needed to be special, but I don't think he realized it could only have been this perfect with him.

He slowly pushes in another finger and begins to scissor them, opening me up while whispering encouragement.

"You're taking my fingers so well, baby."

And: "That's it, sweetheart."

And: "I can't wait to see this pretty pussy stretched out by my cock."

Whoa.

Okay. I was not expecting that. The words should have thrown me. Instead, they settle something deep in my chest, like he sees a part of me I've never had the words for.

I especially wasn't expecting to like it as much as I clearly do. My cock literally jumps in excitement, and a full-body shiver takes over.

I stare at him, wide-eyed, mouth agape, and he smirks.

"I looked up that book you were reading the other night." He smiles, a coy curve of his lips. "I actually took some time to peruse a few of the books you were reading recently and found a trend." He shrugs. "Thought I would take a chance and see if you liked it."

I blush furiously, nodding. "I liked it." I look away from him, my skin flaming. "I've fantasized about it."

"Oh, baby." He smirks, slipping in a third finger, and I am whimpering. "You want me to fuck this tight little pussy?" he asks. I whine in response; all I can think about is his attention and that dick I felt in the club filling me up.

"*Please...*" I groan, because I need him in me. I've never wanted anything more. All I can do is make needy noises as he continues to open me up.

He slowly pulls his fingers free, leaving me gaping and empty. And even though I know he's about to fill me the way I really want him to, I can't help the garbled groan that leaves my throat.

"So impatient, sweetheart," he chastises, tsking as he slides on the condom. "Don't worry, pretty boy, you're going to get this cock."

He lines up the head of his cock with my entrance, and I shudder, the anticipation driving me wild.

When he finally starts to push in, a delicious burn shoots up my spine. I know to expect it, but still it takes me by surprise.

"Fuuuuuuuuuuck," comes out of me involuntarily. I have no control over my vocal cords anymore nor the warbled sounds they're producing. His cock slides over my prostate, and I cry out.

"There he is. Come on, pretty boy, sing for me." Each push and pull hits that perfect spot over and over, and I'm going to come. I'm going to come, and he's not even all the way in yet.

"Oh, baby, fuck, you're so tight." His voice is strained and *rough*. I want it wrapped around me. "Baby girl, fuck, I'm not gonna last." My ears burn when they catch his term of endearment.

His words are music to my ears. My sensitive hole is throbbing in the best way, and heat is coiling low in my belly. I feel that zing shoot down my spine, and I'm coming. I'm coming so hard without so much as a brush of his fingers against my dick.

"Did you just...? Oh god!" I'm suddenly incredibly sad I can't feel him fill me up as he shoots his load into the condom. His hips stutter, and he stills above me.

I mourn that his cum won't be dripping out of my hole.

But then he does the most incredible thing.

This man picks me up, cock still firmly lodged in my ass, and carries me over to my side of the bed.

"How did you..?" I start to ask, kind of amazed he knew without me telling him.

"Your books are over here," he says as if it's obvious, with a tiny shrug.

He pulls out of me slowly, and I clench around nothing, whining *again* because I miss the fullness.

"Give me a second, baby." He walks back over to the other side of the bed and pulls off his mesh top, the only thing left on him. Fuck, he looks so stunning standing there in all his naked glory. I admire him as he crawls back into bed next to me. "Gonna give you the full experience," he mumbles before scooting up close to me.

Before I can ask what he means, he's shoving his half-hard dick back into me. I whimper at the fullness but snuggle back into him.

This is so much more intimate than the sex was. What are we doing?

He wraps an arm around me and holds me tight.

Any chance I had at separating sex and feelings flies out the window as his breathing settles.

As I start to drift, his warm breath against my neck, I know we are truly and utterly fucked.

Chapter 9

Beau

I roll over to warmth. A big wall of muscle is pressed up against me, and I sigh, inhaling deeply to breathe in his tantalizing scent.

Citrus.

Citrus and rain.

Citrus and rain and lingering sex.

I sigh again, contentedly. He smells so much like how I imagine heaven smells.

My arm wraps around his chest, and I pull him flush against my body. He moans and wiggles a little in his sleep as we collide, but curls back into me.

I want to stay like this. I want to stay here with him in my arms. I haven't felt this kind of closeness in, well, ever. I don't think I've ever felt this type of peace and serenity in all of my ten years with Bianca. I have to wonder if that says more about her or Milo.

Milo.

I have what has to be the dopiest smile ever on my face as I think about last night. This morning. Whenever the fuck. Just thinking about him in my arms. Thinking about my tongue on his skin. About my...

Fuck, I could get lost in the thought of him. Of us.

I wish I had taken more time with him, that I had taken the opportunity to appreciate every single inch of him.

My mouth waters a little, salivating at the thought of him.

And what glorious inches they are.

He looked so fucking good spread out beneath me, knees to his ears, my cock splitting him open... Fuck, even just the memory is enough to get me hard. I already feel desperate for a second go, even though I know we shouldn't. Even though I know we can't. Even though I know he won't.

I shouldn't.

We shouldn't.

I doze in and out of consciousness and just squeeze him, feeling the give of his very real flesh under my hand. My fingers find purchase in his chest, squeezing and groping his pec. Fuck, he feels so good. He feels so warm and so real. I love the feel of him in my hands.

I must fall back asleep because, suddenly, my arms are empty. I reach out, trying desperately to find him and feeling only the comforter.

My eyes peel open slowly, crusted with sleep and the lingering weight of my hangover, and I see his side of the bed is made.

I swear, if I find him asleep on the couch, I will lose my ever-loving mind.

Or...

I pause mid-roll out of the bed.

Maybe this really was the one-time thing I said it would be. Maybe that's all he wants. Maybe I should respect that.

My face scrunches up at the very putrid thought.

Fuck that.

No, really, fuck that. We can totally keep having casual sex and not attach any feelings to it. It's fine.

I fling myself out of bed, finding a pair of sleep pants waiting for me on the chest. He's so considerate. I'm pulling them on as I leave the room, hunting down my pretty princess.

Where oh where could he be?

I can hear his voice coming from the dreamy little kitchen. He sounds so agitated. I immediately want to fix it for him, want to make things right for him.

I stretch and feel my muscles pop and flex.

"I promise we spoke two days ago." He pauses, assumedly to let whomever he's talking to respond. I walk out into the kitchen, and he's standing with his back to me at the sink. The muscles in his back are bunched up tight. He's just standing there shirtless in a pair of boxer briefs.

Fuck, his ass looks good.

Bitable.

"Why would I lie to you?" His hand is on his hip, shoulders up by his ears. "Mom, I promise I want to talk to you." He throws his head back, staring up at the ceiling as if it'll be able to talk some sense into her for him.

I can understand a difficult mom.

Based on what Milo told me the other day about her and her little freak-outs when he doesn't answer the phone, and based on the current conversation I'm listening to, she sounds like a bit of a piece of work. I definitely know about difficult moms.

"Mom, please." He sounds so exasperated. I can hear the high-pitched whine of her voice. I cringe a little at the sound. It drags up the worst of memories for me, so I try not to let it take me under.

I wonder if maybe I shouldn't be listening.

Just as I'm about to walk back to the bedroom, he turns and spots me, dropping his phone in surprise. He shakes his head, letting out what sounds like a nervous laugh. Dipping to pick it back up and pulling his phone to his ear, he continues.

"Sorry, Mom, I tripped." I raise a brow at him, and he shrugs. Do his parents not know he has a roommate? Is he keeping a secret from them?

Interesting.

"Look, Mom, I'd love to talk more, but I have to finish breakfast." He turns back to the stove, and I get another delicious glimpse of his ass. "No, seriously, Mom, I'm burning the omelet. I've got to go." He pauses, his hand going back to his hip, and he nods. "No, I'll call you back later, I promise."

He places the phone on the counter but doesn't turn to look at me, instead focusing on the aforementioned omelet in front of him. He grabs the spatula beside the stovetop and flips the eggs with practiced ease.

"You lied to her," I observe unhelpfully. He still doesn't turn around. "That looks perfect." I nod at the omelet, even though he's still not looking at me. "Definitely not even a little burned," I chastise him. I smile even though his back is turned.

I want him to look at me. I want him to see me.

I'm here, Milo. See me.

I shake my head a little. Why does that matter to me? Why does he need to see me? I spent most of my life trying desperately to stand out, trying desperately to be seen. First by my parents, then in my relationship. I guess the need has extended here to my friendships.

"I wouldn't say I lied." I can hear the smile in his voice. "I just jumped ahead a little." He chuckles to himself.

Fuck, Milo, turn around and look at me.

But he doesn't. He pulls a plate down and deposits the omelet onto it before starting to whip up the next one.

I just want his attention.

The weirdest feeling overwhelms me. A tiny voice in my head says that I've fulfilled my usefulness to Milo, and now he'll be done with me.

I walk over and plop down at the table, feeling a little defeated.

We exist in stilted silence, me sitting at the breakfast nook, him standing at the stove. Nothing but tension in the air between us.

"What do you want on yours?"

"Huh?"

He finally turns, holding the bowl of beaten eggs in his hands. "On your omelet." He answers as if that's the most obvious thing in the world.

Oh.

He's making me breakfast.

That's such wifey shit. It immediately makes me feel ... seen. Wanted. Something else I'm not ready to name.

It immediately makes me feel cared for.

I tell him what I want, and he moves to chop the peppers, mushrooms, and onions, the fragrant aroma filling the air. He tosses them into the pan with some butter. The sizzle sounds so sexual, I swear my cock twitches in response.

The sun is shining through the nook window, heating my skin. I lean back in my chair, my abs flexing as I stretch. I look over at Milo, and he quickly tries to hide that he was watching me.

I let loose a wicked smile. I love having his eyes on me.

He's leaning against the kitchen island, his arms flexed and folded. He leans forward, staring down at his hands. They flex and constrict.

I watch as he turns and pours the eggs over, and I picture waking up like this week after week. I picture walking up behind him, encasing his body with mine. Trapping him with my arms on either side of him, kissing his neck.

Breathing him in, licking a line down the column of his throat...

And, there it is, my cock has entered the chat.

I scoot a little further under the table, trying to discreetly palm my dick into submission as it chubs up. Fuck, I cannot keep getting so hard around him. I know he knows how much he turns me on. He has to, after last night.

The silence now is a lot more amicable, just the sound of the omelet cooking and the interruption of our breathing.

"So you cook?" I decide to break the silence, and that's apparently how I'm going to do it. Stating the obvious.

"I can cook a few things," he answers, despite the utter stupidity of my non-question. "You'd know if you woke up at a reasonable hour in the morning instead of flying out the door at the last second."

As if to demonstrate his culinary competence, he flips the omelet onto a plate and walks it over to me.

It smells heavenly.

It looks even fucking better.

"I'm amazing at breakfast." He has a wry smile on his face, something secretive in his eyes. I long to find out those secrets. He walks back over to the stove, pulls out two forks from a drawer, and brings them over along with his plate. He sits across from me, hands me my fork, and we both dig in.

"Holy fuck, Miles." I groan in delight. The eggs are fluffy and delicious. They're seasoned to perfection, and bursting with flavor. "Milo, this is amazing." I dive in, unable to speak or make any noises beyond moans of pleasure as I tuck into the breakfast he made me.

Once we're both done, and I'm still exaggeratedly moaning my gratification, the forks clatter onto empty plates. "If this whole hockey thing doesn't work out, you could make it big by cooking," I tease him.

"If this whole hockey thing..." He chuckles to himself. "Yeah, man, I'll keep that in mind."

The "man" sounds forced, like he's trying to make us bros.

Ugh, the very thought makes me want to cringe, even though I know it's what I should want.

"So you liked it. That bodes well for your time here," he continues as if he's trying to find some common ground for us to stand on. As if I wasn't face-first in his ass last night. He stands abruptly, clearing our plates as he works. "I like cooking; it's relaxing. I don't mind cooking us breakfast."

I nod, a pensive look taking over my face. I want to figure this guy out. Now that I've had a taste...

"Not to ruin the mood you set for yourself," I start, fully ready and honestly excited to ruin this level of calm. "But we should talk about last night."

The plates clatter into the sink, forks bouncing off the ceramic. I rush over to his side and see the plate I used is chipped now.

"Sorry, Milo." I pull his hands from the sink and look them over, checking for any cuts, any hurt. He's bleeding from his thumb, and without thinking, I bring it to my mouth, sucking it clean. His intake of breath is sharp, harsh, and shallow.

Since I'm already here, I meet his eyes, pulling his thumb free and planting a gentle kiss on the tip.

We stand like that for a moment, just staring at each other, our eyes locked, his thumb on my lips. It makes me wonder what'll happen next.

It makes me excited.

But he gently pulls away, pulling his gaze away from mine.

"Yeah, we should talk about last night." His voice is low, and I instantly know that my heart is about to break a little. Even if I know we can't have it, part of me wants everything from last night to never end.

Not to be dramatic, but it's not like I want to date him or anything. I just want to fuck some more. But I guess he's about to do me a favor.

I have my rule for a reason.

Right?

A rule I'd painstakingly broken last night, and I guess I was fully ready to break again. For more of him, I was willing to break all the rules.

But he's right to put a stop to it.

"We can't, right?" He gives me a sad smile. "It would be so bad for either of us to get attached, right?" He begins to painstakingly scrub the plates, pulling those vibrant eyes away from mine.

But god, looking at him now, I'm not sure I care about the rules anymore.

Fuck, he's so pretty. The sun shines through and reflects off his green eyes. They look so pretty, like sea glass.

I could get lost in those eyes.

I must get lost in them, at least for a moment, because I miss what he says next.

"What was that?"

I definitely misheard him.

"I'm just so grateful to you, you know? For making my first time that good." He smiles at me, then reaches into his back pocket and pulls out his phone. "I was just hoping you'd help me set up a Grindr profile." His smile is a little sheepish. "I don't really know what I'm doing."

Oh.

I stare at him, mouth agape.

Oh, fuck no.

Chapter 10

Milo

Waking up tangled in Beau's arms was eye-opening. Or at least, it opened something in me. I want this man. I want him in a way I was not expecting to want someone.

Like, "fuck, please bend me over every piece of furniture in this house, but also hold my hand while we eat together" – type of want.

Like, "call me baby girl, but also call me sweetheart" – type of want.

Like, "spit in my mouth and then kiss me" – type of want.

Like, "oh shit, I could fall for this guy" – type of want.

I have spent my whole life wanting from a distance. Now, for the first time, I want up close. I want something messy. I want it real.

So when he looks at my phone like he wants to smash it to pieces, I know I'm making the right moves. I know he has his rules, that he just got out of a long-ass relationship, that he's not looking for anything serious.

I could wait for him to be ready.

Or…

Or I could help move him along faster.

"So you'll help me, right?" I ask, a sunshiny smile on my face, a very specific app pulled up on my phone. He's looking at my phone like it is the scum of the earth. Maybe I'm going too hard, too fast, but the way he is looking at me is absolutely delicious. I want him to devour me.

We sit there in silence that is too tense to be called amicable. He's busy glaring daggers at my phone, and I'm busy typing in my email where prompted. I feel almost giddy going through this, even if I have no intention of actually using it, even if I fully intend on deleting it the second we finish setting me up.

"So, what kind of picture should I use?" I don't look up from my phone, pretending to be engrossed in the setup process. Finally, I peek up at him. "What kind do you have on yours?"

He seems to shake himself out of it, because he flashes me a too-wide, too-toothy smile.

"You can never go wrong with a good shirtless torso pic." His smile is so forced, but I smile right back at him. "I mean, you want to be discreet, right? Just a hot body. Nothing incriminating." He winks at me, and that wink does things to my insides. They're busy flipping and flopping when he snatches my phone from my hands. "Okay, so do I want to go through these pictures, or should we just take some right now?"

I laugh, suddenly a little nervous. Fuck, am I actually doing this?

But I school my features.

Yes. Yes, I am.

"Yeah, go ahead and just snap some faceless pictures, I guess." It's not like I'm going to use them, but I guess it would be interesting to see how Beau Bennett decides to focus a camera on me.

I stand up, looking down at what I'm wearing, and have to wonder if this is going to be too aggressive. But as I look up at him, he's already pulling the camera back down after snapping some candid shots.

He smiles at me, a wicked little smile. "These are perfect."

I look down at them, and he's right. These pictures would be perfect to seduce faceless and nameless strangers on the internet. The morning light is shining through the window, cascading off my body like ribbons. My muscles are highlighted by the sunlight, and if I were trying to get fucked by anyone other than the guy standing before me, these pictures would do it.

Beau is staring at his feet while I admire the pictures he took. I can tell he hates this. And for a moment, I wonder if maybe I should nix this plan. If I should talk to him man to man about how amazing last night was. If I should tell him I want last night again and again.

But then he flashes me the world's weakest smile, and I know I'm making the right decision. I know that if I tried to ask for what I want, this man would just deny, deny, deny. He would deny until he's blue in the face, and neither of us would be happy. Because I know I won't be happy if I don't get him.

Beau grabs at my phone again, and I hand it over willingly.

"Okay, so we want to bare-bones this info section. Height, weight, position, what you're looking for..." I don't miss the subtle look he gives me as he says that.

What am I looking for, huh? That's what you want to know, Mr. Bennett?

"I mean, you know my stats as well as anyone." I laugh, kind of awkwardly, just letting the silence fall between us.

Beau looks...

Well, in all honesty, Beau looks constipated. He's holding my phone in a death grip, and I want to just laugh. His face is kind of scrunched up, lips pinched in a grumpy little pout, cheeks puffed slightly in his discontent. His face is such an open book, and right now, that book is titled I Hate This.

I want nothing more than to poke at those puffed-up cheeks and tease him.

He's tap, tap, tapping away on my phone, filling out my preferences for me. When he hands it back, I notice that what I'm looking for is listed as "a connection".

My sweet lover boy wants me to be happy.

He's not wrong, I do want that connection. I want to dance badly together at a club. I want to be able to enjoy a wild and passionate night together and just eat breakfast together the next day in easy silence. I want to laugh about that weird time I made him fill out my Grindr profile together.

We haven't had many moments together, but I know those moments are the ones I want more of.

The silence is broken by a barrage of sleek, electronic little chirps.

Chirp, chirp, chirp.

Beau looks down at my phone, his eyes widening at whatever it is that he sees. His fingers swipe, and he drops the phone with a gasp.

I scramble to gather it up from the floor at the same time as Beau. He snatches my phone up just a second quicker than I can reach for it. The look he has on his face is downright feral.

"What?" I ask, genuinely confused by whatever is happening. "What was that noise? What does that mean?" I know exactly what it means. I've been up for over an hour, and I've done research.

Beau looks at me in exasperation, his eyes wild and his lips parted. He looks downright kissable right now, but he's clearly upset.

Fuck, why is he so hot when he's upset?

He kind of shoves my phone into my hands, and I flip it over. I have a ton of messages, or maybe they're just notifications, I don't know. All I know is that there are a lot of them.

"Wow." I'm genuinely shocked. All this for a set of abs? I tap on one notification, and a guy instantly messages me.

Hot4u77: Those tits are perfect for fucking.

Oh fuck. Okay, then.

I guess the guys on Grindr are a little intense.

"Wow," I start, shaking my head at the phone, slightly exasperated. "This is kind of really... Wow, just really a lot." My laugh is void of real emotion, and I think Beau can tell, the way he's looking at me like he's so done with my shit.

I put the phone off to the side, apparently done with my own shit today too.

Beau has decided to move on with his morning, standing up and stretching, the muscles in his abdomen pulling taut as he maneuvers his body.

"I'm so ready for our first game," he says on a yawn, his arms stretched high. He then looks at me and winks. "Are you ready?" he asks like it's a dare.

"More than you know." I'm not just talking about hockey, and from the look he gives me, he knows it.

Hours later, the weight of the morning still sits heavy on my chest. But being on the ice has a way of clearing my head or at least forcing me to focus on something else.

"Let's go!"

Beau is skating circles around my net during morning skate. I laugh at his excitement at actually getting one past me, especially when I have dozens flying at me that I'm supposed to block.

Still, he is the first to get one by me this morning, so I guess that bodes well for us tonight.

"That's it, BB!" Oskar calls out, grinding to a halt next to me and waving at Beau, a big grin taking over his face. He leans in close and pats my mask. "Is good, yes?" he asks me. I'm not entirely sure why, but I nod anyway.

Oskar is an interesting guy. He's funny and loud, a tall Swede who's been playing for the Fury all thirteen years he's been playing professional hockey. He's all tan skin and dark blond hair, blue eyes, and tattoos covering his skin.

Beau is clicking with Paxton and Brennan like crazy this morning. They're practicing passing drills, and I can tell Coach Waldor loves the wordless communication between them. Paxton and Brennan skate up to the bench and pull off their helmets, showing off their sweaty hair, Paxton's a dark, almost black and Brennan's a deep, yellowy blond. They squirt water into their mouths before replacing their helmets and moving back in line.

I watch the three of them move seamlessly across the ice, Oskar and Kirill trailing after them, Oskar smiling and Kirill just sort of scowling. They're all laughing about something funny Beau just said, even Brennan, who until now has kind of had a stick up his ass about Beau.

I don't think Brennan likes Beau too much. He's always scowling at him and never wants to go out with us after practice or on the weekends. Paxton always says he'll talk to him, but nothing ever seems to come from it.

I wonder if he misses Max. I never asked what happened between them, but they were really close when he was on the team. Some things just can't be brought up in the locker room.

Max was the left winger we had on their line before he was traded to Dallas for Beau. They never seemed especially close, but he was always a lot friendlier with Max than he is with Beau now.

Brennan picks up the puck and carries it toward me at breakneck speed. Immediately, I get in the zone, ready for him. Out of the corner of my eye, I can see Paxton.

Brennan breaks in with speed, cutting down the boards before angling hard toward the slot. I square up, tracking the puck, weight set and stick flat on the ice, already reading the shot.

He sells it.

Brennan drops his shoulder and pulls the puck across his body like he's loading a quick release, forcing me to bite. My pads tighten, my glove lifts, and my eyes lock on the blade. For half a heartbeat, it looks like a clean look, the kind that ends in twine.

Instead, the puck slips off his stick at the last second.

A soft, perfect feed slides across the crease, threading through my reach just as Paxton crashes the net. I explode laterally, pushing hard, but I'm already chasing the play now, not controlling it.

Paxton meets the pass in stride and snaps it home before I can recover.

Fuck, our first line circles around, cheering their lucky shot. I point a glove at Brennan, as if to say, *Don't you dare do that to me again*. But I'm smiling with them, laughing.

Our first game is against Chicago. It's a fitting match. Our biggest rival has always been much better than us, but I'm feeling really good about this matchup. Something about how our team is just skating circles around during this morning skate has me feeling good about tonight.

When morning skate is over, I hurriedly undress in the locker room, desperate to get out of there. Beau is with Mia, one of the athletic trainers, getting some soft tissue work,. I probably could use some myself before tonight, but I'm just desperate for time alone with Beau.

"Brunch at my place," Oskar calls out. He lives in this ridiculous house in Saint Paul. It's huge.

I groan internally because I can't miss the first team meal of the season. It's right before a game, so it's not like it's a rowdy party or anything overstimulating, but still., I want the alone time.

More importantly, I want the alone time with Beau so I can flirt with him. Because one thing I didn't account for with this dumb little plan of mine was how much time it would take.

Oskar walks over to me, clad only in a pair of briefs. I focus very hard—bad choice of words—on staring at his face and absolutely no lower than that. He claps me on the shoulder, pulling me close.

"You are coming, yes?" he asks, his voice lower. I appreciate that he's not using his normal booming voice to bring attention to me potentially not going. The last thing I need is a guilt trip.

Beau walks into the locker room in a state of undress, and his eyes land on me and Oskar, narrowing.

I smile my biggest, most sincere smile at Beau before turning it to Oskar. "Yeah, man, we'll be there."

Chapter 11

Beau

Milo begrudgingly hops into Darlene, and we head to Oskar's home. He eyes the dashboard warily, probably noting that a few warning lights may have come to life since we drove her this morning. I'll take her in this weekend. Nothing to be alarmed about.

We're cruising down I-94, windows cracked, wind blowing through our hair. I have the radio blasting some alternative rock, and I'm drumming my fingers on the steering wheel to the beat.

I can feel Milo's attentive eyes watching me carefully. So, so carefully.

"Did you have something you wanted to talk about?" I ask slowly, carefully testing the waters. Milo nods. I can see him in my peripheral.

He pauses for a second, choosing his words.

"Why did you make it seem that anything between us is impossible?" he asks. I can tell his words are careful, that he's testing me just as much as I'm testing him.

"I have a rule," I state matter-of-factly. "It's nothing crazy. I just don't get involved with teammates. It gets messy." I then go into a brief overview of everything that happened with Axel.

I had my first hookup with a guy my senior year of high school. We were on the same juniors team, and on the same club team all through middle and high school. It was our last year because we had both just turned eighteen.

He walked up to me after practice one day and said he saw me checking him out. I was so scared in that moment, terrified of being found out, terrified of being outed to my team and giving up the sport that made me feel alive. But instead of punching me like I thought he would, he kissed me.

I'd never kissed a guy before, and yeah, I did think he was kind of hot, so I kissed him back. I remember the flood of panic I'd felt fading to excitement as the kiss went on. The rub of his body against mine was thrilling.

One thing led to another. We were two horned-up teenagers and our horny brains just took over.

I probably wasn't as freaked out as I should have been, giving my first blowjob in a dirty locker room. I definitely wasn't as stressed about being caught as I should have been. After that, it sort of became a … thing. It wasn't a relationship. We never called it anything. We just fooled around, blow jobs, hand jobs, usually on the road or after late practices when everyone else had cleared out.

It was working fine for a while. But then I met my long-time girlfriend, Bianca, in a shared class. We started as lab partners, and it turned into more. Bianca *did* want a label. She *did* want exclusivity, so I tried to break things off with Axel.

Let's just say that Axel did not take it well.

Any time he got near me, he would chirp at me, calling me every name in the book. He didn't shy away from homophobic slurs either. He aggressively checked me during practices and would purposefully not pass to me in games. It got so bad that our coach wouldn't play us on the same line anymore.

It sucks. I lost a good friend to my horny teenage brain. I don't want to make that same mistake with my horny adult brain.

My chest grows tight thinking about how things ended with Axel. But I know I made the right choice back then. "Things always have the chance to go south, and I don't want to risk that with a teammate again. I don't want to risk that animosity with you."

I sneak a peek at him. He's staring straight ahead, his brows pinched and his lips downturned. I frown, too, because something in me hates seeing that look on his face. Hates making him upset.

"He was in love with you," Milo says matter-of-factly, like there's no room for argument. I splutter at his assertion. There's no way. "He was in love with you, and you were just using him."

"What?" My voice is a little shaky, my hands tightening on the steering wheel. "He was not in love with me." I shake my head, fighting not to close my eyes since I am driving. "There is no chance."

"He was definitely in love with you, and you both dumped him and told him he never meant anything to you at the same time."

Something akin to a million moths takes flight in my belly, and I feel dark and swirly.

Could he be right? Did I do that to someone?

I don't like feeling like this, this feeling of dread. I steal a peek over at my sunshine, and he's frowning. The swirling feeling intensifies. I hate that he thinks I'm this heartless asshole now. I hate that he could have any negative feeling toward me.

But of course he does. I fucked him and then pushed him away.

I shake my head, trying to break free from this clawing need to bring out his sunshiny smile.

Do I distract him?

"I had a lot of fun with you, you know?" I try. "It was incredible. You were incredible."

Milo nods slowly, considering my words, his mouth pressed in a flat line.

"Best sex I've ever had," he deadpans.

Fuck.

I cough, half-laughing and half-stunned. He's never had anyone else to compare it to, but he is comparing it to nothing, and I somehow win.

"Yeah, I'm glad," I say nervously, eyeing him as I pull off the highway.

We sit in a kind of stilted silence as the drive goes on. Fuck, I just need us to get there so we can get out of this truck I accidentally hotboxed with my conversation choices.

The air feels stuffy in here, and I'm suddenly sweltering. My collar feels too tight, much too tight. I roll down the windows even more and yank at my collar a little for some kind of relief—any relief, really.

What should only be maybe a five-minute drive somehow feels like twenty in the uncomfortable silence.

I did this. I made him feel uncomfortable.

We finally pull up to Oskar's ridiculous McMansion and park on the street. I've barely put Darlene into park when Milo hops out and starts walking toward the house. I watch as he walks away, that ass bouncing with every step. My lip worries between my teeth as I ogle him. Fuck, I feel like such a pervert.

I hop out of Darlene myself and trudge up the walkway, taking in the grandeur of this place. It's a Victorian masterpiece, all red brick and intricate architecture.

The door is wide open, and Oskar is waiting for me.

"Welcome, friend," he says, gesturing with an open arm into the huge entryway. I look around the impressive room, my eyes the size of saucers as I take everything in.

It looks like Oskar has leaned into the Victorian features. Smaller, more segmented rooms are connected by high archways. I walk through room after room of intimate, cozy spaces that seem so unlike the Swedish defenseman. The colors are bold, vibrant, so incredibly outlandish.

The living area is down a few steps from the entryway, through this huge, ornate wooden arch. The ceilings are high, vaulted, maybe?

I'm not, like, a real estate expert by any means. I just know it's beautiful, and it's very different from anything I would have actually expected Oskar to live in.

I think about the penthouse apartment that Davis and his girlfriend live in, in downtown Dallas. It's all sleek designs and sharp edges. This place and Milo's place are both cozy, warm, inviting.

I want to spend time here, relax here.

I think the word I'm looking for is "homey".

Yeah, Oskar's place is homey. Like, I could see him having a family here, maybe. Little blond rascals running around and wreaking havoc.

I smile to myself, imagining it.

Suddenly, those little blonds are running through a much different house in my head, their freckled faces breaking into an all-too-familiar smile.

I shake my head, breaking myself free from the dreamy imagery. I run my fingers through my curls, yanking a little just to feel something.

Am I really picturing me and Milo having kids? No, right? That would be wild.

I run into Paxton and Kirill, deep in conversation with one of the guys from our farm team, Clarke something, and two very attractive women. I'm introduced to Viviane, Clarke's girlfriend, and Angelika, Kirill's new girlfriend.

Viviane is all legs and closed-mouth smiles. She doesn't seem particularly happy to be here, but Clarke has his hand around her waist and is pulling her close. His eyes are locked in on the hand Kirill has on Angelika's ass, though. Fuck, you couldn't pay me to deal with that mess.

I know that kind of tension, the kind that simmers just below the surface, waiting to boil over. I'm living it. I make a mental note to stay out of whatever that is. Drama like that has a way of spreading.

Paxton looks completely unaware of the bubbling tension between all four people as he simply picks at the food on his plate and chatters away. I decide I'm not going to touch that with a ten-foot pole and walk past them, throwing up a little wave when Paxton calls out my name.

Brennan is chatting with a few of the younger players. They're on lines further down the list, but not for long. Those kids are fast; they'll be leading the lines in no time.

Milo is in the kitchen, fixing himself a plate.

I step through another ornate arch, and a little gasp breaks free. This kitchen is huge. It's just endless counter space, with a large island, and the fridge is massive. Lining the counters are buffet trays full of breakfast foods, the tantalizing smell of eggs, sausage, and bacon filling the air. I step in next to Milo, who has his plate filled a respectable amount.

I start piling food on my plate and try desperately to ignore the tension between me and my goalie. Normal sexual tension I can handle, but this frustrated tension, I don't like it.

I turn to look around. No one else is in the kitchen. When I turn to face Milo, he's already looking at me.

"Could we sit somewhere, maybe talk for a minute?" I ask, shuffling my feet because of my overwhelming nerves. He nods, and I let out a breath I didn't know I was holding. He turns, and I follow him through the endless rooms of this huge house. We pass so many teammates and WAGs, and we have to say hi to every single one of them. Finally, *finally*, we make it to the backyard. No one is out here, so it's just us as we plop down on the patio set.

I open my mouth to start yapping, and Milo puts up a hand.

"First, if you apologize for sleeping with me, I'm walking away. You made my first time incredible, and I don't regret it." I smile at him because I don't regret it either. I wasn't planning on apologizing for it, but I'm glad to know he doesn't want me to regardless. "Second, I'm sorry for insinuating that you were using Axel. You were just a dumb kid. You didn't know any better."

I shake my head at that.

"No, no, I think you were right. I probably need to reflect on it, like, a ton more, but looking back, there were signs that Axel maybe felt more than he was letting on. And I just wasn't ready for that with him."

"But you were ready for it with Bianca."

"To be completely fair to myself, Bianca was straightforward with what she wanted, even as a teenager. She never played any games. It's why we ended on such good terms." Which is the truth. We aren't going to be best friends or anything, but I know she has my back if I absolutely need to call on her.

"And I wasn't going to apologize for sleeping with you." I chuckle, the sound deep and a little hoarse. "I could never regret that."

He looks over at me, his head tilted down, gazing at me through those lashes. Fuck, this man has me wanting to break every rule over and over again.

Chapter 12

Beau

McFolley's Pub is packed following the game. Fans and players mingle together in the crowded bar. I'm overwhelmed by a barrage of pats on the shoulders, and "nice scoring" and "knew you were a great trade" and "great playing tonight". It's kind, but it's almost too much.

The game ended in a staggering 2–1, beating the Crushers in the final moments. I scored both goals.

I should feel invincible.

Unstoppable.

I should feel like I'm the king of the world right now.

What does not feel incredible, though? What is kind of harshing the vibe I am trying to set for the night?

The hot-as-fuck bartender who keeps flirting with Milo.

I stew in a corner on the opposite side of the bar, watching as Milo orders another fancy little alcohol -free drink from *Jamie*, who's been more than happy to help him out all night long.

Fucking Jamie.

He is a sexy twunk of a man, with a strong jawline and scruff on his face. He's dressed in a short-sleeve black shirt and dark jeans, but his clothing fits him so snugly. I can practically see his pecs. I ordered my drink from him earlier and thought he was kind of cute, even if he's not really my type. But seeing him with Milo all night...

Milo, who's still figuring out what he likes.

Milo, who's still nervous to ask for what he wants.

Yeah, that's why I'm full of bubbling rage. Because I want Milo to feel safe with his next partner. Not because I'm jealous.

Jamie runs his fingers through his curly brown hair as he laughs at something Milo said. His smile is soft, and I can see from here how expressive his dark eyes are. He's leaning over the bar, his pecs pressed against his forearms. He looks every bit the yummy bartender he's playing.

Oh fuck, it's honestly not fair. He gets to just openly flirt with my... With Milo. He gets to make that blush spread across freckled cheeks. He gets to stare endlessly into seafoam-green eyes. He gets to take care of him in front of all these people, and people just think it's his fucking job.

Because yeah, it is, but also, the flirting.

Milo must say something especially funny because *Jamie* reaches across the bar and playfully shoves his shoulder. Milo smiles a thousand-watt smile, and I feel like I'm blinded.

"What's up your ass?" Paxton saunters up to me, two drinks in his hands. He hands me the glass, and I immediately shoot it back.

"Fuck, man!" he exclaims as the burning sensation slides down my throat. "That is a sipping tequila. You do not shoot that shit back."

I start to cough a little, embarrassed at my outburst, but overall enjoying the burn.

"You're just trying to kill me, Matty." I try to laugh through the coughs, making it worse. When I look up, Milo is watching me carefully. Jamie is nowhere to be seen.

I wipe the dribble of spit from my chin with the back of my hand after hacking up a lung, and he watches the movement carefully. It feels almost sensual. As if it's just us in the room, everyone else fading away.

Is it dumb to feel that way while wiping my own spit from my mouth? Yes.

Do I care? Nope.

I let my eyes stray from his, not wanting to be too obvious with this annoying little crush, and watch as Oskar approaches Jamie. He smiles and winks, and I swear Jamie flushes, though it's hard to tell under the warm light. Oskar is such a flirt.

I snort as I scan the room again. Kirill walks over to me, with a stoic look in his eyes and a drink in his hands.

"Behave," he says with a straight face as he hands me my fifth drink of the night. "Yes?" I take a sniff, and it's more tequila. Awesome. I'm about to get wasted.

Kirill is a scary presence. He's tall and tan, with dark hair and tattoos. He's every bit the enforcer off the ice that he plays on the ice.

"Yes, yes." I laugh and hold out my glass to cheers with him. It looks like it pains him to do it, but he does clink glasses with me. Then he turns abruptly and walks away. I watch him go, letting loose a little chuckle.

He walks over to this couple standing in the corner and crowds them like he knows them. I swear I see a smile break out across his face as the three talk. I can count on one hand the number of times I've seen him smile—like, genuinely smile. He steps in close, leaning in so much that I would swear his lips are touching the man's ear.

The woman they're with rolls her eyes at them before sauntering away to the bar.

Kirill is handsome. He and that guy would look so good together.

I shake my head. That's an odd thought to have. Maybe I've had too much to drink?

I chuckle to myself, my internal thoughts rolling like credits through my head.

I stumble toward the bar, and it's fucking *Jamie* who comes over to help me, flashing that gorgeous smile. His dark curls fall in his face. He looks like a goddamn model, not a bartender.

"Jamie," I sneer at him. But my snark is overwhelmed by my drunken slur, so much so that I doubt he can even make out the sneer.

"I think you've had about enough, my friend." He smiles at me, patting the forearm that's resting on the bar.

"We're not friends," I say, hopefully too low for him to hear. The thousand -watt smile he sends my way tells me I'm in the clear.

Phew.

A few of the guys walk over to me, Milo included. I really don't like him seeing me so drunk. Shame rolls through my belly as I think about what a mess I am. Maybe I can convince him otherwise? I'm sure I could act sober if I really put my mind to it.

Milo smiles at me, hoisting my arm over his shoulder, and Brennan takes the other side. "Time to head home, big guy," Milo says, his voice chipper and entirely sober. Did he not drink at *all*?

Brennan rolls his eyes, and they start walking me to the door.

"Let's go, champ," he mutters.

"Guys, I'm not even that... I'm not... What's the word again?" I stop walking with them and ponder for a few seconds before flinging my hand up. "Drunk! I'm not even a little bit drunk."

Which is a lie, because I am, in fact, a lotta bit drunk.

Milo smiles and shakes his head at my antics. Brennan looks annoyed as hell, rolling his eyes again.

"You don't like me," I say to him point-blank. Not even a hint of a slur in my words. "You're mad because they traded Max for me." Brennan blushes furiously before shoving me into the open car door.

I knock my head into the doorframe. Fuck, that's going to hurt so bad tomorrow. Milo falls in behind me.

"I don't want to go home, Milo," I whine. He shakes his head again and smiles before turning and thanking the Lyft driver. "You wanted to take *Jamie* home, didn't you?" He splutters and squawks in indignation.

"No, I did *not*!"

Fuck, I should not have said anything.

Well, Jamie is, like, a gender-neutral name, right?

It's probably fine.

But Milo looks ... He looks unhappy with me.

"Did you really think that I wanted someone else?" His voice is kind of small. I hate when he makes himself small like that.

"I don't know," I say honestly, because maybe he did like Jamie. Or maybe I was overreacting. "I guess I do, or ... did? I don't know." I bury my face in my hands, shaking my head slowly.

I must sit like that, uncomfortable silence encasing me, for quite some time, because we're home in what feels like no time.

I tumble through the front door and head straight for that cushiony couch. Fuck, it looks like heaven. I practically dive onto it and hear a small laugh behind me. I like his laugh. Like, a lot.

"I like your laugh too," he says, chuckling.

Fuck, he can read minds?

"No, Beau, you're talking out loud." He laughs harder, shaking his head like he is disappointed in me. But that smile... Fuck, that smile kills me.

I don't want this moment with him to end. This moment of just us two, sitting here and smiling at each other.

The moment feels so clandestine, just our eyes caught in each other's stares.

"Let's watch a movie," I say, maybe a little too loudly. But suddenly I'm excited.

I'm excited at the prospect of us sitting maybe a little too closely on the couch. Of maybe my arm flinging around the back and pulling him close. Of holding him to me, never letting go.

Fuck, this is getting too mushy for me. I'm not interested in a relationship. I'm not interested in relationship things, like cuddling. But then I think about waking up next to him, holding his body to mine...

I feign getting comfortable, pushing myself away from him because I'm too scared to face what I feel. At least, that's what Bianca would say about me.

Fuck, Bianca.

Did she ever make me feel this way?

I did love her, at one point, but she never gave me butterflies. Not ones that felt more like a flock of seagulls taking off. Not ones that fluttered every time that smile was turned toward me.

When we broke up, she told me I needed to see someone because I was emotionally closed off. And honestly, it feels like she's right. She's always right about these things, and

I never do a damn thing about them. Maybe I should see someone.

The thought gets lost in a drunken fog as the night moves on.

Milo puts on some action bullshit, and we watch in amicable silence. Somehow, as the night wears on, we find ourselves drawing closer. The night finally takes me under, and I feel myself fall back. I can't find it in myself to care as I feel a warm body fall over my own.

Sleep takes me.

Chapter 13

Milo

I wake up to a warm body underneath mine and a painful crick in my neck. Beau, it turns out, sleeps very hot. So hot, in fact, that I am sticky, stuck to him with sweat. I don't even bother trying to pull myself loose, though I doubt I could if I wanted to. Beau's arms are wrapped tightly around me, holding me close to him, nuzzling into my neck.

We're both nearly naked, stripped down to our boxer briefs. Not sure when we did that. Probably around the same time I climbed up onto his lap and lay across his chest, if I'm being honest with myself.

I lose myself in his warmth, cuddling against the wall of muscle and flesh that makes up Beau. My arms squeeze around his shoulders a little. I pull myself closer to him, needing to be in his embrace. Needing to *feel* him.

I breathe in his scent, the delicious warmth and earthy undertones of cedarwood, like a fresh forest. Smoky and sweet. He fills my lungs, and I get the sudden, overwhelming desire to have him fill other parts of me.

My body heats at the thought. I don't know if that's just from rampant lust or embarrassment at my slutty thoughts.

Beau stirs, his chest rumbling as he yawns. His arm around me squeezes, and I'm suddenly incredibly aware of my bladder.

"Fuck, Beau," I groan, wiggling to get loose so I can go relieve myself. Then I feel him under me, and it's as if my wiggling has awoken the beast. His cock is rigid, and mine is plumping up to match. He begins to grind against me, and I immediately stop my wiggling. This isn't okay.

But he hits just the right spot, and I let loose the moan I was holding back.

Our clothed cocks slide against each other, and the delicious friction zaps up my spine.

I know I should stop. I know I should try harder to climb off of him. Because I know that the second Beau wakes up, he's going to freak out about this. He's going to freak out, and I'm going to get my feelings hurt.

Speaking of which...

His eyes suddenly fly open, and he scrambles to sit up, which is really fucking uncomfortable. I roll off him, my ass hitting the rug with a *thud*.

"Fuck, Beau," I groan again, but in a less fun way.

"Ha—hey." His voice is startled and his eyes a little crazed. His hair is flat on one side and sticking up on the other. His dick is still rock hard.

"Hey," I say from the floor, smiling up at him like a big blond lump. I feel so stupid for letting myself enjoy that moment with him.

"What are you...?" He gestures to me down on the ground, and I simply shake my head. I'm trying not to laugh. Or maybe I'm trying not to cry? I can't really tell.

All I know is my eyes burn and my chest is a little tight. But I'm smiling at him. I'm smiling at him, so he smiles back. And I quickly look down and let a tear fall for this ruined moment together.

"Fuck, last night was brutal." He reaches his arms up in a stretch that expands his chest beautifully. I want to lick the divots of his abs and around his pert pink nipples. I watch the muscle ripple, and the layer of fat he has looks so biteable.

Instead of acting on my frankly carnal desires, I nod slowly.

"Yeah, last night was a lot of fun." I let loose a yawn, which in turn gets him yawning.

"Did you... Do you not drink?" Ah, that was one of the questions I was waiting for. It came a lot later than I thought it would, but I'm ready all the same.

"Yeah, I don't drink."

"During the season?"

"Ever."

"Oh."

A pause, a beat.

"Damn." Beau looks at me with wide eyes. "I had my first drink when I was eleven." He laughs at my look of shock and waves it off. "I wasn't drinking like crazy. My dad just would pour me a drink whenever he had one." He sighs. "Which wasn't that often because he really wasn't home much."

"Your dad would..." I trail off, unsure of how to respond to that. "He would pour you a drink when you were eleven?"

He waves me off again, letting out a bit of a chuckle at my concern.

"Really, it was nothing. You're making a bigger deal than it needs to be." He continues to smile, but I can see the strain in his eyes. I know he doesn't want to talk about this. Just something in me is screaming to keep poking the bear.

He stretches again, all that beautiful muscle extending and lithe before my very eyes, and I've suddenly forgotten what it was I wanted to bug him about.

Horrifying parenting, who?

It explains the heavy drinking, I guess. It's completely normal to mirror what you saw growing up, and if you haven't been told that's not normal, why would you think any differently?

"Why do you look like that?" Beau asks, his face twisting slightly in confusion. "You're making the same face you make when you find all the edge pieces for your puzzle." That makes me laugh.

He's fighting what we have so hard.

"Nothing, I just didn't really understand why you drank so much last night, but I get it now."

"Whoa, what?" he asks, eyes bugging and brows furrowing. Did I say that wrong? "What do you mean by that?" His arms cross over his chest. He looks so upset.

Fuck, I definitely shouldn't have said that.

"I didn't mean anything bad." I throw my hands up in defense. "I just meant you were mirroring your dad's behavior. That's totally normal. I do it."

His eyes squint, and his face gets red. It's not a sweet blush, though. It's absolute rage.

"I am *nothing* like my dad," he shouts, hands clenched into fists at his sides.

My hands fly up to protect my face. I don't even think. I just move. I don't know why I respond like this, but something about his shouting makes me feel like I need to protect myself. I haven't seen him angry before, and I don't like it.

"I'm sorry," I whisper. His face relaxes slightly from the pinched rage.

We both stand there for a moment, letting the heated air between us cool off. He's breathing hard, and I'm holding my breath. Finally, Beau speaks.

"I'm sorry I yelled." His voice is steady, calm once again. "I shouldn't have yelled at you."

I nod slowly.

"I'm sorry I said that about your dad," I whisper. He shakes his head.

"It's not that. I just don't want to be like my dad." He plops back down onto the couch, throwing his head back and closing his eyes. "My dad is just not a good man. His drinking wasn't even the worst thing about him. It was mostly that he was never there. Growing up, he was never home." He sighs and rubs his face vigorously with open hands. "When he was home, he was mean." His head pops up, and he looks at me. "He never hit me, but his words cut fucking deep."

I nod slowly, absorbing his words, letting them fill me.

I hurt him.

"I won't say anything like that again," I promise.

But I think to last night. To his drunken jealousy. What am I getting into?

An hour later, I'm asking myself the same question, this time while staring at Darlene's rusted frame.

"Why do you need to drive?" I ask, eyeing *Darlene* and scrupulously seeking out any reason for us to not take this old-as-sin truck. Beau rolls his eyes.

"I need to drive her every once in a while, or her battery craps out." That's not the only thing that's gonna crap out... I eye the old rust bucket, nervous to get in but not wanting to piss off Beau any more than I already have. So I climb into the truck, and send up a little prayer to whoever the fuck listens for those.

Our car ride is tense. Silent, save for the sound of Darlene's tires tearing across gravel. I want to talk to him. I want to say literally anything to him. I just worry he was too vulnerable last night with me, then again this morning. And now he's closing himself off.

Suddenly, a loud *ruh... ruh* sound comes from some-where in Darlene's belly. It's like a weird, hesitant cough, or maybe like she's (fuck, I sound like him) clearing her throat to say something important. I look around us, glad we're almost at the arena, because I would bet money that the important thing she has to say is that she's going to die.

There's this weird hiccup in the engine, as if Beau's let off the gas. I look over and see the RPM needle twitching. The power dips in waves, surging and dropping. There are these uneven chugging and metallic rattling sounds, and something misfires in the engine.

A squeal, like a stuck pig, sharp and angry. My hands fly to my ears, immediately overwhelmed by all the sounds and stressed by the impending doom of a vehicle careening to its end.

Even if that careening is probably overdue and definitely expected.

With a clunk and a shudder, the engine cuts out while we roll to a stop right in front of the arena.

Dead silence.

I chance a look at Beau, and his eyes are wide. He looks fucking devastated.

"Darlene?"

His hands grip the steering wheel like he's clinging to his own life and not the life of his truck.

"Beau?" I ask carefully, worried to startle him. Our teammates, all walking into practice themselves, stop to watch the spectacle.

He's trying to turn the key, but nothing is happening. No click, click, clicking. No turnover.

He looks over at me, big fat tears in his eyes. Fuck, I guess I didn't realize how much she meant to him.

His eyes say all kinds of things as I look into them.

But mostly, they say what we both know.

She's gone.

Chapter 14

Beau

Milo leans over and whispers to me, "You know, you could probably pay to have her fixed." His hand finds the small of my back and gives it a tiny, almost squeeze, like reassurance. He's interrupting my phone loudly blaring *Ave Maria*, which is rude, but he's cute, so I'll let it slide.

"Shhh," I hiss back at him, finger to my lips.

We're standing side by side at a scrapyard, dressed in our funeral best. Honestly, we probably look kind of ridiculous. Milo is wearing a black cashmere sweater with black suit pants. I'm wearing a full black suit, down to the black button-down and dark wool overcoat.

I'm sweltering.

We look laughable. I realize that, but ... but I'm sad. Like, genuinely sad about this truck.

Darlene got me through one of the toughest years of my life. And then she got me through the subsequent difficult years. I still remember the day I got her.

That was one of the single best and worst days of my life.

I had been saving for months to finally be able to buy myself a car. It had been a difficult few months, especially when big chunks of my earnings kept disappearing. I knew where it was going, but I didn't dare call him out on it.

I took the bus to the dealership that day. The sun was high in the sky. Montreal is beautiful in June. It was my big night, and I wanted to reward myself for the accomplishment.

Drafted at eighteen—not a miraculous feat by any means, but there were rumors that I was one of the best rookies coming into the league. I knew what that meant. I was stoked about all the possibilities.

But I was there alone. So I decided to do something, alone. I made a decision to head to the nearest used car lot and buy myself something with my own money, money that I had worked hard to earn. Money that I'd managed to keep hidden from my dad.

My dad has always been impossible, not just with his incredibly brilliant drinking ideas for his child, but with money too. He would constantly steal my money for his extracurricular activities, gambling his life away.

So when I got there ... there she was. This beautiful, dark green 1994 Ford F-150 XLT. She drove like a dream.

I had exactly enough money to buy her. I remember feeling so grown up driving out of that dealership in my amazing new ride. I drove her straight to the draft, where I was the number three draft pick.

I named her for my grandmother, my mom's mom.

I only knew my grandmother as an adolescent. She passed over ten years ago, but she was a good woman when she was alive. The kind of mother figure I desperately wanted my mom to be. The kind of mother figure who wanted me around.

So, of course, I named the symbol of my independence after her.

It was when I drove her home that I found out my mom had left. It was in her that I drove for hours looking for my mom. It was in her that I got the call from my mom telling me she never wanted me, that she was going to start over and I should just forget about her.

I should say that now.

I should say all of that now, here, with him. With someone I'm quickly considering one of my closest friends. But my words feel stuck.

I steal a peek at Milo, and he smiles at me. It's a sweet, tender little smile. It's a smile I don't want to ruin by talking about my mom.

I don't want to let her ruin anything anymore.

My ringtone blasts through the silence between us, interrupting the song.

I look down at my ringing phone and see *his* name. The sun is beating down on the back of my neck as I stare at the phone in my hand. I stare at the caller ID.

Dad.

Dad.

Dad.

Fuck it, I guess. I pick up his call, unsure what even to say. I point to the phone, and Milo nods as I step a few feet away, standing on the opposite side of Darlene's carcass.

"Dad." My voice is strained.

"Squirt!" His voice is so jovial, he must be on a winning streak. He's also never called me "squirt", not once in my life. "Hey, buddy, how are you?"

I hate that he does this. Every time, he does this. Tries to shoot the shit with me. Tries to talk to me like we're a normal family who just talks to each other.

"I'm great," I lie. No, no way. He wants to talk to me like a normal-ass dad, then he gets the real shit. "Actually, no. No, I don't know why I said that." I sigh, running my hand down my face in exasperation. "I'm really not doing too hot right now. I'm actually kind of bad, I guess."

"Oh." He's not used to reality sneaking its way onto our calls. He's going to have to try and pivot to keep up. "What's going on? You want to talk about it?" I can practically hear him begging me not to. But he asked, so I'm gonna tell him. I walk back toward Milo because I suddenly feel so dumb for walking away.

"Darlene died." My eyes tear up again, and Milo reaches out and hands me a goddamn handkerchief. I side-eye him, but I'm grateful.

"Your grandma?" he asks stupidly. "She died, like, nine years ago."

"Ten years, actually, but no. I meant my truck." I can feel when I start to curl in on myself. My hands start to shake, and my stomach feels flippy. But more importantly, I feel Milo standing next to me. I long to just lean into him, have him put his arms around me and just hold me.

Instead, he stands close. So close I can reach out my pinkie and loop it around his.

"Your truck?" he asks slowly. I know exactly what he's going to do. He's going to treat me like an idiot, like a moron. He always does this to me.

"Yeah, Dad, my truck. The truck I've had since I was drafted." The truck I got when Mom left. But I don't say that because I can't form the words with my useless mouth.

"Okay…" The silence draws out. I guess he's not going to just come out and say it.

"What do you want, Dad?" My voice is clipped. I don't really have the patience for whatever it is that he needs, but I know I have to help.

"I just need an advance this month." I sigh. There it is.

"Yeah, Dad, sure, whatever." I'm more consumed by my finger entwined with Milo's than I am with my dad's desperate plea for my money. My pinkie slides up his, along the side of his hand before sliding back down and entangling itself again.

He doesn't even sound ashamed to be asking like this. I guess when I'm enabling him the way I am, he has no reason to feel shame with me. Maybe I shouldn't…

"Thanks so much, kid." His voice has an edge to it. "It was just so expensive putting you through hockey when you were growing up. I appreciate you paying me back."

And there we go. That's why I always put up with his bullshit. His guilt trips.

"I already said I would send it, Dad," I bark into the phone, annoyed and embarrassed. I don't know if Milo can hear what my dad is saying. "I'll send it tonight."

"No, no," he barks right back. "I need it now. Like, right now."

Fuck.

That means he's in deep and probably about to get his kneecaps busted. I pull my hand from Milo's, suddenly feeling incredibly empty, and I move back around Darlene.

I pull my phone from my ear and get to sending my dad the money. Anything to get out of this uncomfortable situation. I peek over my shoulder, and Milo is being very intentional about not looking at me. I pay the man and walk back around Darlene.

Bless him, Milo is standing where I left him on the other side of Darlene.

I suddenly feel exhausted.

My dad has hung up, and *Ave Maria* is playing again on my phone.

Suddenly, all of this feels stupid. I want to leave, and I want to pretend we never came.

I say as much to Milo, but he puts a hand up , the other grabbing my arm gently.

"I think it's making you feel better to say goodbye to her."

Her.

Not it, her.

I take a deep breath. He's right, of course. Having this dumb little funeral does make me feel a tiny bit better. Having him here with me, though, makes me feel like I can actually move past this.

I walk a little closer to Darlene and run a hand over the dark green paint of her hood. She was a great truck. She got me where I needed to go, and she helped me land on my feet when the rug was pulled out from under me.

I pat the hood.

"Goodbye, Darlene. Thank you."

The drive home was quiet. The days after were quieter. The days come and go without incident. I sent the money to my dad as soon as we got home from the funeral. He doesn't thank me. What's new?

But as it always does, the ice calls us home.

Grief, I'm quickly learning, does not pause for hockey, but hockey helps the grief.

It is a new day, and we're set to play against the Columbus Mammoths tonight. Our rivalry with them isn't huge, but they've always been better than Minnesota. Than us.

I have to start thinking of myself as part of the team because I am. This is my team; this is my family. And if we're going to keep winning, I have to mesh with this team like they're my family.

These are my brothers.

I push onto the ice, ready to face off against the Mammoths. I look back to where Milo is mucking the crease. He slides back and forth, his skates roughing up the ice. He looks like a sweet little kitten making biscuits. I smile, my cheeks heating as I continue to watch him. I smile despite myself.

That one is definitely not my brother.

Definitely.

Chapter 15

Milo

We're back at McFolley's Pub to commiserate over an embarrassing loss against Columbus. The Mammoths skated circles around us tonight.

I let in seven—*seven*—*goals*.

Embarrassment creeps up my neck as red-hot heat overtakes my face. As I look around at my teammates, the ones who decided to come out tonight, I can't help but commiserate.

At the end of the game, everyone came to give me head pats and hugs, and I felt so dejected that I didn't even get to enjoy it like I usually do.

I've never really felt the need to drink, and tonight is no exception, really, but I kind of get it. I get why the other guys are drowning their sorrows. I long for something, anything, to numb my embarrassment.

I feel like a failure. Number two draft pick? I'm sure Minnesota is regretting their decision tonight.

"Tough night?"

Jamie's voice is a cool balm on my frayed nerves. I don't know what it is about him, but this guy is seriously soothing. Something in his presence? It was the same after the game against Chicago. He just walked over and soothed me with his sweet words. I wasn't quite on edge like I am now, but it feels nice all the same.

"You have no idea." I groan, dropping my head against the bar with a thud.

"Shit." He chuckles, the sound low and honey-sweet. "That bad, huh?"

"Was bad night for us all." Oskar comes up behind me, patting my shoulder solemnly. "We all have off nights, yes? Is not your fault."

I look up at him and smile. He's a good teammate. It's nice of him to try and make me feel better, but his kind words aren't really the ones I am needing tonight. They aren't the ones I long for.

But when I look at him, Oskar isn't looking at me. He's watching Jamie, who is, in turn, refusing to make eye contact with the giant Swede. My eyes skate between the two for a minute, trying to sus out whether this is animosity, indifference, or something more.

"You want another club soda?" Jamie catches my eye, and for a second, I worry I'm caught being nosy. But he just winks, and I sigh in relief before nodding.

Since when do I care about my teammates' business? Especially something as private as whatever is happening between these two. It's literally none of my business.

But something is definitely happening between them. Oskar is practically mooning over Jamie, hearts in his eyes. I guess I can't really blame him. Jamie is incredibly handsome. His dark curls and bright eyes, and that smile. Not my type, really, but handsome all the same.

Speaking of smiling, I search the bar for my favorite smile. My favorite smile on my favorite face.

I could use any kind of pick-me-up.

But I don't find it. What I find in its place is an ugly scowl.

He throws back a shot, and the scowl takes over his whole face. Eyes pinched and lips downturned in almost a snarl. My lips curl downward, incredibly displeased with his reaction. The loss was ugly, for sure, but does he blame me?

But he's not really frowning at me. Our eyes aren't meeting. Where is he looking?

"You hungry, handsome?" Jamie has a tray in his hand, looking at me over his shoulder. His brow is raised, and

I'm acutely aware of Oskar's eyes on me. They're boring a hole in the side of my head that I'm trying to ignore.

"A basket of fries for me and my friend." Oskar smiles at Jamie again and winks, but Jamie ignores him, looking at me for confirmation. I nod, and he flashes me his pretty smile. It's all teeth and almost too wide, like he's trying to prove a point. Like he's trying to say his smile is for *me* and not for *anyone* else.

Oskar sighs as Jamie walks away, watching him wistfully. I want to tell him he's being obvious, to warn him, but a small part of me wants him to step out into the spotlight. For him to be super obvious so that maybe I can hold Beau's hand in public. So maybe I can kiss his cheek and have it not be the end of the world.

I want everything that comes with coming out. I'm just so scared to be the first. So, yeah, selfishly I want Oskar to be thrust into the light so that I can stand in the sun and enjoy the rays on my face.

But do I really want him to be burned so I'm safe? That doesn't feel fair.

Jamie brings the basket of fries and plops it down between me and Oskar, who immediately tucks in. I pick at them gingerly, suddenly not very hungry. I feel distracted by a scowl and angry eyes.

I still haven't seen Beau smile tonight.

What is he mad at?

I steal another glance back at him, but he's still not looking at me. He still is not looking at me, and he still has a nasty scowl on his face.

I may not have seen him smile, but I have seen him throw back drink after drink. I know he's a grown man who can make his own decisions, but I'm starting to worry.

He does a line of shots with the rookies, all of them laughing. But he's swaying, as if the wind outside is carrying him to and fro.

He stumbles a bit, running into a booth, where a couple looks up at him warily. Everything in me itches to go save him from the embarrassment. Because, fuck, he *is* embarrassing himself. Someone needs to get him out of here, and I want it to be me.

I push myself to standing, and Oskar turns to look where I am facing. When I go to move, he puts a hand on my shoulder. He's shaking his head.

"I think that would just make things worse, my friend," he says to me, voice low, not wanting to bring attention to the spectacle. I cringe a little. He's right. If I tried to walk over there, it would just draw attention, but I hate seeing him like this. Seeing him fall apart and lose himself to drinking.

I wanted to numb myself tonight.

Beau apparently wanted to forget tonight entirely.

It seems like, win or lose, he wants to lose himself to the drinks and the night. I think back to that game we played a while back when he absolutely destroyed the other team. We were on fire. Still, he drank himself to oblivion.

Is this something we're close enough for me to concern myself with?

I peek over my shoulder and watch him. He's talking with Paxton, who's not quite as trashed, but still drunk.

The two are laughing together, each holding a drink—some kind of beer, maybe? I can't believe they're really still being served. They're absolutely sloshed.

When I turn back around, Oskar is watching me. I raise a brow, and he shakes his head.

"You are judging him," he says. He doesn't ask because he doesn't need to. He just knows. "That will not help him."

Fuck.

He's right. Of course he's right. I stare down at the half-eaten basket of fries in front of me. I'm being a bad friend to him. If I can't even be a good friend, how the hell can I expect him to want me to be a boyfriend? The thought lands like a slap. I want to be more than his friend, and being more starts with being better.

I pick up a fry and pop it into my mouth, letting the salty flavor distract me. Instead of focusing on the negatives of him drinking, I can just work to make him feel better. I can work to show him how well I'd take care of him.

Because I'd take such good care of him. I'd treat him so right.

I decide once and for all that I'm going to take this man home and take care of him.

"Oskar." I turn and look at the Swede. He smiles at my use of his actual first name. He's told me in passing he hates his nickname; he thinks it's stupid. "I'm going to gather Beau up and get him home before he accidentally does something he regrets." Oskar lifts a brow. "I'm not judging him, but I know he's going to judge himself."

And he will. I know he'd hate to know how he was behaving.

I push myself up from the bar and turn toward my man. He's still laughing with Paxton, but when he catches my gaze, his eyes turn to molten heat. I feel my body react to the absolute blazing stare we are under, but he's not getting any action tonight, not from anyone but my own hand at least.

When I'm finally standing in front of him, he kind of just collapses into me, as if he finally feels safe enough to let himself fully fall apart. Paxton, drunk off his ass but not so much that I can't wrangle him to help me, gets one of Beau's arms over his shoulder. We're hoisting him out of here.

As I'm walking out, I make eye contact with Jamie, who winks at me and stifles a little smile at the giant hooligan I'm helping out of here.

I drove tonight, so Paxton helps me get him into my car. I started it ahead of time, so the BMW is blasting cool air, and the water bottles in the front seat are waiting. Once I have Beau buckled in, I gently coax the water into his hands and then into his mouth.

Fuck, he's going to be hurting tomorrow.

The drive home is quiet, Beau not having as much to say this time around. He's just looking down at his hands in his lap.

After a few minutes of complete silence, he finally speaks up.

"Are you upset with me?" he asks, his voice kind of quiet, a little scared.

I shake my head vehemently.

"No, no, of course not," I try to reassure him, but I can't really look at him. I can't see if my words are hitting their mark, if I'm making him feel better at all. I drive a little fast, pushing the speed limit so we can hurry up and get home, so I can take him in my arms and make him feel like everything is okay.

"Jamie likes you." He says this matter-of-factly, and I don't care for it because I don't care for Jamie the way I care for him.

Jamie is cute, but he doesn't set off butterflies in my stomach the way Beau does. He doesn't light up my day with his smile. He has a nice voice, but his laugh doesn't make my heart skip a beat.

He's not Beau.

He'll never be Beau.

I wish there were a way for me to say that without scaring him off, without potentially ruining everything.

"Maybe he does, but I don't really care for him." I hope that gets my point across without going into the deeper bits.

"Oh," he says, a secret little smile upturning his lips. "But you talk to him all night."

I chuckle a little.

"He's the only one who knows how to make my mocktails." I throw a smile Beau's way. "I may not drink, but I still want to fit in on nights of such epic fucking losses." I groan and pat the steering wheel in my frustration. "Seven. Fucking. Goals."

I let in seven goals. Seven. The number circles my head like a vulture.

His hand skates down my back, running in soothing circles. Even when he's blasted out of his mind, he's so kind and caring.

I wanted to show him how I could take care of him, but it turns out he's the one taking care of me.

Chapter 16

Beau

I wake up feeling heavy. Heavy *everywhere*. My limbs are weighted down by my choices from last night, and my gut is churning like the open ocean is sloshing around in there. Most importantly, though, my eyelids are glued shut, fused together with gunk and sleep and bad decisions.

I try to stretch, to yawn and force my eyelids apart, but the movement makes my stomach lurch, and suddenly I'm scrambling to the bathroom. My feet slide comically against the hardwood and across the tile as I fall to my knees with a crash. I empty the contents of my stomach into the toilet, which, if I remember correctly, consist purely of bottom-shelf vodka and cheap beer. I don't think I even got a greasy hamburger to soak up the alcohol at any point in the night.

"Are you okay?" Milo stands just outside the open door, not really looking in. I wouldn't want to see this mess either, so I can't really blame him. But fuck, what I wouldn't give to have him running his fingers through my hair or in big circles on my back.

"I'm—*burp*—" I lose the internal battle again, spilling my metaphorical cookies into the toilet. I was going to tell him I'm fine, but clearly that's not true. Clearly I'm a sloppy, hungover mess.

To my surprise, Milo actually walks into the bathroom and crouches behind me. He rubs soothing circles on my back, shushing me and my incoherent blubbering. Tears run down my face, and he wipes them away. I want to lean back into his touch, but another bout of vomit spills out of me. The tears spring back to my eyes.

I hate throwing up.

So much.

"Let me go get you something that'll make you feel a million times better." He abandons me, and I continue to groan into the porcelain bowl, burping and puking in tandem.

I hear a loud whirring that feels like nails rattling around in my head and continue to upchuck every ounce of alcohol I threw back last night. Fuck, I feel disgusting.

When hangovers were created to punish us for having a good time, I wonder if anyone imagined it would feel like the reverse of the night before. Instead of throwing drinks back, I'm throwing them up.

Lovely thoughts to have with my head buried in a toilet.

When I'm finally, *thankfully*, done vomiting everything I've ever eaten or drunk, I stumble out to the kitchen. The romantic sunlight is practically blinding. I cover my eyes and hiss a little.

His laugh, normally one of my favorite sounds, screeches through my skull.

"Shut up, you banshee."

"Hurtful," he mutters, but I swear my hearing is supersonic right now. I can pick up every hitch of breath, every clink of kitchen equipment, and every whispered word.

He slides a glass of the nastiest-looking liquid I've ever seen toward me. I lift it to my nose and give it a cautious sniff.

Huh.

It smells pretty good, actually.

I pinch my nose, ready to throw back the most disgusting-looking drink ever.

He walks around the island and pulls my fingers away from my nose. I try to shake him off, but he laughs again and really looks at me. His eyes say *trust me*, and I want to. I want to believe he won't hurt me, that he's safe. So I do.

I let him hold my hand as I throw back a drink that looks exactly like what I just threw up.

The drink is shockingly bright, spicy, fresh, and smooth. There's a sweetness that tastes almost tropical, followed by a warm, zippy sharpness. He lets go of my nose and I keep gulping.

"What is this?" I ask, staring down at the half-full glass.

"It's this hangover cure I've made for the guys after a particularly rough night." He lists off the ingredients. "The ginger helps with nausea, and orange and lemon help with liver support. Turmeric does too. The pineapple helps with inflammation, and the cucumber helps with hydration. Finally, the coconut water and salt bring the electrolytes." He lifts the container of juice again, and I nod fervently, holding out my glass for a refill.

I sip the rest of the juice while he messes with something on the stove.

"What are you making?" I ask, walking up behind him and leaning my head against his back. He's shirtless in the kitchen again, like he is every morning, but something about this morning hits me differently. My mouth waters a little as I take in my roommate's bare, muscled back, glistening in the morning sunlight. Sunlight that was excruciating to look at only a moment ago.

He pauses, his arm halting mid-motion with the spatula, and I can feel him take a deep breath before he starts moving again, shuffling something around in the pan. I lift my head and rest my chin on his shoulder, looking at the source of the delicious, salty smell.

Hash browns.

Thank all that is holy and good.

I grab his face and kiss his cheek with an exaggerated smack.

"Thank you, Milo. Thank you, thank you, thank you." I need greasy potatoes like I need to breathe this morning.

He laughs, looking at me out of the corner of his eye, a wicked grin taking over his face. It curls his pretty lips and crinkles his eyes. His face looks so naturally lovely like this.

"Seriously, this is exactly what I needed this morning." I look down at the open carton of eggs and start peering around for another pan.

"What are you looking for?" he asks.

"I'm going to help with breakfast," I say matter-of-factly. I crack an egg into the pan and immediately the shell crumbles in. "Fuck." I reach in and fish it out. "I swear I can handle scrambled eggs."

I feel the flush starting at my chest, like a warm hug that rises up my neck and blooms across my cheeks. I tuck my chin, trying to hide it from him. He doesn't seem to notice, so I keep breaking *eggs* into the pan.

We stand there, side by side, in a gentle silence. My head no longer feels like it's ringing like a bell, and I can simply enjoy the company I'm in.

He continues to push around the fried potatoes while I push around the scrambled eggs, and I feel fucking good just standing here next to him.

"So," Milo starts. I can hear the wariness in his voice. He's bringing something up that he desperately doesn't want to talk about, something he thinks I don't want to hear, and I have a feeling I know exactly what it is.

"Don't—" I try to start, but he raises a hand to stop me.

"I know"—he tries again—"that you probably don't want me to bring this up." And he's right. "But I think we should talk about it."

I roll my eyes internally, maybe externally too.

"I know," his voice is a bit exasperated, "that this is the last thing you want to talk about this morning."

"So why are we talking about it?" I ask, throwing my hands up in irritation. He's not wrong. I really don't feel like talking about it. Something about last night just brought out something bad in me, and I drank too much. That should be the whole conversation.

"It's not good to hide behind drinking, Beau," he states matter-of-factly.

And I know he's right. Mom would always hide behind her chardonnay, and Dad certainly still does. But that's not what I'm doing.

I've always enjoyed a drink with the boys after a game, win or lose. Celebrate or commiserate. And I want to be friends with these guys, not just with Milo.

And sure, yeah, I was a little heated watching *Jamie* flirt with him. It made my blood boil. But that's normal, just jealousy. Not something deeper.

I'm an only child. I don't like sharing my toys.

I tell Milo just the bits about wanting to make friends, not the parts about Jamie. I'm sure he got enough of my sad blubbering about that last night.

Our moment is interrupted by the sudden, blaring ring of my phone. I jog back to my room to grab it from the side table and groan when I see Christian Grady's name lighting up the screen.

I almost don't answer. I want to stay here in this bubble of hash browns and gentle silence. But the name on the screen makes my stomach drop.

Fuck, my agent.

I slide my thumb over the answer button and bring the phone to my ear.

"Grady, hey," I say, feigning interest in whatever the hell he's calling about. Honestly, he's probably about to lay into me for last night's game. Who needs shitty parents when I've got a shithead agent ready to pick apart everything I did wrong?

"Benny," he starts, and I don't correct him. It bugs me, sure, hearing the old nickname, but not enough to pick a fight with a fifty-year-old man. "We've got some things we need to talk about."

I sigh and brace myself, ready for the hit.

"Look, kid," he says, sounding... nervous. And suddenly, I'm not so sure where this is going anymore. "I can't be your agent anymore."

Everything screeches to a halt.

Because I may not like the guy, but he's been my agent since juniors. He was a friend of my mom's who signed me as a favor to her.

And until now, he's kind of been my only connection to her.

"What—"

I can practically hear him lift a hand to stop me.

"Kid, I don't want to get into the logistics of it. Just trust me, I can't be your agent anymore." He sounds exasperated, as if *I'm* the one causing problems here. As if he's not the one dropping me without a single explanation.

"I know I played kind of shitty last night..." I start, but he cuts me off.

"It's not your gameplay. You were on fire."

He's not wrong. We may have lost, but it wasn't because of anything I missed. The other team just played better. But...

But now I know for a fact something is up. He never compliments me, and now I know why. He's been waiting for an excuse to cut me loose.

"What is this?" I ask, determined to figure it out. Determined to understand why this man is firing me completely out of left field.

There's a long, drawn-out silence. So long I almost ask him again.

"I'm seeing Bianca, and it—" He's still talking, but nothing else is registering. All I can hear is this faint buzzing as his words settle.

"Wait, what are you saying?" I press the phone hard against my ear, my face pinched. There's almost no way I heard him correctly. Because if he really is saying that he, a man in his fifties, is sleeping with Bianca, a woman in her mid-twenties, I'm going to lose my shit. Did he take advantage of her?

Of fucking course he did. The old creep. God, I should have fired him ages ago.

"It's a conflict of interest," Grady's smarmy voice explains. Fuck, has he always sounded like such an asshat?

"You probably should have been more conflicted about fucking my ex." I somehow manage to keep my voice calm despite the fact that I'm teeming with rage. I can feel my face getting hot and my brows pinching.

"Please don't talk about Bianca—" His voice is dripping with condescension, but I'm not about to let him continue.

"I'm not gonna shit on B for being taken advantage of, you old prick."

This conversation isn't going anywhere, so I hang up on him. I guess I need a new agent.

I don't know if she wants this. If he pursued her, or if she... No, I can't think like that. She deserves better than me assuming the worst.

I dial Bianca, the number still memorized from years together.

"B, I just got a call from Grady. Can you call me back? I'm not mad, just concerned." I try to keep my voice level, but I know some of the frustration is leaking in.

I was wrong earlier. Turns out this was what I didn't want to talk about.

Chapter 17

Milo

I sit at the table, tucking into bland eggs because Beau forgot to season them, and listen as he chats with his old teammate. He's asking some guy, Davis something, to have the Dallas WAGs check in on Bianca.

"See you later, man."

Oh fuck, we're playing Dallas tomorrow. I wonder how weird it must feel to play against former teammates like that. To forecheck former linemates. To chirp at players you once considered brothers.

I obviously have nothing to compare it to, but I can't imagine I'd be gracious about one of my exes sleeping with my own agent. Though Miranda is incredibly professional, so I doubt she'd actually do that to me.

Beau finally sits down and throws his head back in frustration.

"Fuck, what do I do now?" he asks no one in particular, but I'm all he's got, so I give him an answer.

"We need to get you a new agent, I guess." I shrug, already planning to type up a message to Miranda and see if we can set up a meeting.

"We?" he asks.

"Of course." I look up, and he's staring at me. "What, like I'm just going to let you scramble through this alone? We're friends, Beau." I roll my eyes, but secretly hope he doesn't latch onto the word "friend" too hard.

We're not just friends, baby. We are much more than that. So much more.

He takes a big bite of eggs and makes a face at me.

"What the—"

"You didn't season them." I shrug, having already decided mine were a lost cause and sticking to the greasy hash browns.

"Jeez," he huffs, "like, at all? This tastes bland as hell." He tries another bite before shoving them aside, like I did, and tucking into the potatoes. Once he gets a big, crispy bite into his mouth, he moans. "These, you did perfectly."

"Nuh-uh." I put my fork down with a loud clink. "You are not blaming those eggs on me. You made them." He stares at me, eyes wide.

"Oh fuck. Yeah, I did, didn't I?" He smiles, eyes crinkling at the corners as he laughs. He tries mixing them with the hash browns and makes a face. "I really fucked these up, huh?"

I laugh with him because it's dumb, but making bad breakfast together was nice. A lot nicer than I thought I could have for myself.

"Okay, look," I say after a few moments of amicable silence. "My agent is great. Miranda Mason. She's taken great care of me, and she represents several of the other guys on the team. She's also married, so I doubt you'll have to worry about her sleeping with your ex."

"Well, I only have the one ex, so unless Miranda suddenly moves to Texas, I think we're in the clear." Beau smiles, and I'm glad he can be so open talking about something that made him uncomfortable only moments ago.

"Practice is this afternoon. Let's swing by early and see how much we can talk about. I'll message her and ask if she's available to meet us." I pull out my phone and send that exact message to Miranda.

We get into my car, and I think Beau must get some kind of flash of déjà vu from last night, because he's suddenly acting very shy, very quiet. He's blushing, pink spreading across his cheeks and down his neck. I keep my eyes on the road, not at all distracted by the gorgeous man beside me.

"I'm sorry about last night," he says quietly. I nod slowly, unsure which part he could possibly be apologizing for. I ask him as much, and he gets even redder. "How drunk I got. I was jealous."

"You were jealous?" I ask carefully. I'm unsure where he's going with this. Could we really have made a breakthrough already? There's no way, right?

"I was jealous of how much attention Jamie was giving you. Of how much attention you were giving him."

Oh.

Oh.

This is better than I could have hoped for.

"I see."

"Especially after last time, when you assured me you didn't have feelings for Jamie, there was no reason for me to go off on a jealous bender the way I did." He sighs, slumping into his seat a little. "I'm sorry."

Fuck, this is some serious growth. I hold all my excitement inside and just nod along.

"I forgive you," I say finally. "Maybe next time, just come sit with me instead of stewing from across the room. We can share some fries."

"We shouldn't, though, right?" he asks, and I'm confused. He just admitted that he likes me. That he was jealous last night because a bartender was flirting with me. "We should just be friends, right?"

I laugh, trying to keep the pain out of my voice when I respond.

"We're just sharing fries, not swapping spit."

Fuck, why does this hurt? Two steps forward, one step back. The cycle, over and over, and I'm willing to put in the work, but my feet hurt. I just need to sit for a moment and rest.

"I'm glad you came in." Miranda is staring at her laptop, keys tap tap tapping away as she edits a contract for Beau. "Christian Grady isn't a huge name in the industry by any means, but I've heard of him." She makes a face, wrinkling her nose. "He did you a favor. You're better off without him, in my professional opinion, and I'd say that to his face." She points at Beau, making sure he's listening to her.

Miranda Mason is a powerhouse of a woman, all five foot four of her. I'm a big believer that size isn't everything, and she's the reason why. She's saved me from being screwed several times in major endorsement deals, and she's a fucking wiz with my finances. Watching her face off with major brand-name lawyers has been a really fun pastime of mine.

Her skin is an umber hue, darker toned, and her hair is cut short. She once described to me what went into caring for Black hair textures. I was blown away by the amount of product she said she needed just for the pixie cut she keeps hers styled in.

Her large, red-framed glasses sit on the very tip of her button nose. She's young, only in her early thirties, and one of the people I admire most.

She finally stops typing and prints out the contract before walking it over to the desk we're sitting at.

"You take whatever time you need to look this over." She pulls out a highlighter and begins marking different sections. "These are the terms of our professional relationship, this is the commission structure, and this here outlines my responsibilities." She hands it over to Beau.

He looks over at me, question in his eyes.

"She's not going to screw you. She takes great care of me and some of the other guys—Paxton, Brennan, Oskar. But we can get the team lawyer to look it over if you'd like."

He shakes his head.

"No, I trust you." He sets it down on the desk and signs.

Miranda smiles at both of us.

"You know, you both are so nice to look at. We should look into some joint endorsements. I bet some of the heavy hitters would be interested." She walks back around and sits at her desk before launching into a list of brands that we should try to sell to together.

I can picture it, us doing commercials together, ad campaigns, photo shoots. We could build an empire.

I watch Miranda carefully, trying to take in her words as I picture the universe she could help us build.

I wonder if I should come out to her.

I wonder if Beau would want to come out to her.

"Can we have a moment alone?" I ask, interrupting her spiel. She stops and smiles at me.

"I'll step outside. Just holler when I can come back in." She walks out the door and it clicks carefully behind her. I turn to look at Beau.

"We should tell her," I say with gusto, suddenly very excited about the prospect of coming out.

"Tell her what?" he asks, wariness in his eyes.

"About us!" I exclaim. I might be a little too excited about this.

"Us?" he asks, eyes widening.

Oops. Too excited. I mean about us being queer, obviously, but the words slip out before I can catch them. Us. Like we're already something.

"Not us us. Us being queer," I say quickly.

"You think she'd be cool?" he asks, raising a brow.

"I think her wife would have some issues if she wasn't," I retort, laughing a little. "She can help us come up with a game plan, a worst-case scenario plan. Come on." I grab his hands and squeeze. He stares down at where our hands are joined, and I almost let go, but he squeezes back.

"Okay, yeah," he says, nodding slowly. "Let's do it."

"Miranda?" I call out. She comes back in, nudging the door shut with her hip before walking over to her desk. Before she can even sit down, I blurt out, "I'm gay!" If she's surprised, she doesn't let it show.

"Me too," she says. "Well, I'm bi."

"Me too," Beau adds for good measure.

She looks between us. I can feel my face heating with embarrassment at my outburst. I was excited a second ago, but was this too much for one day?

"So," she asks slowly, carefully, "do you want to come out publicly?"

"No," Beau and I say at the same time.

"Okay then." She settles into her chair and begins typing again. "We'll just make a game plan for if and when you do. If you're outed, any scenario you can think of, we'll plan for it."

I let out a breath I didn't realize I was holding.

The game against Dallas has settled into a tense, grinding rhythm. There haven't been any goals yet, but definitely not for lack of trying. I watch line after line form their attack against Dallas's goaltender, only to be stopped short every time.

The rest of the team is feeling the heat, the pressure piling down on them. But me? I'm soaring.

I'm locked in, tracking the puck cleanly, squaring up to every shooter. My rebound control has never been sharper, swallowing pucks and steering shot after shot away. But we're in the third, and I know Dallas is about to get desperate. The number two team being shut out by the number seventeen team? Unheard of.

I'm quickly proven right. Dallas keeps sending shot after shot, all designed to test me harder and harder. Point shots through traffic, quick low wristers looking for rebounds, one-timers off the rush. Nothing gets past me.

This is the game of my life, one that will be shared on highlight reels for years to come. I've had clean, beautiful save after save.

I've never felt better than I do at this moment. I feel on top of the world, like this game would fall apart without me.

The clock is ticking down, but I know not to count them out for even a second. It's late in the third. I'm still in top form, but Dallas is turning up the pressure.

I see the rush. I know it's coming, but I still don't expect what happens next.

One of Dallas's defensemen drives the net *hard*. He crashes into the blue paint, spraying me with ice. Honestly, he's much too close for comfort. I try to stay focused on the puck and not on the giant body in my space.

I keep my stick down, my pads tight, eyes tracking a loose rebound.

But this man... He *wants* attention. He plants himself firmly in the crease, crowding me. His shoving is subtle but effective, pushing and prodding me. His stick knocks against my skates, trying to throw me off balance. It's blatant goalie interference, but no calls are being made.

He shoves me again, and I stumble a little before catching myself.

I'm five seconds from losing my cool and decking the guy when Beau explodes out of nowhere. His hand digs into the defenseman's jersey, yanking him backward. He pulls him clear of the blue paint and shoves him hard.

"*You don't touch my goalie,*" he seethes, his teeth bared.

Chapter 18

Beau

"Protecting your boyfriend, Benny?" Erickson taunts, spitting onto the ice and shoving into me. "I always knew you were fucking queer, you fag." I see red. I never got along swimmingly with Erickson, but jesus christ. The guy never said anything like that to me before.

We skate around each other, circling like hungry sharks. I smell blood in the water.

Gloves hit the ice, and we crash together, all fists. I shove into Erickson again, grabbing at his jersey. He's easily got a few inches on me, but I drive my helmeted head toward him anyway. I throw punch after punch, catching his temple, his jaw. Just pounding into him.

"Benny!" I hear the familiar voice of my former teammate and best friend, but I can't stop myself. I feel Davis's hands digging into my jersey as he tries to pull me off of Erickson. "That's enough, man..." he says, but I turn, fueled by adrenaline and lost to tunnel vision, and I deck him. It's a clean punch, straight across the jaw.

I feel bad, sure, but I mostly feel rage.

I turn back and keep wailing into Erickson's face.

Whistles are blowing all around me, the crowd rife with cheers, jeers, and boos. I'm so lost in my rage, I can barely register them as more hands grab for me. The linesmen pile on, trying to yank me off him. He's on the ground, his face bloodied and swelling in an odd way. It's very possible I knocked a tooth loose.

I'm finally yanked away from Erickson, a linesman using a solid, firm grip on my collar to maneuver me back. Fuck, when did I punch Davey? I see my best friend—former best friend now, I guess—clutching his nose as it gushes blood. Fuck, I did that?

I don't feel regret, per se.

But I feel...

I feel not great about it.

The ref is down at center ice, calling the penalty and calling for my ejection.

Fuck.

Yeah, I should have expected that. Or at least, I would have if I'd been able to see anything beyond red rage. Watching Erickson rough up Milo the way he had...

I skate toward the tunnel, a scream building in my throat.

I can't protect him from here. I can't do anything from here.

The roar of the crowd fades to a dull hum as I push through the gate. Each step down the tunnel feels heavier than the last.

I feel all the rage drain out of me with each step. I head to the locker room where Mia is waiting.

"Beau, what happened?" she asks, shaking her head. She eyes me warily, her arms crossed.

"I don't want to talk about it," I reply grumpily.

"You're going to have to get over that real quick, buddy," she says, pushing my face down into the massage table's face hole. "We were tied 0-0 with the number two team in the country. Your coach is going to have some words with you, and they're going to be loud and they're going to demand something."

She's right, and the rubdown she gives is the least re-laxing massage I've ever had because all I can think about is the reaming I'm going to get when Coach comes back here.

Fuck, the last thing I want to think about is how mad Coach is going to be when he gets back here.

I can already hear his voice. Not yelling, never yelling, but that disappointed tone that somehow feels worse.

When she's done, I rush back to the shower, ready to just enjoy the steaming hot water and some time alone for once.

The water cascades down my sore body, hot and red against my skin. I push my face under the stream and groan. It feels incredible. My body aches from the fight, muscles tight and rippling under the stream.

My mind wanders as I stand there. My hand wanders, too, dragging soap and suds down my abs and stopping just short of... No, I can't do that here.

My hands slide the suds back up my abdomen, enjoying the slick glide of my wet skin.

But then there he is. I can practically see him, a stunning vision. My mind paints a vivid picture of him. I see his pretty pink lips part on a gasp. I can perfectly envision him laid out on his bed, the sheets a rumpled mess beneath him. His blond curls fall wild around his flushed face.

The look on his face when I pushed his knees up, the gorgeous sounds he made as I worked him open with my tongue.

I have no control of my body. My hand grips and squeezes my aching dick. I give it a slow, languid stroke as my mind continues to wander.

Fuck.

Suddenly, I can see it, him, almost perfectly, on his knees here in this shower with me. The hot water turns his pale, freckled skin a heated pink. He looks up at me with those wide, princess-green eyes. His pretty pink lips are parted slightly, his chest rising and falling with each stuttered breath.

I reach out and would swear I can feel his face, those wet curls beneath my fingers.

For a moment, I let myself believe it. That he's really here.

I hold my dick out for him, painting those plump lips with my precome. His tongue slips out to lick it clean before the water can wash it away. We didn't get to do this the other night, but it's all I can think about.

Milo.

On his knees for me.

Ready and desperate for my cock to slide down his throat.

Ready and desperate to swallow my come.

I bet he'd be just as eager to take my cock in his mouth as he was to take it in his pretty little ass. I bet he'd have a smile on his face, his eyes hungry as I slide past those luscious lips.

My grip around my dick tightens, almost punishing. When I let go, it bobs and jerks like it has a mind of its own. It feels possessed as I think about Milo.

I shake my head, trying to break free from the pretty vision of him on his knees, but I can't.

I can practically feel the tiny, featherlight kisses he presses all over my hip bones, my pelvis, and my balls. They tighten, and my hand pulls back. I want this to last. I want this dream to never end.

Just like I never wanted it to end when I sank into him that night. I haven't even been looking for an apartment the entire time I've been staying with him. Not once have I even browsed the list that Paxton gave me when I first moved here. I've never called a real estate agent. I have no plans to.

Dream Milo meets my eyes as he *finally* flicks the tip of his tongue out, connecting with my slit, licking up the bead of precome.

"That's it, baby," I say to my fantasy, "don't waste a drop."

Gripping my cock in one hand, I tap it against his lips again, loving the feel of that lush flesh. They part, and I push into the red-hot heat of his mouth. My hand tightens as my imagination runs wild. Fuck, I can practically feel his eyes on me as I start to fuck his face.

I look down, and sure enough, he's watching me through his lashes.

Fuck, why does this feel so real?

His tongue swirls around the tip, licking and sucking at the head before taking me deep, all the way to the back of his throat.

I know my time here is limited. The game is almost over. None of this is real. I can't have it, even if I want to. Even if I'm desperate for him. Even if I'm so desperate for him that I'm conjuring him in the locker room shower for one of the best blow jobs of my life.

Is that sad? That the best blow job I've ever had exists only in my imagination?

That I can almost perfectly feel his mouth wrapped tight around my cock?

Fuck, but I want him...

I want him so bad.

I know I can't have him.

I know, I know, I know.

But why can't I? Why can't this moment be real? Why can't every little moment with him be real and mean something?

I mean...

It does mean something.

It means something to me.

Does it mean anything to him?

The rule. The team. The fear of ruining this the way I ruined things with Axel. There are a thousand reasons. But right now, in the steam and the silence, none of them feel heavy enough.

I push my cock all the way into his mouth and I swear I can feel it hit the back of his throat. I swear I can feel that.

That this is real.

That *he* is real.

As my hand slides over my drenched cock, over and over, I get closer and closer to the edge. As I get closer, my fantasy becomes less and less tangible. His mouth becomes my hand. And as I spill over the locker room shower floor, I know that I would give absolutely anything to make this real.

I stand there, water spilling over my head, my curls drenched and my skin flushed from the heat. I watch as my come slides down the drain.

I can't believe I actually did that in here. I walk toward the bench and dry myself off, getting dressed in my suit. My hair is still sopping wet, soaking the collar of my shirt. I can't hear the cheers and jeers from the crowd all the way in here, so I sit and imagine the worst.

I left my team in a tricky spot against one of the best teams in the league. They're going to be so mad at me.

Milo is going to be so mad at me.

I drop my head into my hands and sigh.

What have I done?

Chapter 19

Milo

The locker room is somber as we dress down from the game. Sad men in various states of undress surround me.

We ended up losing in overtime, 1-0.

It was, of course, Davis who got the game winning goal.

The puck rimmed hard around the boards and popped loose at the bottom of the circle. Davis collected it on his backhand, head up just long enough to sell the shot. And I bought it, dropping early, sealing the ice.

All it took was one quick toe drag, pulling the puck through Oskar's skates, shifting it from backhand to forehand in one smooth motion. Oskar's stick swept through empty air. I lunged across, scrambling to recover, but he was already sliding past the post.

The fucker, instead of shooting, delayed, just a fraction too long for me to reset.

Then he slipped the puck in between pad and post, banking it off the inside of my skate.

I felt like I let down the whole team.

It was my fault. I know it was. After watching Beau walk down the tunnel, I was a wreck. They probably could have just skated right up and slid the biscuit in the basket with no problem. I couldn't focus, not with him gone and his teammates *knowing*.

Because they were acting like they knew exactly what had happened between us, like they somehow knew every intimate detail. They teased and poked at me, chirping about something they knew nothing about.

Because they didn't. They couldn't.

There is no way they know anything. Not anything beyond speculation.

Beau wouldn't have told people like that. He wouldn't have trusted them with our secret. I honestly don't think he's trusted anyone but me with the fact that he's bi. Definitely not anyone on his former team, in the homophobic capital of America, Texas.

I don't think he would have, not the way he wailed into Erickson.

Erickson, who was the most unbearable all game. He had a lot of slurs he wanted to throw at me.

I just look at the swelling where Beau punched him and take a deep breath. I picture Beau there, punching him again and again, and it makes all the slurs roll off like water off a duck's back.

Honestly, it's a miracle I didn't let in more pucks with how hard Dallas went after my apparently *faggot* ass. But this fag locked them out for a whole game, and it was only in overtime, only because Beau was gone, that they got one past me.

They were feeding off the energy on the ice. The energy Beau put out in the rink with the savage way he protected me.

Fuck, the way he threw Erickson off me was so intense, so heated. Thinking about it now makes my cock jump a little. Thank God I'm still mostly dressed at the lockers and not completely naked, dick swinging in the showers.

I can only imagine how embarrassed I'd be getting caught hard in there.

I'm only in my base layers, a moisture wicking compression shirt and leggings, my cup hiding the obvious chub I have. The pressure against the plastic builds as I keep daydreaming about Beau.

The rage in his eyes was electric, a jolt straight to my groin and, somehow, to my heart too.

There's movement to my right, and Kirill is there, shuffling nervously. He has his phone in his hand, typing out what looks like a full paragraph to someone. I must be feeling some kind of nosy because I recognize the name.

Clarke.

He's a player on our farm team that I've seen hanging out with Kirill and this tall woman I assume is one of their girlfriends.

He's kind of adorable, with big, unassuming eyes that look like they see everything, even things that may not be there. His smile is small and secretive. His hair is absolutely wild, not curly, just a longer mess on his head.

Kirill is typing a mile a minute, and as I watch him, I suddenly realize I'm basically eavesdropping. I immediately school my features and look away, back toward my locker.

Kirill is an interesting man. Tall, covered in tattoos, but so quiet, always keeping to himself.

He looks up and catches my eye, dropping his phone to his side and meeting my gaze.

"What?" he says, his accent thick. I smile at him, but he doesn't return it.

"Nothing, just... Sorry. I accidentally saw your phone." I point down to the offending piece of technology. "Haven't seen Clarke since we recalled him a few weeks ago, right? How's he doing?"

Kirill's eyes narrow, his shoulders squaring.

"What?"

"Sorry, Kirill, I just saw you were texting him. Clarke Wyatt, right?" I take a small step back, because somehow I keep saying the wrong thing if the ragey look in his eyes is anything to go by.

"What do you mean by that?" he asks, his voice steady, quiet but firm.

"Um..." I start.

Kirill's eyes stay on me, waiting. I have no idea what to say.

Then I see him out of the corner of my eye. Beau. He's standing, talking to the PR team and Coach Waldor. I'm sure they're trying to come up with a way to spin this as a positive.

I apologize to Kirill, who just grunts at me and goes back to his phone. Typing a mile a minute.

I hear "highlight reel" thrown out, and I know that'll fix it. Hockey fans love a highlight reel of anything, even fights. Even if they'll have to dig for quite some time to find any other fights of Beau's, because Beau doesn't fight. At least, he never did when he was playing for Dallas.

I could probably count on one hand the number of fights he was in when he was in Dallas.

But here, in the land of hockey, he's suddenly a different player. A player who fights. A player who fights former teammates. A player who fights people he was once friends with.

Our gazes meet as I walk to the showers, and I feel a thousand pounds lighter.

His eyes say *I'm sorry*.

And I believe him, but part of me is sad about it. What is he sorry for? Is he really sorry for protecting me? Maybe he's just sorry for the mess he made?

I can barely hear Coach laying into him. That's one of the things I like about Coach Waldor. He is always able to get the point across without eviscerating your entire being.

Don't get me wrong, his tirades are devastating. They are just at an appropriate volume. There's nothing worse than being screamed at in front of everyone.

"I know no one touches the goalie, but maybe leave that type of mentality to Volkov or Jagger." Coach pats his shoulder gently, as if he's afraid he'll spook him. "We just can't risk losing you in a game this tight."

I know it wasn't just that mentality. I heard all the nasty vitriol Erickson was spitting. Not just at Beau, but at me as well.

I go through the motions of undressing as I think this through, walking toward the showers for a quick rinse before we leave.

I stand under the hot stream of water and let my mind wander. Beau isn't the kind of guy to get into fights just for the sake of it, right? So I need to chill the fuck out and accept that he got into this fight for me. He fought his former teammates for me.

He has feelings for me.

Now I just need to hear that from him.

An hour later, and I'm still waiting to hear that from him. The silence in the truck is louder than any words. The car ride home is tense, the air between us heavy. Beau has been heavy-handed on the wheel like this ever since driving home in his brand-new F-150. I tried explaining to him how bad of an idea it was to get another truck, even a strong, capable one like Buck (his words, not mine) for the icy winters of Minnesota. I tried explaining fishtailing to him, only to be extremely alarmed to find out he not only knew about it but was, quote, *very good at getting out of it*, unquote.

Beau alarms me, in almost every way imaginable. The way he behaved during the game tonight. The way he came to my rescue. I think what alarms me the most, though, is how much I wanted it, how much I want him. Because I want him.

I want Beau.

Fuck, I want him so bad.

I know I want him, obviously. That's what this whole plan was about, wanting him. Teasing him. Showing him exactly what he could have if he'd just admit his damn feelings.

If he would just say he wants me just as badly.

If he would just be honest with himself.

If he would just be honest with me.

I think his feelings were pretty clear tonight. Pretty obvious in how he protected me. In how he burst into the crease like a demon -possessed man. The rage I saw in his eyes. The rage I saw as he pulled Erickson from the crease. The rage that overtook him as he pounded his face, into someone that just a few short months ago, he was teammates with.

He did that for me.

He did that because of what he feels for me.

He didn't just do it because he's a passionate player. He's not that kind of guy.

I guess the only way to know for sure is to test the waters.

I look over at him carefully, and he's staring daggers at the car ahead of us. I want nothing more than to reach out my hand and take his, squeeze it, and tell him I'm here. Tell him I *saw* him tonight.

"So," I start, dipping my toes in. "That was some game tonight."

He scoffs—legit scoffs—at me.

Wow.

His shoulders are tight and high, and he clearly is not happy about tonight. I guess I should leave it be?

The night air is cold, but he has the windows cracked anyway. Icy air blows around our faces, filling the cab. My eyes tear up, but it's only because of the air blowing in my face and has nothing to do with that scoff.

I should have guessed that he wouldn't want to talk about it. That he would be about as thrilled to talk about his outburst as I was to see the aftermath.

But I don't want to let him get away with simply scoffing away his problems. I want him to face them, and I want him to face them with me. I'm not going to let him shut me out. Not tonight.

I open my mouth to say something else, but it turns into a scream. The hum of the tires vanishes, replaced by a thin, hollow hiss, as if the road has turned to glass. The truck sways, just slightly but enough that my stomach drops before my brain can catch up.

My scream is all I can hear as the truck slides.

Chapter 20

Beau

Milo is screaming, his eyes glued shut, and his hands have the "oh shit" handle locked in an iron grip. He looks so damn scared. The wind is rushing through the crack in the windshield and blowing through his blond curls. His cheeks are flushed a dark pink from the chill, and maybe from fear, and his mouth is dropped open in a wide grimace. I don't want this to be the last time I see him. I don't want this to be the last way I see him.

A lot of thoughts run through my head, scary thoughts and big declarations that I'm nowhere near ready to admit to even myself, let alone the man next to me. So I try to tuck those back into my brain before they somehow make it out of my mouth and into the open space between us.

We're careening down a short hill when the brakes suddenly decide to start listening to me, and we stop at the very bottom. We don't crash into anything. We simply stop.

Milo is still screaming. Maybe I'm screaming too? I don't know anymore what's going on. All I know is that heat is flowing through my veins, and I feel both terrified and also incredibly alive.

The screaming melts into the rush of the cold wind.

We've both quieted, the cab full of our heated breaths. We both are just staring ahead, not really looking at anything, but feeling everything. I know he feels it too. He has to. How could he not?

Even though the windows are cracked and it's a brisk night, I feel nothing but heat coursing through my limbs. Every inch of my skin feels electrified, and I want to zap him with my touch.

"Are you okay?" I ask, my voice barely a whisper, but in the quiet night air, I know he can hear me. I've rolled the windows up slowly and locked the doors. My adrenaline is pumping furiously, coursing through my veins. My breathing is heavy. *In and out, breathe, breathe.*

The windows slowly fog with each heated breath.

Fuck.

Looking at Milo...

The way he looks just sitting there, breathing every bit as hard as I am, a bead of sweat dripping down his temple... I watch that drop of sweat with fervent hunger. He swallows, audibly gulping, and my eyes flick to watch the way his Adam's apple bobs.

I want to bite it and then lick the marks.

I want him.

I want him *now*.

His eyes meet mine. In the fogged-up cab, with our hearts still racing from the crash, there's no space left for doubt. Only want.

There's a loud click, and then my seatbelt flies free and I lunge across the truck cab, our mouths crashing together. His hand snakes around my head, holding our faces together as his tongue plunders my mouth. We explore each other, hands mapping out our bodies.

His hand gropes my chest, tweaking my nipple through the flannel. He gives the piercings a gentle tug. I cry out.

Fuck, these clothes have got to go. Now.

I begin pulling at his shirt, yanking it up and away from his body. He recognizes what I'm doing and begins to help me, pulling it over his head and tossing it into the back seat. My own shirt I rip open, the buttons flying all over the console and the dash, but fuck it if I care. When his hands finally press against my bare chest, flesh against heated flesh, I practically growl my approval.

The pants are another story. I push off him, back to my own seat, and begin furiously unbuckling and pulling down my pants. I motion with my head that he better start doing the same. In my mind, I imagine ripping them from his body, and my cock twitches at the thought.

Fuck, I'm so turned on thinking about this man.

Once we're both entirely undressed, I jump back into action. The center console, thank goodness, is pushed out of the way, and I pull Milo with me back to my seat. Pushing the seat back as far as it'll go, he straddles my lap.

"Is this okay?" I ask, gripping his ass and rubbing him against my swollen length. He nods his approval, and I groan. "Fuck, baby girl, I've been wanting to do this all night. I've wanted you all night." I moan into his ear. I rifle through the door-side compartment and pull out a small packet of lube. Milo raises a brow at me.

"Were you expecting this?"

"I'm a regular boy scout, baby, always prepared." I wink at him, before pulling his face back down to mine to meet in a searing kiss. He laughs against my lips, and I smile back, pressing our joy together.

I like laughing with him. I like making him laugh. I like this, us, more than I should.

I lube up my finger before running it through his crease until I find his slutty little hole.

"Is this pretty pussy hungry, baby girl? It wants to gobble up a big fat cock, huh?" My finger runs tight circles around and around his hole before pushing against the ring of muscle. He mewls at the sudden and delicious pressure. I know he loves it, the pressure, the sting, so I push until it pops into him.

"Fuck, baby, yes," he whines.

My finger moves in and out of him, fucking him open. Passing over his prostate and making that pretty boy sing for me. Both of our cocks are at full attention between us, weeping and begging for any kind of touch.

I press another finger against his entrance. "Okay?" I ask. He nods, and I push into him, his whine answering the stretch.

"Ride my fingers, baby, take what you need from me." I whisper the words, my voice hoarse with desire. He begins to bounce on my fingers, and my cock loves the view. It's weeping so much there's a pool of precome on my belly. I cannot wait for him to slide that delicious hole down my dick and bounce like that on it.

"I need your dick," he begs so beautifully, and fuck, I immediately want to comply.

"One more finger, baby girl," I concede, a little desperate myself. "You need to be all stretched out so you can take my cock."

I push said finger into him, and he howls, grinding his hips back and forth, pressing my fingers against his swollen prostate over and over.

"Please, baby." His begging, fuuuuck… Yes, it does it for me. I'm about to shoot my load all over myself just from listening to his pretty words. "Please, please fuck my pussy."

"We don't have condoms, sweetheart," I tell him, and his eyes fall open. He looks at me with fire in his eyes.

"I haven't been with anyone else," he says hurriedly. "My last test results were negative."

"Mine were too." I pull him in for a kiss.

I pull my fingers free and whip out another packet of lube. He laughs, the sound loud and free, because this time I pull it from the door handle. What can I say, I really am always prepared. Lubing up my cock, I line it up with his welcoming entrance.

As I push in, my head knocks back against the headrest, and I let out a fervent moan.

Fuck, he feels like sliding home.

"This okay?" I ask, pushing in inch by inch. He nods and mewls, happy little sounds pouring out of him.

I'm buried balls deep in no time, and he squeezes around me.

"Fuck, baby girl, give me a second before you do that. I don't think I'm going to last." He responds by *squeezing again*, the little shit. "Baby, I swear, this will be a lot less fun if I blow my load in point two seconds."

He chuckles. Such a little shit. A brat if there ever was one.

Finally, *finally*, I'm able to start moving. I give my hips an experimental pump, thrusting up into him, and he throws his head back and groans. I bite my tongue, smiling at him as he starts to bounce. His cock bounces and slaps against his stomach with each bounce. His hands find my thighs, and he bounces harder, riding me like I've never been ridden before.

"That's it, baby girl, ride 'em." I whoop loudly, and he throws his head back and laughs, bouncing harder, faster. He looks so beautiful like this, so free. A lovely flush spreads up his chest and across his face. His freckles stand out like beacons in the pinkening skin.

My hands find his hips, and I maneuver his body from bouncing to a steady grind. He whimpers as his ass moves steadily back and forth against my hips. I let out what sounds suspiciously like a growl into his ear, and he shudders.

I'm so dangerously close to the edge already, the adrenaline pumping viciously through my veins, this sexy man bouncing on my cock...

"Milo, sweetheart, I'm right fucking there. You gotta slow down."

"No," the little brat counters. "I'm right there too. Fuck, please, literally just breathe on my cock and I'll come" my pretty brat demands of me.

"That's right, baby girl. Of course you're right there. My little come-hungry slut is so ready for release, isn't he?" He whines in response, staring down at me, flushed all over, and his cock leaking precome so much that, if I didn't know better, I'd think he already came. His balls are drawn up, and I know he's right. All I have to do is look at his bouncing dick and it'll go off.

My fingers wrap roughly around his dick and give two experimental pumps, and sure enough, he screams, ropes of come shooting all over my chest and face. I let out a surprised burst of laughter as I'm covered in his release. A loud gasp, almost.

His orgasm causes my own to shoot off as his tight hole begins milking me for every last drop.

The thought of my seed filling his hole does something deep to me, my chest swelling a little at the thought of stuffing him full and making him keep it in there. I wish I had a plug with us.

A truly prepared scout.

I'm storing that away as a thought I should maybe keep to myself.

I want to own him. In every way.

A flush that I'm hoping I can just write off as the exertion of sex spreads across my face, but I know it's so much more than that. Fuck, I want to mark this man in every way possible. I want him to be marked as *mine*.

I want him, I want him, I want him.

Milo, unaware of my internal turmoil, crashes down on top of me, my softening cock still stuffed in his ass.

His chest is pressed against my own, his hard nipples rubbing against my pierced ones.

"Fuck, you were amazing," he says, and I swell with pride. Car sex is no easy feat. *Anal* car sex at that. It did feel incredible for me. I'm just glad it was as good for him.

He kind of flops off me, sliding into the passenger seat lazily. I let out a tiny whine at the thought of my come sliding down his thighs. I want to push it back up into him.

I want him well bred, stuffed full of my seed, dripping and desperate.

I reach down and slide my pants back up, not bothering with my shirt. Milo does the same.

Do we talk about it?

I pull us back onto the road, and we're sitting in amicable silence for quite a few minutes.

Right when I'm about to give up on us talking, Milo takes a deep breath and blows it out slowly.

"So that was…" He pauses, collecting his thoughts. I wish I could see the expression on his face. "That was good, right?" He sounds almost shy about it, as if he's scared of my answer.

"It was so good, baby," I say, ready to reassure him, but he cuts me off.

"No, not the sex. The sex was great, obviously, but … we … we're good?" he asks, kind of slowly. I'm not entirely sure what he's asking, what he needs from me right now for assurance.

Does he mean…

Are we…?

We pull to a stop at a red light, and I look over at him. I watch his eyes as he watches mine, reflected in a pool of red until that light flashes to green. It's only then that I know exactly what he means.

And I have to wonder that myself. Are we good, the two of us together?

What are we becoming?

Chapter 21

Milo

"You look nice." Beau is spread out on the couch, one of my books in his hands. He has these slutty little glasses on, and I internally groan.

He's shirtless, gray sweatpants slung low. His belly button ring is in, and it glints in the low light of the lamp on the side table, as do those slutty nipple piercings.

He sparkles.

He's going to look so mad when I tell him where I'm going.

It's been a week since the truck sexcapades, and Beau has been especially quiet. I assume I stressed him out with my questions. Now it's time to amp things back up and get him back on track.

My heart clenches up as I think about just telling him. About maybe being honest with him about this whole thing. About telling him how I feel and how I want him to feel about me.

About how I know he feels about me.

Because after that night in his truck, the way he held me as he fucked me, I know he feels something for me.

He has to.

And then I think about what we've talked about. About his rules. About his fear of connection, and I decide to stand tall and continue with my plan. I know he'll be upset, but I know this is the push he needs.

"I, uh … I matched with someone." Despite my desire to be resolute, my voice is barely above a whisper. I guess I'm a bit more chicken shit than I realized. I stare down at my toes, watching them shuffle absently.

"You what?" His brows shoot to his hairline. My eyes meet his, and I swear I see hurt in them. But I blink, and it's gone, replaced by rage. The anger takes over his whole face, and I barely recognize him.

"I… I have a date." I flinch at my own words, suddenly hyper-aware of how I might be hurting him. Am I hurting him?

I don't want to hurt him.

"A date?" he asks. The hurt mixes in with the anger.

"A date." I nod, almost solemnly.

"A date." The question is gone, and all that's left is quiet indifference.

Fuck.

Okay, fuck.

That actually hurts.

I knew he would be upset, but for him to act like he doesn't care? That stings so much more.

I turn and rush from the room, not wanting to look at him anymore. Not wanting to see him hurt. And worse, not wanting to see him not care.

"You don't drink?"

Wilder looks at me, his green eyes large and expressive and confused.

"I would have picked a different place if I knew."

I wave off his concern.

"This is great. Don't worry about it." I gesture around us at the bar we're in. Mara is bustling around us, filled with the tangy and spicy smell of Mediterranean food and delicious drinks. Wilder laughs a little, the sound deep and warm, like a hug.

"I mean, thank god for their mocktail menu, but I figured based on the club we met at that a bar was a safe bet." He picks up the menu again, and I take a moment to admire him.

He's good-looking in an easy, unstudied way, with his messy auburn hair, a sheared short beard, and broad shoulders filling out a faded shirt. He stands out, hair wind-tousled and green eyes sharp. Handsome in a textbook way, but definitely not my type.

No, my type is dark curls and amber eyes, warm skin and smiles.

But despite what I told Beau before I left, this isn't a real date, and everyone here is aware of that.

Wilder is the guy who tried to dance with me at the club. He's "poked" me on Grindr, whatever that is supposed to mean, and I recognized him. We chatted, and it turns out we have quite a few things in common.

We talked at length about our older siblings. His brother, fifteen years his senior, acted for him as Violet did for me. He made all the mistakes growing up and told little Wilder about them. What Wilder learned was very different and ended up not being as big a lesson for the young and very gay man. Though, I suppose "be careful about having unprotected sex" is a universal truth. The only difference is that Wilder won't have to worry much about knocking anyone up, since he's a big ol' beefy bottom.

Still, he got a really cute niece out of the deal, so not the worst lesson to come out of that.

It was when we started talking about our parents that things got a little too uncomfortably similar.

"Coming out to my parents was a disaster." He laughs, clearly not too traumatized by it. "My mother cried."

"My mom cried too!" I exclaim excitedly, maybe a little too loudly. The people at the table next to ours side-eye us, but the woman smiles, so I can't have been too disruptive. "My dad was all stoic and disappointed."

"Yeah, my parents are kind of a piece of work." He chuckles, shaking his head. "But obviously you understand the woes of unsupportive parents."

"My parents aren't necessarily unsupportive." I laugh nervously, thinking about the phone call I had with my mom earlier today. She laid into me when I accidentally let the gay-friendly club incident slip.

"You seriously want to come out that way?" she asked me. Like I could be clocked immediately going to a bar that's queer-friendly. I still haven't even told them about Beau, so as far as she's concerned, I went alone, but I guess somehow that's worse in her eyes.

"They would think you're going to pick someone up," she whispered, as if Dad hearing would be the worst thing in the world. When I pointed that out to her, she scoffed. "You really want your dad embarrassed?"

The "more" in that sentence was implied.

But was that how I wanted to come out to the world? After all this time hiding in the closet? Was that how I wanted to be outed, to be thrust into the light like that?

No, I thought. No, I want to come out on my terms. I want to come out because I want to come out. I want to call a press conference or post a statement, give an interview with a magazine, I don't know. I just want to be able to live my life. I want to be able to fall in love and not have my mom freak out on every phone call.

I want to tell my family about Beau, even if there's nothing to tell about. I just want to share with my parents that I might be falling in love. And more importantly, I want them to be happy for me.

"So." Wilder smiles at me mischievously. "Obviously this isn't a date because of a certain someone." He winks at me, and I can feel myself blush furiously. "What does he think you're doing tonight?" He tucks into the meal that's just been placed in front of us.

"Uh…" *How do I explain this?* I think to myself, suddenly realizing I might be kind of an asshole.

Wilder stops with his fork inches from his mouth, staring at me.

"What does he think?" he asks again, putting down the food. His brow is up in his hairline, and his lips are quirked in question.

"Um..." I start again, schooling my features and playing with my plate. "He maybe thinks I'm on a date," I say, my words barely above a whisper.

"Milo Hall, he does not." His words aren't loud, but damn, they are stern.

I lift my hands in panic, trying desperately to shush him.

"Did you really tell him that?" he asks again in complete exasperation.

I explain the whole plan to him, starting from the Grindr setup and every subsequent idea. Although, I'm starting to think of them as bad ideas from the way Wilder is rolling his eyes at me and shaking his head.

"Milo, no!" Wilder stares at the ceiling, his head thrown back in exasperation. "Milo, I understand that the situation you both are in is not ideal, but you have to be honest with him about how you feel."

"But what if he—"

"Good point, yes, but also what if he doesn't?" He crosses his arms and stares at me, drilling the point in through sheer will.

Well, he has me there.

I sit back and ponder his words. Am I being unfair by automatically assuming that Beau can't change, that he can't grow? Maybe, this past week, he was waiting on me just as much as I was waiting on him.

I have to tell him how I feel.

The drive home is blue. All I can think about is his face when I said the word "date". The hurt I caused. The hurt I felt when he didn't seem to care.

I push through the front door slowly, suddenly nervous about what I'm gonna find. I can hear him pacing, the shuffle of his slippered feet against the hardwood. I'm suddenly a lot more nervous than I was.

"Beau...?" I call out, unsure if I have any other words for him beyond his name. What do I do? Do I beg for his forgiveness? Do I tell him everything first?

I've never felt so nervous in my life. Not before my first game as starting goalie. Not before the day he moved in.

Then I think about the moment we met. I think about turning around to amber eyes and dark curls. I think about that thousand-watt smile. Will I get to be on the receiving end of that smile ever again? Will he forgive me?

Do I forgive myself?

I won't if I lose him over this.

He's starkly quiet from the living room, and I'm stuck stagnant in the entryway.

Fuck, I can do this. I can do this.

I can tell him.

"Beau?" I call again, my voice a little surer. The shuffling has stopped, he's gone quiet and I'm sure I can feel his anger radiating throughout the house, bouncing off the walls. It bounces around and around, circling my head as I take a step forward until finally it hits true, smacking me in the face, and I blanch.

I'm standing in the entrance to the living room, and there he is. He's standing there, and he's staring at me. His jaw is clenched, and his eyes are narrow. And he doesn't even know yet. This is just... this is just because he thinks I was on a date.

There's this part of me, a super teeny-tiny, small part, that's kind of relieved that he feels like this because he thought it was a date.

Fuck, the relief is so tiny, I swear.

"Beau," I say again, and his eyes close. His eyes close, and he sighs, like my words are a balm.

"Milo," he says slowly, carefully. My name is a whisper on his tongue, a balm to my own burning heart. "How was your date?"

The word "date" is filled with so much contempt, so much anger, that it feels like ice has been poured over my head.

I stand there, absolutely doused, my emotions flaring. I notice that Beau is swaying a little, and then I notice a half-empty glass sitting on my side table. Fuck, is he drunk?

I take a stuttered step toward him, reaching out a little with my hand, wanting desperately to feel him. To feel the warmth of his skin. I wonder if he was drinking. He's angry, and I want desperately to fix it. I want to make him feel whole and happy and, honestly, sober. I want to take away the pain he needed to drown in a drink.

Why did I do this? Why did I mess with his feelings like this?

"So how was it?" he asks again, his voice still contentious. I hate hearing him like this, the sound of his voice grating on my nerves. Fuck, this hurts.

"It ... um ..." Fuck. I can do this. "It wasn't a, uh, a date," I kind of whisper, my voice low and anxious. "I ... um... It was just a friend."

Beau is just... standing there, just staring at me. I swear I see his brow twitch a little.

"It wasn't a date." He says the words slowly, as if he's trying to feel them out as he says them. As if he maybe doesn't believe them. As if he doesn't believe me?

But maybe that's me making it about my lying. Maybe I should...

But before I can make any staggering confessions, Beau takes a deep breath and walks toward me. He's walking toward me, and he grabs me.

He's grabbing me ... and he's...

He's kissing me.

Chapter 22

Beau

Our bodies come together, flesh meeting flesh in a violent dance of passion and maybe some rage.

At least, on my end.

I'm so angry with him for trying to trick me. So angry with him for going out tonight and letting me think he was actually going on a date. But mostly, I'm so angry that it is working.

That his sneaky little plan to get under my skin and make me fall for him is absolutely working.

Because it is.

Because I am absolutely falling for this man.

I'm falling for sea glass-green eyes. I'm falling for blond curls. I'm falling for thousand-watt smiles.

I'm falling for him.

Because all of this rage, all of this anger, simply melts away as our tongues dance together. It melts away, and all I feel is soft. Soft for this man in my arms. Soft for *him*. Soft for his kisses, for his touch, for *him*.

"You thought you could tease me tonight, huh?" I ask, my nails digging into Milo's flesh, into his back, and into his ass. "You thought you could *trick* me." I chuckle into his kiss. He has the courtesy to at least look ashamed of his little ploy.

"Beau..."

But I cut him off.

My fingers dig into his ass, hauling him up and against me. He gasps, but obeys. He jumps into my arms, powerful thighs wrapping around my waist and holding onto me tightly. His achingly hard cock presses against my abdomen.

My own throbbing dick presses against his ass.

"Do you feel that, baby?" I ask him, thrusting my hips and pressing my dick against him. I obviously am pushing blindly, but in my head, I'm hitting that tight little hole dead on. "Is this okay, sweetheart?" I ask gently, my head bent in close as I whisper in his ear.

Milo throws his head back and moans, the loveliest sound drawn from those pretty, pink lips. Rolling his neck, he moves back in close. His arms are circled around my neck, holding me close to him. Our noses press together, and our lips are just millimeters apart.

I pull his face back to mine and devour his kiss. He tastes so honey-sweet, a hint of mocktail on his tongue maybe. It's my chance to toy with him.

"Ah." I chuckle again. "You indulged a little tonight?" He looks at me through those thick lashes, his freckles popping against his rosy cheeks. "Needed something sweet to get you through your little deception?" I ask him, a teasing lilt to my voice.

He buries his face into my neck as I carry him to the bedroom, licking and kissing along the column. His tongue, the wicked little muscle, traces a line down my throat to my shoulder, moaning against my skin. Fuck, it feels so good.

He bites into the muscle, and I groan, stopping as my cock twitches in response.

"Naughty, naughty," I croon before I begin walking again.

I whisper praises to him as we stumble into his room. "Right there, baby" and "yes" and "good boy". The lights are dimmed because I planned for this. I didn't plan for the lie, and I do feel like I should punish him for it, but all in all, I planned to get this man into bed again.

If he wants me, I am going to give myself to him. I am going to give him everything.

When he left earlier in the evening, I was in a state of absolute distress, pacing the floor with my fingers buried in my hair, thinking of some nameless and faceless man running his fingers through Milo's blond curls.

I grip those curls now and shudder, knowing how close I was to losing it. How I thought I was so close to losing him. The Grindr setup was one thing. The bartender was one thing. A real and fleshed-out date? I was convinced I was too late to figure out my feelings.

And why would he wait for me? I certainly wouldn't.

I throw him on the bed and toss myself on top of him, crawling up his sexy, long body, peppering him with kisses as I go.

"My naughty boy," I whisper when I finally reach his ear, and I can feel him shivering under me. I begin pulling at his clothes to get him naked as fast as possible. His shirt, a nice button-down, rips a little as I yank it over his head.

"I'll buy you a new one," I whisper against his skin as I continue to bite and lick at his exposed flesh.

"I don't care," he groans. "Not even a little." His voice is breathy, and he stares down at me. His hair is a shiny golden halo around his head, curls wild. His freshly kissed lips are pink and plump. His skin is covered in a sheen of sweat, making him glow, a heated pink flush spreading across it.

Fuck, he looks so sexy like this, just laid out for me and desperate to be devoured.

His hands stretch up over his head, and he raises his hips—unspoken permission to continue with unbuttoning and tearing off his pants. Still, when I grip either side of the denim, I look at him and raise my brow. He nods fervently. I slide his jeans off, and his erection presses against his briefs obscenely. My face is already there, so I do the logical thing and mouth at him over the fabric, the wet of my tongue drawing out the wet of his precome.

I can taste him through his briefs, and it's so filthy.

He's whining and moaning, squirming beneath me. I stand up slowly, enjoying the imbalance of being completely clothed and messing with his almost naked body. He stares up at me and watches, enraptured, as I slowly pull off my clothes, peeling off my sweater and sliding down my pants. I don't have to look down. I know my erection is pointed directly at Milo.

It wants him just as badly as I do.

Now naked, exposed, I crawl up his body once more. I kiss up his legs, his calves, his thighs, right to the crease of his groin, where I lick him fervently. He practically purrs for me. I lick and suck and lave at the skin surrounding his cock, refusing to pull down his briefs and give it the attention it desires.

"Please, please, please, *please*," he begs me, the sweetest sound I've ever heard.

The head of his cock is poking out the top of his briefs now, needy and angry and red, and I smile at it lasciviously. Bending over, I give it a pointed lick, dragging my tongue over his slit.

He howls, his whole body bowing in response.

I love eliciting these sounds from him—the moans, the groans, the *whimpers*. They're a balm to my aching chest, where my heart is beating too hard and too fast.

I slip my fingers into his briefs, admiring the vision of him all laid out and flushed once more, before unceremoniously tearing them off. I apparently use a little too much force because there's a ripping sound as I pull them down his meaty thighs.

"I'll—"

"I know, I know," he laments, rolling his eyes. "Buy me a new pair. Please hurry." His voice is so breathy and desperate.

"Roll over." I help push him onto his belly and pull his hips back toward me. With a hand on each cheek, I pull him open so I can admire that pink hole. It winks at me, and he whines in response. Using my pointer finger, I gently probe at his hole, just to see what noise he'll make.

Fuck, he keens at the pressure and his hole has a little give.

"Oh baby, this hole is so desperate to be filled, huh?" My finger runs lazy circles around the ring of muscle. It quivers under my touch. "Look at it dance for me, just needy for attention." His face is buried in the comforter, but I can imagine it all flushed and sweaty. I nod toward the bedside table, even though he can't see me. "Lube."

The bottle is in my hand, and I stare down at him again. He's laid out before me, on his stomach, his ass in the air. He looks like such a slut like this.

Such a slutty little feast.

It would be ludicrous to pass up such a delicious opportunity.

I lean in and begin licking at his hole, my hands firmly gripping his hips to keep him exactly where I need him. He cries, his voice hoarse, and I work him open with my tongue.

Fuck, his hole is pink, wet, and sloppy.

Exactly how I want him.

I work on him carefully, opening him up with lube-slicked fingers. He moans and whines, pushing back onto my fingers, fucking himself on them.

"Naughty boy." I tsk at him, and he whimpers in response, but he doesn't stop. I let my fingers stay where they are while he continues to fuck himself, edging closer and closer.

I can tell he's about to come, his balls drawing up and his back tightening as the tension builds. I pull my fingers out before he can get too close and topple over.

He sobs real tears when I pull my fingers from his ass, making sure to give his prostate a generous rub. His hole winks up at me, sad and empty.

"*Please, please, please!*" he begs so prettily.

I lube up my cock and press the head at his entrance. He keeps trying to fuck himself back onto me, but I hold his hips steady, groaning.

This man, this powerful machine of a man, is broken down and desperate for me.

I slide into him, and once again, it feels like I am coming home.

I look down at him, the lust fading into something deeper, something more tangible. I feel connected to him beyond just where our bodies are joined.

He feels like home.

This doesn't feel like fucking anymore. As I hold his face in my hands and kiss him gently, it feels like making love.

I'm holding him close, my face buried deep in his nape, inhaling his citrus scent and the smell of sex. My arms are wrapped around the curves of his muscles, and I squeeze him as close as humanly possible.

What is this feeling? What is it that I feel so deeply for him?

I know I'm falling for him; I know that. But have I already fallen?

Am I really already there?

I don't know if I'm ready to face that yet.

It took me a year to say those three words to Bianca, and we still ended up falling apart. Maybe I should give Milo and myself more time to really cook, to be together and grow together, before I potentially ruin it.

What are the chances he feels what I feel? I mean, he felt like he had to trick me to get me into bed. He can't feel all that attached to me. What if I say it too soon and he decides I'm not worth it?

Wave after wave of doubt crashes through my head, my grip loosening on Milo's chest. My nose is still buried in his hair when he finally speaks up.

"Beau, what's—"

But we're interrupted by a knock at the door.

A knock at almost midnight on a Wednesday.

What the fuck?

"I've got it," I answer hurriedly, rolling away from him and heading out the door. I pull on my sweatpants but don't bother with a shirt. Why the fuck would I need one?

The knocking continues, a vigorous pounding as if they know it's an ungodly hour and we should be asleep.

"Yeah, yeah, I'm coming." I chuckle at my little innuendo and reach for the front door. I can hear Milo shuffling behind me.

I swing open the door, and there's an older couple standing on the other side. The tall, pale-haired man has his hand raised, ready to pound on the door again. His partner, a shorter, more golden-haired woman, is standing just behind his shoulder. They look painfully familiar.

"Can we help you?" I ask, unsure if Milo has made it to the entryway yet. They're both staring at me hard, and the woman's eyes narrow into a glare.

"Who are you?" she asks with a sneer. I sneer right back, but before I can ask her who the fuck she is, I'm interrupted.

"Mom? Dad?"

Chapter 23

Milo

My parents are standing in my doorway on this dark November night, glaring at Beau, and I'm standing behind him, hiding from their animosity like a fucking coward.

"Miles Winfield Hall, who is in your house at this late hour?" Mom is glaring daggers at Beau, as if he's the whole reason I'm gay.

And in all fairness, if I didn't know I was super gay before meeting him, I would now. Beau would absolutely "turn me", so to speak.

"Winfield?" is all Beau asks, turning to look at me with a devilish smile on his face. He's ignoring all the heat coming from my parents and just giving me this dopey, lopsided smile, like he won the lottery by hearing my stupid middle name.

"Yeah, it's a family name," I tell him, fighting the smile. My brain is firing on half cylinders because one, I just had earth-shattering, life-changing sex, and two, my parents are here and I need to be panicking. I just know if I smile right now, they'll take that as a personal attack.

"Miles!" my father huffs at me again. Their hands are literally on their hips, and I could almost swear there's steam coming out of their ears. They look like the trademark image of disappointed parents.

"Mom, Dad, come in." I wave them in, unsure of what else to do. It's not like I can ask them to leave. Beau walks away from the door, shaking a little with each step from silent laughter. They watch his retreating form with more malice in their eyes. "Please come inside," I beg, shivering as the cold air flows past them into the house, surrounding me in a freezing embrace. Mom huffs at me and shakes her head. I see literal tears in her eyes.

Oh my god, it's going to be one of those talks.

Sure enough, when Mom and Dad stomp all the way into the living room and turn on Beau, who's just sitting on the couch, Mom already has tears running down her cheeks. I can feel the eye roll coming and have to force it deep, deep down.

"What are you both doing here?" I ask once I've shut and locked the door and made my way into the living room. Mom spins on me.

"Don't you think this should be a *family* conversation?" Her voice is full of contention and malice, and it's all directed at Beau. Again, like I wasn't already gay before I got here. Like he's personally responsible for this development.

"I think—"

"What kind of conversation are you expecting to have at eleven fifty-eight?" Beau asks matter-of-factly. I look at the clock, and he's right. It's fucking late. As if to emphasize his point, I see my dad fighting a yawn.

"I don't think that's really any of your business," Mom snaps, but she's trying not to yawn herself, so it doesn't come across as fiercely as I'm sure she would've liked.

"Mom, Dad, why are you here?" I try to keep my voice stern and direct and to the point, but it's hard. When Mom swings those teary eyes my way, I almost fold immediately.

"You haven't been answering your phone!" she bellows.

"We talked. This morning!" I reply, trying to keep my calm and failing miserably. They've done this a few times. I miss a call or two, and they just show up, even though Colorado is a thirteen-hour drive from Minneapolis. I'm really starting to understand where Beau is coming from when he says they don't respect boundaries.

They have suitcases. They must have planned this trip when we talked this morning if they're already here.

That's so frustrating. They planned a whole trip out here without even telling me.

"There's no way that's true. I would remember," she says with a sharp nod.

"Mom, we talked about the club. You were pissed at me. Remember?" I'm trying to keep the exasperation from my voice because I know that's just going to piss her off more.

"What club?" Dad asks, but Mom interrupts him.

"I don't remember any of that, honey." She waves me off with a dismissive hand, and I want to groan. How does she always do this? How does she always blow me off with so little care?

If she doesn't remember, it must not have happened. At least that's how things work in her mind.

"Son." My dad's voice is low and gruff. He's pissed. "Are you going to introduce us to your little friend?" He quirks a brow and nods at Beau, who's just smiling at me. He mouths "little friend" like it's the funniest thing in the world, and he's not wrong.

"This is Beau." I gesture at him halfheartedly, not really wanting to turn their ire onto him. "My teammate."

"Teammate?!" My mom half screeches. "What were you thinking?"

"What was he thinking about what?" Beau asks with faux innocence. He turns to look at me and bats his lashes, getting more comfortable on the couch.

"Son, I really think this is more of a private, family matter." My dad is playing friendly, always worried about appearances. "Would you mind excusing us?"

"No, Dad," I start, stopping Beau from standing up and leaving me alone. But he doesn't look like he's willing to move an inch. "Beau was right. What kind of productive conversation can we expect to have this late? We should get some sleep." I grab their suitcases from where they were left haphazardly by the door and start to move toward the big guest room, before stopping. That's where Beau's stuff is, but is that where he's sleeping tonight?

I stare longingly at my room and think about sleeping beside him again. I think about dozing off in his arms and waking up wrapped up in him. But can we really do that with my parents here, breathing over our shoulders?

"Beau is in this room, so y'all will be in the other guest room down the hall." If Beau is surprised by this announcement, he doesn't say anything. My mom is grumbling behind me. I can hear her steaming and stomping as we make our way down the hall.

Once I've deposited them, my mom grabs my collar and yanks me to her level.

"We are *not* done talking about this, Miles," she hisses in my ear. I turn toward the door, only to see that Beau saw that interaction.

I feel myself flush with embarrassment at her actions. She doesn't know how to behave.

Once we've left them to their own devices, Beau pulls me back to the kitchen.

"What the fuck—" He looks at me with wide eyes, checking me over as if he's looking for an injury. "I didn't realize it was that bad. Are you okay?" His hands continue to pat over my body until I huff out a laugh.

I know what he's doing. I know he's trying to make me feel lighter, something that seems almost impossible when my parents are around, but he actually succeeds. I feel a weight lift from my shoulders.

"I didn't know they were coming," I gasp out, bent over, resting my hands on my knees. "What do we do?"

"What do you mean?" Beau asks.

"They can't stay here. We're not going to be able to do anything," I say as if he just asked the stupidest question.

"What do you mean, we can't do anything? I thought you said they knew you were gay?" He quirks a brow at me, daring me to say it, daring me to be open with him about just how shitty a situation I'm in with my parents, daring me to tell him that I don't feel comfortable being myself with them here.

"We, ah…" I start, but I'm embarrassed.

"If you're about to tell me we can't be together around your parents, in your own home, you're gonna get popped upside the head, I swear, Milo." He chuckles low. "Also, can we talk about *Miles*?"

"Milo is short for Miles."

"No duh." His laughter is light. "Your parents are so damn condescending to you. You hear it, right?" He puts a hand on my shoulder and pulls me close, almost close enough to kiss.

"Yeah, I think I'm starting to." I chuckle low. Suddenly, I'm overwhelmed with this hot embarrassment as want simultaneously overcomes me. I don't know if we're there yet, but I know what I need. "Hey, will you… I mean, can you…?"

"Do you want me to come sleep with you tonight?" he asks me, and I flush red-hot before nodding slowly. "C'mon." He swings an arm around my shoulder, pulling me close and smacking a kiss on my forehead. "Let's try and get some rest before we tackle this mess with your parents tomorrow, yeah?

"Yeah."

Later, when we're curled up together in bed, his body draped around mine, his arms holding me close, I feel so content. As I drift off to sleep, I realize I want to be here in his arms forever. This is home.

I wake up to a loud and honestly quite angry gasp that sounds annoyingly familiar.

"Mom, get out." I groan into my pillow. Beau is still curled into my side, but he's groaning, too, and shoving his rock-hard morning wood into my hip, grinding into me with little thrusts.

"I was just…"

"Get out!" I call out again. Beau and I are both scantily clad in only our briefs, and this is such a gross violation of privacy on my mom's end. I'm a fucking adult, god-dammit.

I hear her shuffle out of the room, slamming the door shut behind her.

"There goes any hope of sleeping in," Beau mumbles against my ear, his breath tickling my skin. He nuzzles into my neck, and I sigh a contented sigh. "Do they always do that?"

"She's never barged into my room before," I answer honestly, because she genuinely hasn't. Not before. Something about this trip must have really set her off for her to be overstepping this much.

What is it about Beau that makes them so mad?

We move around the room in lazy silence, just kind of brushing against each other and peppering gentle kisses as we get ready for the day.

When we finally step out of the bedroom together a few minutes later, my mom is making her way back toward my room in a huff.

"Finally!" She waves a wooden spoon at us. "Breakfast is getting cold."

I can smell the scramble hash she made, and I wonder for a second if maybe this morning won't be a total shit-show.

But then we finally meander out to the kitchen, where my very upset father is sitting with his arms crossed and a deep, angry scrunch to his brows.

"You've scarred your mother," he accuses.

"If seeing two adults cuddle is scarring, she probably shouldn't have barged into our room like that," Beau says matter-of-factly, and both of my parents swing on him, glaring all their malicious intent as hard as they can.

Our room.

I love the way that sounds, especially coming from his mouth, the way his lips curve around each word. I just want to jump on him.

"Your room?" my mother shrieks. "How long has this been going on?" She turns quickly to me and throws up her hands. "And with a teammate, Miles?" She shakes her head, blonde curls wildly flouncing in the morning light. "What are you going to do when this blows up? You think he's going to keep your secret when he dumps you?"

Each word feels kind of like a dagger. *When* this blows up. *When* he dumps me. Sounds like my parents have a clear view of how this is going to go.

"Even if things didn't work between us, I would never out Milo. That's not okay." Beau's brows are pinched, and I can tell he's growing more and more frustrated. He looks over at me with an exasperated look in his eyes, and I can tell he's teetering close to the edge.

"We are just worried about you, Milo." My mom's voice is chock-full of what feels like faux concern. It's dripping with condescension and false niceties. Nothing about the way she's behaving feels genuine. "Honestly, Son, what is your plan here? Just continue to screw each other in private?"

I flinch at her crass words.

"I don't know, I was kind of thinking it would be nice to..." I look at Beau, and even though he doesn't know what I'm about to say, he nods encouragingly. "I was thinking it would be nice to maybe come out?"

"WHAT?!" Mom is screeching like a banshee now, her arms flailing as she continues to squawk and crow.

"You cannot be serious, Son." Dad has his face buried in his hands, and Mom is full-on sobbing now. "Nothing good can come from it. I mean it, nothing. You'll get booted from the team, and you'll go out an absolute disgrace."

"What will people think?" Mom cries, big crocodile tears rolling down her cheeks.

And there it is. That's all they really care about: appearances.

What will their friends think about them having a gay son? What will random hockey fans think about them having a gay son?

I'm just about done with her crocodile tears when Beau puts his hand up.

"That's enough," Beau shouts, bringing everyone to silence

Chapter 24

Beau

We're all standing in the kitchen, Milo's parents' jaws dropping open like they're ready to start yapping again, but I throw a hand up to stop them.

"Seriously, y'all can't continue to flap your lips like you know how this works. You need to stop. You know nothing." I sound so serious and so forceful. Milo reaches out and squeezes my arm. I look back at him, and he smiles.

"Milo is currently one of the best goalies in the division, in the whole league probably. The PHL really only cares about players playing well. They would be stupid to count him out of the league entirely just because he likes dick." I shake my head, closing my eyes. "The fact that you don't believe your son's talent can carry him says way more about you than it does about him." I level them with a glare before continuing. "I would never jeopardize Milo's career or my own career if we didn't make it. That's incredibly selfish and goes against everything I believe in as a person. If you had gotten to know me at all before walking in here and just shitting all over us, maybe you would know that."

Milo's mom is loudly sobbing, big, angry tears flowing so hard she'll be dehydrated in no time. I roll my eyes, and his father scoffs. I can tell he's gearing up to clap back, but I just don't have the energy for their bullshit.

"Look, your son is incredible. He's an amazing goalie, yes, but he's an even better person. If y'all had even a modicum of respect for him, you would trust that he knows his own journey, that he knows the path that he needs to follow here. You should trust that he knows himself." I sigh because, based on the looks on their faces, they're not quite getting it. I finally look at Milo and shrug. "You'll do whatever it is that you need to do, and I promise I'll be here for you. I promise I'll support you. I promise I'll..."

"We've heard quite enough." Mr. Hall, surprise, surprise, is glaring at me.

"You clearly don't value our input," his mom chimes in, incredibly unhelpfully. The tears are still waterfalling down her face like she thinks they'll help her cause.

"It's not that I—" Milo starts, but his mom shoves past him, pushing him into the island like a little bowling ball of fury. He cries out, and I rush to his side, unsure of how to help, just knowing that he needs it.

His ribs are all red and angry, and I feel all red and angry. His parents are such shitheads. They don't care about their son at all. They only care about hearing themselves yammer on and on about things they don't understand. Yet when their son cries out to them, just wanting to be heard, they can't return the damn favor.

"Are you okay, baby?" I whisper to him, wiping away the tears gathering in his eyes. He nods carefully, his hand gripping at his side. There's a huge red splotch where he hit the island. It's for sure going to bruise.

"I'm fine. It's not that bad." His voice is low, and he flinches a little when I run my fingers lightly over the bruising skin.

His dad scoffs and shoves past us. We just stand together, huddled in the kitchen, listening to his parents shuffle around in their room. I'm selfishly hoping they're packing their bags to leave, but I don't know how that'll make Milo feel.

"Do you think they're leaving?" he asks, and I search his eyes for any sign of how he genuinely feels about that. His eyes are hooded, and he refuses to meet my gaze. I take him into my arms and just crush him to me.

"Yeah, baby, I think they are." I pull back and cradle his face in my hands, forcing him to look up at me. "How do you feel about that?" I search his face for any sign of discomfort, for any sadness. My fingers feather over the red blotch on his ribs, and he flinches. "Fuck, baby, are you going to be able to play tomorrow?" He rolls his eyes hard, forcing a laugh out of me, and I can hear one of his parents scoff again. "Seriously, baby, this looks pretty angry. We should talk to PT about this."

I go to move to the freezer, but his hand grips my arm, holding me in place.

"I'm just getting you an ice pack for that bump, sweetheart. I'll be right back." He squeezes me again, but nods and lets me go.

Ice pack in hand, I maneuver him to the living room and sit him down. We just sit huddled together, me pressing the ice pack against his ribs and him full-on hissing at me. My chuckle is low and smooth. I'm trying desperately to keep him distracted from his parents' huffing and puffing, heard loudly from the guest room.

Finally, after what is much too long for two people to need to pack up after only one night, his parents roll themselves out into the living room. Mrs. Hall bursts into tears again, and Mr. Hall makes a big show of comforting her, patting her back and really just being an overall douche. I want to sneer at the two of them but don't want to stoop to their level.

"You really are just going to let us walk out of here like this?" his mom asks between sobs before pulling out a tissue and obnoxiously blowing her nose. I can't stop the eye roll that takes place at that, though I definitely try.

"Mom, what do you want from me?" Milo asks, throwing his head back in exasperation. "You're choosing to leave like this. I didn't ask you to leave. This is one hundred percent your decision." He throws his hands up to match his energy. "So seriously, what do you want from me?"

"I want you to *listen* to me," she all but screeches back. He stands up with a huff and begins to usher them out the door.

"Well, when you're ready to have an adult conversation with me about the possibility of me coming out, I'll be ready to talk with you. Until then, I think maybe we should take a break from each other and cool off."

His parents blanch at that.

"You can't take a break from being our child," his dad hisses.

"I can, and I will. Either y'all can respect that and give me some space, or I can block you." He walks around them and opens the front door. "Please leave."

I've never felt so proud.

His parents literally stomp out of the house like two petulant children, and I have to remind myself of his bruise before I pounce on him. He slams the door shut and walks back over to me. I may be so proud of him I'm horny, but he has tears in his eyes, so I take a deep breath.

He plops back down on the couch, and I grab his hand and give it a squeeze.

"That must have been really hard," I say softly, trying to keep my voice low and soothing. "I'm really proud of you."

His head is flung back against the back of the couch, but he turns and squints at me, a smile spreading across his face.

"That sucked, like, a lot," he says slowly, thinking about his words before he says them, "but all I really feel is relief. Like maybe I can actually do this. Maybe I can actually come out?" His cheeks blush as if he's imagining the prospect, and I hope it's a flush of excitement.

Part of me wishes I could come out first, take that leap for him, but I think he needs this. I think he needs the opportunity to be brave. And who am I to take that away from him?

Before I can voice my thoughts, Milo is rolling over on the couch and is suddenly straddling my lap.

"It was so hot watching you stand up to them, sweetheart." He nuzzles into my neck, and I groan. I can feel him plumping up, and before I know it, he's rock hard and grinding his erection against mine. I reach up and bring his lips down to meet mine in a searing kiss.

What starts as wild and fervent turns sweet and tender as we just rock into each other. He's cradling my head, and I'm holding him close. We sit there like that for quite some time, just kissing, just being close, just holding each other.

I want to tell him how I feel, but I still don't have the words for it. I still can't find it within myself to say them, so for now, I'll show him exactly how I feel.

I stand up from the couch, bringing Milo's legs to wrap around my hips and his hands around my neck. I start to move to the bedroom, but he stops me.

"No, fuck me in the kitchen. On the island." His words are breathy and desperate. I change course and do exactly as he asks, moving toward the kitchen as quickly as I can manage with this big, beefy bottom in my arms.

I sit him on the island, and we continue to kiss from this new angle. But as our lips move together, I grow more and more hungry for his body. My fingers tangle in his curls as I hold his face to mine. Finally, *finally*, I move down the column of his neck with the reverence of a prayer, licking and sucking at each juncture, desperate to elicit the most provocative sounds from him.

My hands are suddenly very busy tugging at his pants, very grateful we're already in such a state of undress in the early hours of the day.

He maneuvers out of his pants and sits on the island in all his naked glory. I pull out my cock slowly, already achingly hard and dripping precome. I hold out a hand to him.

"Spit."

And he obeys so beautifully.

I wrap my hand around our throbbing cocks, giving them a gentle squeeze and moaning at the delicious pressure.

"You like that, pretty boy?" I ask with a sugary sweetness, leaning in close and letting our bodies press together. "You like rubbing that gorgeous cock against mine, like feeling how much I want you? Such a pretty slut for me," I coo at him, one hand wrapped around our dicks, the other on his face, forcing his eyes on mine. For a moment, we stand there together, dicks in hand, eyes locked on each other.

I'm entirely enraptured by him.

Entirely caught up in this beautiful man.

This man that I long more than anything to call mine.

His pupils are blown with lust, and he's worrying his bottom lip between his teeth. His cheeks are flushed and covered in a sheen of sweat, those gorgeous freckles standing at attention. I want to lick a stripe up his chest, really taste him.

We get lost there for a while, just enjoying each other's space and air, foreheads pressed together. My hand moves leisurely over our shared erections, in no real hurry to come, just whispering sweet nothings to my man.

Mine.

Mine, mine, mine.

All mine.

I pull his mouth down to mine and lose myself in his kiss, his lips so soft against my own.

Those three words are on the tip of my tongue. I literally have to eat my words and swallow them to keep from saying them aloud, to keep from scaring him off.

This is so real, so fast.

When we finally come, it's together and on an exhale.

This is real.

Chapter 25

Milo

Things between Beau and me have shifted in an astronomical way. Something from the other night fundamentally changed us. It changed how I see him. It certainly changed things I want to say to him.

It changed how I feel for him, really cementing my feelings into something tangible.

I think I might love him?

I know my feelings for him are running deep, coursing through my veins, because they don't leave me even as I settle into our game.

I settle between the pipes, and all I can think about is Beau. All I can think about is confessing to him, to telling him how I feel.

But tonight is not the night for those kinds of declarations. Tonight, we have a game, and we have to stay focused.

We're playing absolute bruisers this evening, and I need to be on my A-game. I need to be in peak form. So for the millionth time tonight, I shake all thoughts of loving Beau loose from my skull, and focus on the game in front of me.

We're in deep against the Boston Guardians. 2-1, we're ahead.

I've never liked playing them. They play dirty, always too rough when they don't have to be. Rough in ways that make you wince just from watching. Rough in ways that could potentially involve me.

They've never been above roughing a goalie, so I have to stay sharp. And I'm glad for my sharpness. They are all up in my crease the first two periods before they finally back off.

We're in the third period, and so far it's been a relatively clean game, just some shoving and general annoyance, but we're all sitting on edge, just waiting for that other shoe to drop.

Waiting for them to bring down the metaphorical hammer.

I'm on the opposite end of the action right now, watching as the team silently communicates and, fuck yes, manages to put away another biscuit right over the goalie's shoulder.

3-1.

Each point makes me more and more nervous because I know it's another reason for Boston to become unhinged.

I know it's just another excuse for them to start coming after us, for them to start going after my teammates.

I nervously watch as the puck drops, and we win the faceoff.

I can see everything from the crease, the whole rink laid out in front of me like a chessboard: lanes, gaps, bodies in motion. I track the puck as Paxton curls low through center ice, head up, stick loose and confident. He always looks confident when he's in his flow like this, chasing a puck and flying down the ice. Brennan streaks down the right wing, calling for it, while Beau slides wide on the left, timing it perfectly.

It's a good rush. A perfect rush.

Paxton feeds Beau through the neutral zone, clean and fast. I tap my stick once against the ice, a warning more instinct than sound.

"Boards!"

Beau doesn't dump it. He never does.

I drop my stance as Beau crosses the blue line, knees flexed, glove hand set while the defense pinches in. Oskar and Kirill hang back at the red line, already reading the play, ready to retreat if it turns.

The opposing defenseman steps up on Beau, forcing him toward the wall. Brennan cuts toward the slot, stick down, looking for the dish. Paxton trails high, ready to support.

Then there he is.

Fuck, he's right there.

The second defender accelerating in from Beau's blind side.

Too fast.

Too late.

But I cry out anyway.

The hit lands with a violent crack, echoing through the arena.

Beau gets crushed into the boards, skates flying out from under him as his upper body takes the full force. The puck kicks loose behind the net, but my eyes never leave the corner.

Beau is lying there, motionless.

There's screaming. Someone is screaming.

Someone should tell them to stop.

Oh.

It's me.

Brennan is there by Beau's side instantly, dropping his gloves halfway as he shoves the defenseman back, shouting something that I can't hear, or maybe I'm just not listening. I'm too busy willing Beau to move, to open his eyes, anything.

I don't realize how far out of the crease I am until I'm crossing the red line. I just need to see him, need to make sure he's okay.

His eyes peel open slowly, and I breathe out a sigh of relief.

Paxton skids in right behind him, arms out, barking at the ref, furious.

"What the fuck was that?!"

The whistle finally blows, but Beau still isn't actually moving.

Oskar and Kirill skate in together from the blue line, sticks down but bodies tense. Oskar positions himself between Brennan and the opposing bench, Kirill looming just behind Paxton like a silent threat.

I finally see a little movement. Beau is curling up on the ice, arm tucked tight against his chest. In the stark silence of the rink, I can hear him groaning in pain.

Fuck, that's not good.

Beau moves to try and sit up, but he immediately slumps back down, his face twisting in agony, his breath hitching sharp and shallow. Paxton drops to a knee beside him, talking fast and low, one hand hovering like he's afraid to touch him. I'm close enough now that I can hear him.

"Hey, BB, you're fine just like that, man. Don't move." Paxton crouches down, but looks away toward the bench, where the trainers are springing into action. "Just stay still, okay?"

Oskar pushes away from where everyone is huddled. His face is red with anger. His wild eyes keep flying between where Beau is lying crumpled on the ice and the defenseman who rocked him. He looks like maybe he wants to risk the suspension. Right now, I can't really blame him.

Not when they cut Beau's jersey open, pads shifting, and I see that unnatural swell of skin near his clavicle.

My stomach drops too low in my belly, and I immediately feel as if I'm going to be sick.

I've wandered close enough now that the ref is telling me to stay back.

Brennan and Kirill are huddled together, swearing under their breath.

The arena has gone completely silent, no music, no chatter, just that horrible, collective hush.

I grip the top of my stick like I'm trying to choke it, my breathing shallow. My face is wet. Why is it so wet?

The stretcher is brought out, and they carefully put a neck brace on him.

Why am I just standing here?

I push closer, still wanting to see him, to let him know I'm here, but scared to get too close, scared that all it will take is one look at me and it'll be so obvious how I feel.

"Is he okay?" I ask, over and over. "Is he okay?"

I want to scream. No one is listening to me. No one is answering me.

But then...

Then I hear him.

"I'm okay," his voice is hoarse and strained. "Tell him I'm fine." His voice is so low it's barely a whisper, but I'm straining to be near him, and I hear him. "Tell him to go. Tell him to play."

My vision blurs, stinging from unshed tears.

I'm going to play for him. These fuckers aren't getting anything past me.

Chapter 26

Beau

I don't remember anything but blindingly bright lights and the most sickening pain in my arm. Or maybe the pain isn't in my arm. Maybe it's my shoulder. Possibly in my neck. I just know it hurts to move, and I'm on so many drugs it's unbelievable.

It feels like my head is in a bubble as I look around the hospital room. It's so sterile and boring here.

Well, it was, until some people started sending flowers. Then there's a small garden in the corner, all these beautiful flowers showing up. The nurse said some were from the team management, the owner, the Boston management, et cetera, et cetera.

The morning sun manages to shine through the closed curtains and directly into my eye. I blink and cringe at the brightness.

The nurse this morning said my concussion was so bad and I should rest, but my head is pounding and my arm, shoulder, neck, whatever, is aching.

Out for the season.

Fuck, I bet the higher-ups are cursing this trade now that they can't use me to get to the playoffs like we planned. I wanted to show them that we could so badly. I wanted to show that I was a good choice, that bringing me on was a good move for them, and then this happens.

This happens, and I can't prove shit to anyone.

The door clicks, and I swing my head back to see who's coming in. The head swing was a mistake, because holy shit, that hurts.

Oh.

Oh, it's *him*.

Milo.

"Milo," I say on a whisper, as if I'm afraid if I speak too loudly that I'll scare him away, or maybe that he's not real and if I acknowledge him too fervently that he'll disappear.

"Beau," he says just as carefully, almost like he's afraid of all the same things.

My vision is swimming, and all his features blur together, and I'm not sure why.

"Oh, baby."

He's moving then, suddenly and so quickly, by my side. His fingers brush my wet cheeks.

Oh.

I'm crying.

When did I start crying?

Wetness drips onto my hand.

He's crying too.

"Why are you crying?" I ask him, my voice not really mine but drenched in heavy medication. I sound woozy, and I feel woozier.

"You scared me, sweetheart." He keeps brushing the wetness from my cheeks, only for the tears to keep pouring. "I was so worried about you," he says, the tears overflowing and streaming down blotchy cheeks.

"Shhh, baby," I try to soothe him as I cry harder too. I try to reposition myself in bed, scooching slightly, and he immediately moves to take up the open space. He curls his body around me, gentle with his touch but desperate to feel me.

We lie there together for quite some time, kind of unaware of how much time has passed, just enjoying each other's company.

We must have fallen asleep because, the next thing I know, the loud creak of the opening door stirs us. Milo is drooling on my uninjured shoulder, and Paxton is standing in the doorway.

Paxton.

Captain Paxton "Matty" Mathews.

Captain of the Minnesota Fury.

My team captain.

Oh fuck.

"Matty." I try to adjust myself in the hospital bed, pushing myself up to a seated position and jostling Milo in my wake. He stirs slowly, cuddling into me and rubbing his face into my chest.

I shake him a little, causing him to look up at me, and he gives me a sleepy smile. I smile back at him because I just can't help it. He's so beautiful like this, the morning light blasting through the curtains and causing his golden curls to glow like a halo.

"Milo," I whisper to him, kissing his temple, because we're already caught, might as well go all in. "We have company."

"Huh?" he asks, still blinking the sleep out of his eyes. He looks too cute like this, but his eyes go wide when he registers my words. He pushes himself to standing much too fast and wobbles like crazy. "Paxton," he says sharply, and for a second, I think he's going to salute him.

"Milo," he says slowly, obviously still processing the scene he walked in on. "Beau." He's looking between us, careful consideration in his eyes. "Management wanted to come check and see how you're feeling. I offered to come because I was worried about you."

I've never been more thankful in my life because, despite how okay I feel about all this, I am definitely not ready to face management. I look at Milo, and he's looking at me, confusion on his face more than fear. I nod, because if he's okay with this, so am I.

"So," Paxton starts, "how long has this been going on?" He kind of vaguely gestures between us like we are unaware of what this looks like. More importantly, like we're unaware of exactly what this is.

"I just want to clarify," Milo pipes up, albeit nervously, "just exactly what this is."

Paxton makes a face at him and shakes his head fervently.

"I really don't need to know the gory details, guys." He waves us off hurriedly.

"No, no, Paxton, god, I would never." Milo's eyes are bugged out of his head, and I laugh at him. He smiles easily at me, taking my laugh in stride. "No, I just mean, this isn't some... fling. At least, it isn't to me." He looks at me again with just the biggest, most hopeful eyes. I can't help but match his smile with one of my own.

"It's not a fling for me either. I don't think it has been for a long ass time. Not to me." I smile a secret little smile, and Milo matches it.

This is the first either of us has actually said anything of the sort aloud. We both just look at each other and smile , a little more broadly.

"Okay, I get it, guys, really." Paxton is chuckling, his arms crossed over his broad chest. He's dressed as casually as the first time I met him, athletic shorts and a long -sleeve compression shirt under a hoodie. His black hair is flopping into his face over and over as he keeps trying to brush it back.

He really is a handsome guy. Too bad my type is tall blonds with big princess eyes and bubble butts, with smiles that light up every room he walks into.

"So," Milo starts, staring at the floor and shuffling his feet, "I guess this is us coming out?"

Paxton seems to think about this carefully, looking between the two of us before staring at his own feet.

We stand there in stilted silence for a few minutes. It's not uncomfortable or anything. I think Milo and I can both tell Paxton has something to say, and we're both just patiently waiting for him to open up.

Finally, Milo speaks up.

"You don't have to tell us anything if you're not ready." He says this carefully, as if he's approaching a cornered animal, trying so desperately to be a safe space for him to land. But he's right; whatever Paxton is gearing up to share doesn't have to be this earth-shattering moment.

"No, guys, it's fine." He takes a deep breath and smiles at us both. I'm still not entirely sure he's going to say anything when he takes another deep breath. "I'm pan," he says. Followed quickly by, "Pansexual."

Oh.

Oh.

Wow.

"I'm bi," I decide to pipe in. "Bisexual."

"I'm just gay." Milo shrugs, and laughter bubbles from my chest. I don't know what it is, but something about that is just so hilarious to me.

Paxton and Milo join me in raucous laughter.

The laughter dies down, and it's just three queer men standing in a somewhat awkward silence.

"So what does this mean?" Milo asks after the laughter has died down. "Do we have to come out now?"

I can visibly see the captain switch flip on in Paxton.

"This doesn't have to mean anything. I don't really feel the need to come out right now, you know? It's not my time yet." He gestures to himself, and we both nod, because who are we to tell this guy what to do. "But I fully support you two, and the team will give you their full support as well." I raise a brow because, the whole team? Really?

Milo nods, though. He looks at me, and the corners of his mouth tilt up.

"Yeah, I'm pretty sure coach's daughter is gay. I think Davidson has two dads?" He nods but still looks pensive, like he's trying to conjure more queer connections on the team. I'm honestly not one hundred percent certain who Davidson is. I think maybe a D-man? "Yeah, I think Jo and Dre in marketing are both queer." I definitely don't know who they are.

"There's more than just that, but what matters is: do you feel ready to come out to the team? Do you feel ready to come out to the fans?" We look between each other, and back at our captain, who throws a hand up. "Look, dude, you're concussed. Why don't you take some time to think about it. You're gonna have nothing but time while your collarbone heals up." He laughs again, backing up toward the door slowly. "I'm gonna let you both get back to your nap, but maybe just keep the cuddling to a minimum until you get discharged?" He winks and walks out the door.

And then it's just the two of us. The light is still shining through the small opening of the window. The world didn't end.

But I'm still pretty hopped up on pain meds, so I check in with Milo anyway.

"Did that really happen?" My voice is incredulous. "The drugs they gave me earlier were really good. The doctor turned into a walrus."

"A walrus?"

"Yeah, a walrus. So I'm thinking really anything could happen."

We both laugh at the absurdity, but Milo reassures me anyway.

"Yeah, that really just happened. Our captain came out to us." He turns and looks at me, eyes still wide. "Like, actually came out to us." He shakes his head, smiling to himself before sharing it with me. "Go back to sleep, baby. You should be getting out of here soon." He leans over, kissing my temple. I feel so at peace with him here with me. "I'm gonna go talk to the nurse, okay, sweetheart?"

I nod slowly, a sleepiness overwhelming me as I watch that bubble butt walk out the door.

Fuck, this is all so real.

I must have dozed off because, the next thing I know, there's a loud ringing. It's incessant and never-ending. My head is absolutely pounding, but I manage to peel my eyes open.

The light in my room is absolutely blinding, and the ceaseless ringing is reverberating in my head. It stops and then picks up immediately again.

I finally am able to move enough to find my phone, the source of the ringing, but I'm surprised to see the caller ID.

"Bianca?" I answer, my voice staggered.

"Beau, thank goodness." Her voice is not the most un-welcome sound. While we did go our separate ways, we didn't part on the worst terms. I just assumed she hated me since she never responded to my voicemail about Christian Grady. "I was watching your game last night and saw what happened. But no one knew anything! I was so worried about you!"

"B, I was worried about you." My voice is a little slurred from the copious drugs in my system, but I try to fight it. "I tried to call about Grady."

"Ugh." I can hear the eye roll in her groan. "Christian was a one-time thing who cannot take a hint." She tsks at something on her side of the phone before continuing. "Really just a thorn in my side more than anything, so nothing to worry about. I don't know why he quit with you, honestly. You're his biggest client. Or you were." She snickers.

I shake my head. She's always been so outspoken and independent. It was one of the things I liked so much about her. One of the things I still like about her. We may have been a bad match, but not because she was a bad person.

"Do you need a restraining order? I can help with a lawyer," I offer carefully, knowing almost immediately what she's going to say next.

"You know I can handle my own shit, Beau." She sighs. "I'm just glad you're okay, That hit looked so fucked, and I was so worried. Thanks for answering me. Thanks for letting me check on you."

And she's gone with a click.

Just then, Milo walks in with the nurse in tow. A smile on his face and my heart in his hands.

Chapter 27

Milo

I get home late after a game against the Toronto Vortex. We were demolished in overtime after holding them at bay, 0-0, all three periods. I'm dragging as I walk through the door, my feet shuffling, and I'm fighting back a yawn.

Beau is where he usually is when I get home, sitting on the couch and watching me walk through the door. The television is decidedly *not* on, so I can't yell at him for watching it when he should be resting his poor concussed brain. Even though we both know he's going to magically know a lot about the game as soon as I sit down.

He looks nervous tonight, something shifting in his eyes as I move across the room.

"Look," I start, a smile creeping up my cheeks. It feels fake, false, like I'm trying to stamp happiness where it doesn't belong. "Let me get out of this suit, and you can tell me everything we did wrong tonight." I start to laugh, but Beau just kind of hiccups and turns quickly from me.

He hiccups again, and I'm staring at the side of his head.

Is he...?

He wouldn't...

But did he actually...?

I peek around the space and notice a bottle sitting on the counter. The lid is off. There's a clean whiskey glass in the sink.

He didn't.

"Beau..." I stare at him sideways, narrowing my eyes to a distrusting slant. Because he wouldn't be stupid enough to be drinking less than a week after a concussion diagnosis. And he especially wouldn't be stupid enough to mix alcohol and his pain meds for his collarbone fracture.

He wouldn't.

So do I ask him?

I stare down at him for a moment while he looks anywhere but at me. Something in my gut is fluttering, and not in the good way. This feels bad. This feels like deception.

No, I walk away, slipping my jacket off as I go. Now not only stressed and angry at myself for letting in that goal tonight, I'm also stressed about whatever is going on with him. I'm not sure I'm emotionally in it enough to be able to confront him tonight. I'm not sure I have it in me to be that person tonight.

I recognize the behavior. I see it in him, and it scares me. Because I know what's going on.

My heart twinges a little.

I slide out of my suit and into a pair of sweats. I look down at the shirt in my hand before tossing it on the bed. It lies there in a rumpled heap as I leave to head back to the living room to find out what the hell is going on with my... Beau.

Maybe it's sleazy to try and use my body to win over this argument, if it even becomes an argument, but sometimes you have to fight dirty.

I saunter back out to the living room and plop down beside Beau, who's still decidedly not looking at me.

We sit there for some time, silence falling over us. For the first time in a long time, the silence doesn't feel amicable. The silence feels stilted and heavy, and I really don't like it, but it has to be done.

"Beau, you know this isn't okay, right?" I ask slowly, trying desperately to catch his eye. He hiccups again before blushing furiously and looking over at me shyly.

"I don't—"

"You have to know exactly what you're doing." My voice is harsh, direct. I don't mean for it to sound as brash as it does, but he flinches.

Fuck.

This isn't how I wanted to bring this up, but I know I have to. I can't keep watching him drink his life to oblivion. I can't keep watching him hide behind inebriation.

I think back to the bar and meeting Jamie. Jamie, who is incredibly sweet and flirty and not at all my type. And then looking across the bar and seeing Beau seething at us. It was great for my scheming and plotting and whatnot, but looking back, Beau was painfully drunk every time.

Win?

Drunk.

Lose?

Drunk.

Sitting at home with a fractured collarbone and a concussion?

Drunk.

Maybe I'm projecting. Maybe this is all in my head, and Beau doesn't display alcoholic tendencies.

Maybe.

Maybe.

Maybe.

Maybe this is biting off more than I can chew. Maybe I can't be enough for him. Maybe I can't... Fuck, maybe I'm not enough.

He's looking at me now, and ... and I think those are tears in his eyes. A very obvious drop drips down his cheek, and now I know he's crying.

"I'm sorry," he whispers, staring down at his lap, tears piling up and overflowing.

We sit there in a staggering silence, unable to move and unable to grasp what's happening.

Am I really mad at Beau for drinking? Any other time, I'd say no, but this time, so fresh off a concussion... Yeah, I'm actually mad.

"Do you have any idea how bad this could be?"

Hiccup.

I groan and wrap my arms around him, pulling him closer. His body shakes a little as his tears really begin to flow.

"Fuck, Beau, you're scaring me, you know? When you do this, you scare me." I squeeze him a little, still trying to be cognizant of the fracture. I'm upset, but I don't want to hurt him.

"I just hate the way this feels, the way I feel." He slumps forward in a way that can't be comfortable for his shoulder. "I feel so useless like this, like I'm nothing if I'm not contributing." He vaguely gestures around the house. "I tried to clean, but it fucking hurt, and I felt like you would see how useless I am. I'm afraid that the team will realize how useless I am, and they'll trade me again, and then I'll lose everything."

I look around the house as he speaks and see where he attempted to clean, but my brows scrunch together. How could I possibly see him as useless?

"Beau," I start, my hand running in large circles along his back, "my feelings for you are not tied to your usefulness. They're not tied to what you can offer me."

We sit there for a while, silence squeezing us, more like an awkward embrace than anything.

My *feelings* for him are suffocating me. I want to tell him exactly how I feel, but I know he's only just accepted that we're an item. I don't know how long it'll be before he's ready for any grand declarations of feelings.

"You don't have to hide behind drinks." I try to get him to look at me. "You don't have to hide behind getting drunk. You don't need to be numb. Not with me."

I climb up on his lap, cradling his head in my hands and holding him close to me. His body is shaking a little, like maybe he's crying. I try to shush him, to bring him comfort. My fingers run through his dark curls, and I tilt his head up to look at me.

Large amber eyes, swimming in tears, wet lashes, but he tries with a sad sap smile. I wipe at those teary eyes, and they close. He leans into my touch.

I hate that he feels that he has to numb his emotions. I hate that I haven't made him feel safe enough.

I hate that he's felt this alone.

I can't help but feel little bouts of anger bubble up in my stomach as I slide off Beau's lap and pull him to his feet. I don't feel like anything is resolved. If anything, I feel more confused than ever.

Beau stumbles behind me as we make our way to the bedroom—our room, if I have anything to say about it. The drunkenness combined with the concussion is a recipe for disaster.

"Oh, baby, you want me to rock your world?" he asks, still sniffling and wiping away at his tear-streaked face. His cheeks are red and splotchy, but I turn back and smile at him, because of course that's where his mind goes.

Flicking on the lights, I pull him into me and give him a push toward the bed. He starts purring and moaning at me, clearly still thinking this is going to lead to sexy fun times. I roll my eyes skyward.

He runs his fingers through my hair as I kneel down and help him out of his sweats. Yanking them down bit by bit while he wiggles his hips to "help" me is quite a feat. And then I'm treated to a fun little surprise.

He's gone commando.

Although, he must be pretty drunk because his dick is still hanging limply between his legs.

"If you suck it, I'll be good to go, I swear." I try not to laugh at his charming offer. He's standing pressed against a bed in a sling, a T-shirt, socks, and that's it. Pooh Bear-ing it has never looked so good.

"Come on, baby." I urge him into the bed, and he grabs at my ass, leaning into my body, his forehead resting against my chest.

"Mine."

I chuckle at his drunken declaration.

"Yes, sweetheart, yours."

I'm all yours, forever, if you'll have me.

He cradles my head in his hands, tilting my face down to look at him.

"You're so beautiful," he says, eyes glassy, words slurred.

"And you're so drunk." I laugh, hiding the scoff.

"Yes, I'm drunk." He nods, hiding his face against my abdomen. "And you're beautiful. But tomorrow I'll be sober, and you'll still be beautiful."

Chapter 28

Beau

I hate what yesterday became. I hate it so much.

I wake up in bed, half-dressed and in pain, all alone. A glass of Milo's hangover juice is waiting for me beside the bed, along with some aspirin, but Milo is already gone. Already on his way to practice this morning. I'm currently banned from the arena, but I had every intention of begging Milo to at least bring me along so I can watch practice.

I'm so embarrassed by my behavior last night. So embarrassed by how drunk I got watching the game. Because, yes, obviously I watched the game. Okay, I listened to the game, so that doesn't really count as screen time, and Milo can't really get mad at me for that.

I sip the juice slowly, letting its crisp coolness run down my throat and soothe my stomach, and swing out of bed, desperate to get some pants on.

I keep myself busy making breakfast. It turns out cracking eggs is even harder when you're down an arm, so really I just manage to make a mess of the kitchen. My scramble is more shell than egg, and I spill hashbrowns everywhere when I try to open the bag.

I look around at the mess I've made, and I have to laugh. This is ridiculous. I snap a picture and send the chaos to Milo. He replies seconds later. They must not be on the ice yet.

Me: *image of mess* don't leave me alone in the kitchen lol

Milo: LOL

I smile down at my phone. I can practically hear his laugh ringing in my ear, a sweet, melodic sound. It makes me feel warm all over just thinking about him.

I down the rest of my juice, my stomach settling easily, and bring the plate of crunchy eggs and mushy hashbrowns to the couch.

It's quiet in the house without Milo's happy energy. He makes me unbelievably happy, so happy I can feel it in my toes.

The couch is warm and comforting, and I long for Milo's embrace. He is warmth and comfort and makes me feel like all the little pieces I shatter into can be pieced together again. He doesn't just hold me together, though. It feels like he helps me hold myself together. He helps me find all the tiniest lost pieces and put them into the open wounds of my soul.

God, I'm getting mushy about this guy.

I think I'm feeling things about him that I never even felt for Bianca, and honestly, that's really scary.

Do I love him?

Fuck, I think I do.

Do I tell him?

A beat passes, and my belly fills with butterflies and hope.

I think I have to.

I sit with those thoughts for quite some time, letting them ruminate in my head. Letting them grow roots.

Before I know it, it's midday, and Milo is pushing through the door. He has a big smile on his face when he sees me, and I try to match it, but I swear there's this little worm digging around in my brain, telling me everything is moving too quickly.

Despite the little worm, I manage a smile at Milo.

"Hey, sweetheart." The hairs on the back of my neck stand on end at the term of endearment, but when his hand brushes my cheek and he leans down for a kiss, I meet his lips earnestly. The kiss lingers, him licking the seams of my lips a little before I invite him in.

Before long, Milo is straddling my lap and kissing me fervently, exploring my mouth with his insistent tongue.

He suddenly pulls back at the sound of a honk outside.

"Fuck, I was supposed to get you ready." He looks down at what I'm wearing and shrugs. "We just need to get a shirt on you."

"Get me ready for what?" I ask, a little alarmed. "Who's here?"

"The community relations manager, Dre—I told you about her last week—set the team up with a visit to the hospital to see the kids there." I definitely don't remember who Dre is, but I nod anyway because I used to love these kind of team outings with Dallas. "I thought it would be a good way to get you out of the house."

I nod gently but excitedly. Getting out and cheering up some kids sounds like the perfect way to spend my day. It will definitely help me stop stressing about the man I may or may not be falling in love with.

I'm not going to think about it or anything.

Milo helps me up, and I'm not thinking about it. He gently helps me undo my sling and put on a shirt, and I'm not thinking about it. My head pops through the shirt hole and he's smiling at me, and I'm definitely not thinking about this.

It's Paxton and Brennan waiting outside for us, sitting in the front seat of Paxton's Volvo XC90 Plus. Paxton smiles and waves at us. Brennan doesn't look up from his phone.

I'm really empathetic, so I can tell from everything about the way Brennan acts around me that he doesn't like me. I just can't really understand why. Maybe this little trip will show him I'm not that bad a guy.

Dre pairs me up with Brennan to talk to the kids, and I'm not even kidding, he rolls his eyes.

I follow behind him at a slight distance, suddenly very aware of how I'm acting around him, and go to do just that when we walk into a room with two kids and their parents.

Brennan is a fucking natural with these kids. He jumps in immediately, making the perfect jokes and making them smile. I shake hands with the parents because it's what I'm familiar with. I love kids, don't get me wrong. I just don't know what to do with myself around them.

Finally, I turn my attention to the kids.

They're cool kids. We talk about hockey, and they shockingly know their stuff. One of them brings up Max, the winger who was traded for me, and I see Brennan look down and smile a secret smile.

I could almost swear his eyes glistened a little.

Maybe...

Oh.

Brennan and the feelings he may or may not have for his former line mate don't matter to me. I guess the possibility of having yet another queer teammate should mean something to me, but more importantly, I understand Brennan's animosity toward me.

I understand why he may hate me a little. If someone came and took Milo's place...

Fuck, I don't even want to think about that.

My own eyes glisten a little as the thought rolls around in my head. It makes me want to come out now and be open, scared I might lose him if they don't know he's mine.

The next room we wander into has two kids, but one of the kids is in a bed by herself.

Something about her draws me over. I sit on the edge of the bed, and she shoots me a shy smile.

"You're Beau Bennett," she says matter-of-factly. She looks up at me, and her shy smile grows. I chuckle and thrust out my hand to meet hers.

"I am," I say, matching her tone, "and you are?"

"Priscilla Pailor." She takes my hand. The size difference is astounding. She's a tiny little kid, though I don't know if that's from her illness or her age. My hand swallows hers, but I steadily shake it. I can tell she's really trying to squeeze, but her grip is weak.

"It's really nice to meet you, Priscilla."

I can hear Brennan talking with the parents of the other little girl in the room. I hear words like *abandoned* and *alone* and *deadbeat*, and I know Priscilla is just like me.

"So, Priscilla, do you like hockey?" I ask, digging around in my pocket for the little cardstock headshots they brought for me to hand out. I wish I could get her tickets to a game or something.

I sign the card of my stupid face, to *my friend Priscilla*, and my signature looks dumb, but she lights up when I hand it to her.

"We'll have to get y'all to a game sometime," I say, to both kids in the room, but really to Priscilla. She smiles a sad smile and shakes her head.

"I wish I could, Mr. Bennett," she says solemnly, "but I'm waiting on a new heart." She puffs up her chest a little.

"The nurses say that they're looking for the perfect one for me. It has to be just right."

Brennan goes to talk to her and gives her a card of his own, while the mom in the room pulls me aside.

"Her parents have sort of abandoned her here, so she has no way to be approved for an outing like that." She looks at me with a sad smile, as if to say what I was offering was sweet, but...

I turn back to look at the sick little girl, and sit down on the edge of her bed. Brennan pats my shoulder to indicate that he's moving to the next room, but I wave him off. This is where I'm staying for the rest of the visit.

Priscilla and I play Go Fish for quite a while, laughing and talking. She tells me all about how much she misses school and her friends. Her favorite subject is math, and she likes hockey, but she's never gotten to learn how to skate.

She doesn't bring up her parents once.

Finally, a familiar presence enters the room.

"Hey, Beau." Milo's voice is soft and warm, the sweetest sound. "Who's your friend?"

"My name's Priscilla Pailor, I'm eleven," she says proudly, jutting out her hand to shake his, just like she did with me.

"It's nice to meet you." Milo takes her tiny hand in his. "I'm Milo…"

"I know who you are," she says again, so matter-of-factly. "You're Milo Hall, starting goalie for the Minnesota Fury."

"I am." His smile at her is so warm. I wonder what he's like with kids. I bet he's so patient with them.

He looks over at me, placing his hand on my good shoulder and giving it a little squeeze.

"We've got to go."

I don't want to leave her all alone again. I don't want to abandon her.

I turn back to Priscilla and give her my strongest smile, zero wobble to it.

"We'll come back and visit, okay? I know you cheated at Go Fish, so we're going to play for real next time." I give her a wink, and she giggles.

"I didn't cheat, Mr. Bennett," she says faux sternly.

"Sure you didn't." I ruffle her hair and stand up. My eyes start to burn a little as we turn and walk out.

"Goodbye, Beau!" she calls.

I turn at the door and give her a final wave.

We're back home, and my heart is racing. I know Milo can tell I've been feeling sad since we left, but I'm scared to just trauma dump all over him. The last thing I want is to be an emotional burden on him.

He walks over to the couch and pats the spot next to him. I plop down, my back creaking as I get myself comfortable. He pulls my head down to his shoulder and begins running his fingers through my curls.

My cheeks burn, and I rub them, my hands coming away wet. Why am I always crying?

"Do you want to talk about it?" Milo asks softly, his hands a gentle caress. I nod slowly because I really do. I don't want to talk about *her*.

But I have to.

"My mom wasn't the best," I start, because where else can you start? "She was only fifteen when she got pregnant. She lied to her family about her pregnancy with me, for who knows what reason. The reason changed every time I asked. She didn't want them to force her to abort, she didn't want them to force her to get married, she didn't want them to force her to give me up, et cetera, et cetera." I roll my eyes. "One day, she decided she didn't want to be pregnant anymore and decided to try to self-abort. She failed and was put in the psych ward, where everyone finally realized she was pregnant with me. She was force-fed all the vitamins she hadn't taken in the previous months. When she finally had me, my father married her because 'it was the right thing to do', which is such bullshit." I scoff before continuing.

"She babied my father growing up, did everything for him. But me…" I pause, kind of stuck on how exactly to word this. "She treated me like I was nothing to her. I was a burden to them. She never missed an opportunity to tell me how difficult I made their life." I sigh, breathing in Milo's citrus-and-rain scent.

"I got to play hockey, and everyone kept telling me how good I was, and I thought, 'Hey, here's my chance to pay them back.' I kept working hard and getting better and got drafted when I was eighteen." The tears are starting to well up at this point, overflowing down my cheeks and soaking Milo's shirt sleeve. "The night of the draft, my mom just left. No note, nothing. I used my first paycheck to hire a private investigator to try and find her. He found her." It's starting to get harder to talk as I cry harder. "She was with a new husband, one that didn't gamble away all their savings and was taking care of his two kids. A proper little family."

Milo is straddling my lap, holding my head close to his chest and whispering soothing words to me.

"She said she deserved a chance at a real family," I sob. "I still only hear from her once in a blue moon when she asks for money for her stepkids." And I give it to her. I have nothing against these kids, and if she just wants them to go to a good college, who am I to hinder that?

"That wasn't fair of her to put on you," Milo says, pulling me close. "Her inability to be a mother to you was on her, not you."

Milo takes me to the bedroom, and we curl up together, me crying and him holding me.

"I feel safe with you," I whisper into Milo's neck. He responds by covering my face in kisses.

Chapter 29

Milo

I wake up the next morning, and my heart is aching for Beau.

What he told me about his parents... I know mine are really a piece of work, but his mom clearly did a number on his self-worth.

I wake up with my arms still wrapped around him, holding him close. He looks so peaceful in my arms, so serene. Nothing like the sobbing man I saw last night. I think about his tears, just the endless tears as I held him and he wept. I think about those tears, and I feel helpless. What am I supposed to do?

I know that his strong emotions and his shitty childhood are why he numbs his emotions with alcohol now. I'm sure he grew up seeing that shit on the daily. And just because he recognizes that what his parents did wasn't okay doesn't mean he doesn't see drinking like that as normal behavior.

I don't want to see him hurt himself, but I don't want to be that guy who starts out a potential relationship by delivering an ultimatum.

My thoughts turn to Coach. To what he's been through. Maybe he would understand what I'm thinking. Maybe he would understand why it's so important that I handle this. He would get why Beau's self-medicating is a problem.

It may be risky, talking to Coach, but I know that all he wants is for his team to work cohesively. He wouldn't hold something as trivial as drinking against Beau.

When I first joined the team, I never went out with the guys after games. Why would I go to bars and shit when I don't drink? But he told me it's not about drinking with everyone; it's about the camaraderie built in time spent together. It's about being a team, always.

It took me quite a few tries to get the hang of a mocktail menu, but eventually, I figured it out. Now I go to every celebration with my teammates because they're my brothers.

I roll out of bed, leaving Beau, planting a kiss on his forehead before slipping into sweats and a T-shirt.

I need to talk to our coach.

When we were talking about my own hangups with alcohol, Coach Waldor told me about his own past with alcohol.

He was a center for the Minnesota team back in the day, top of his game, in his absolute prime. He was married back then, to a pretty young woman named Jackie. He was drinking one night to celebrate after a game and got behind the wheel. He hit ice and then hit a tree, concussion, pelvic fracture, foot crushed. Jackie died on impact.

They slapped him with a DUI, took away his license and he lost the love of his life.

He never drank again.

Coach knows how much alcohol can fuck up your life. He'll know exactly what to say to Beau.

I pull up to the rink and park in the garage.

When I finally walk up to Coach's office, you'd think I would have some idea of what I'm going to say, but no, of course not. I have nothing. Nada. Zilch.

But I knock on the door anyway.

"Come in." His voice is booming, always so stern and strait-laced. I push open the door, and he smiles at me. He's a handsome older man, neatly trimmed hair cut close, dark eyes. He walks with a slight limp, but that doesn't take away from his powerful presence. "Milo, what can I do for you?"

I pull out the chair across from his desk and sit myself down. This is not going to be a standing conversation.

"I'm worried," I say quickly, maybe too quickly. "About Beau."

I'm suddenly ashamed, embarrassed to be airing Beau's dirty laundry like this to our coach of all people. I feel my cheeks heating, the flush blooming across my face.

"Worried? About what exactly?" He quirks a brow, clearly taking in my blush but thankfully not addressing it.

"His drinking." I've come this far, might as well get some insight. "I'm worried about how much he's using alcohol to numb his emotions. I'm worried about him, and I don't know how to talk to him about it."

"I see." Coach Waldor is watching me carefully, a serious look on his face. "It's not my place to talk to him about things that aren't affecting him on the ice."

"It's affecting me," I say quickly. "I worry about him constantly. I can't focus during practice because all I can think about is if he's at home getting buzzed. I know he's only out for a few months, but I worry about him so much. I l—"

I come to a screeching halt.

I'm not saying that for the first time out loud to my coach.

But it's true. I do love him.

I love him so much I'm sitting in my coach's office, trying to figure out how to tell a boy that I love him. Because when it comes down to it, that's what I really want to tell him.

"I'm scared he's going to end up really hurting himself," I finally continue.

"I see," Waldor says again, very slowly.

We sit like that for quite some time, stilted silence between us. I think he knows exactly who I am, and I think I have to tell him.

"I'm gay," I spit out, my words coming out much too quickly. There's a beat of silence between us before.

"I figured," he answers self-assuredly, nodding to himself, because of course he knew.

There, that wasn't so hard.

"You have to be honest with Beau about how you're feeling, son," Waldor says slowly, like he wants to make sure I'm following every word so carefully. And I am. "If you can't do that, then you're not starting your relationship out with open communication and honesty. That's so important. Jackie always said that communication and honesty were the key to any happy and healthy relationship."

"But this isn't just about our relationship," I counter. "This is about him as an individual."

"Then you'll have to appeal to him as an individual."

His attention turns back to his computer, and for some reason, I feel as if our conversation is done here. I push myself to stand.

"Milo." Waldor doesn't even look up as he types, but he has a secret smile tilting his lips. "Tell the boy how you feel. I think that'll be enough for him."

I nod slowly, but internally, I'm battling. Because Beau is still so skittish. What if I tell him how I feel, that I love him, and he bolts? What if he laughs?

No, he wouldn't do that. He wouldn't do that to me.

The car ride home is so tense that I am pretty much white-knuckling the steering wheel the whole time.

I walk through the front door, and Beau has on those glasses, and he's reading one of my smutty books. He looks up when I walk through the door and smiles.

"Did you know some of these books are, like, emotional porn?" he asks with the loveliest smile that I try to match. I must not do the best job because his falls, and he sets the book down. "What's wrong?"

"I wanted to talk to you about something," I say slowly, unsure really of how to start.

"Okay." Beau nods and pats the couch next to him. I plop down beside him, and he scooches closer to me. Our sides are touching, and I instantly feel a little better, a little braver.

"I want to talk about what you told me last night," I start. "Just a little bit," I hurry to continue when his face kind of falls. "I don't want to make you uncomfortable at all, so we can talk about anything else if it starts to feel that way, okay?" He nods slowly, a wary look on his face. "You told me about how awful your mom was, but I want to ask about your dad."

Beau laughs a shallow laugh.

"What about him? He's a deadbeat who is always asking for money." He scoffs a little and looks straight ahead. Fuck. Have I pissed him off already?

"Why is he always calling you and asking for money?" I ask carefully. I think I know, based on what I've overheard, but I don't want to assume.

"He's a fucking addict," Beau says matter-of-factly. "He gambles his life away and then I have to bail him out because I owe him. I wouldn't be a big hockey star if it wasn't for him." I can tell he's repeating words he's heard over and over.

"You know that's not true. Children don't owe their parents anything." I reach out to touch him, unsure if he even wants that, but he leans into the touch. I take the opportunity to wrap an arm around him and pull him to me. "I … I want to talk about his addiction."

"What about it?" He gives me a killer side-eye, and I blanch a little. "He was a shit father." He leans back into the couch, crossing his arms with a vexed expression on his face. "He was always busy driving up to Oklahoma to gamble away his life. We never played catch or whatever cheesy dad stuff he was supposed to do."

Like not making you feel like a burden? I think to myself.

"Have you heard about addictive tendencies being genetic?"

"Genetic?"

"Yeah," I continue slowly. Not because I don't think he can keep up, but because I don't want to miss anything. "Basically, children of parents with substance use disorders have a higher risk of developing addictive tendencies, despite how they were raised, and you were raised in the thick of it." Beau is nodding as I'm talking, and I suddenly feel like I'm talking over him. "I don't want to just steamroll you. I want your input. I want this to be a conversation."

"I don't really have anything to say. Besides, it sounds like you think I'm an alcoholic."

"No!" I say, maybe a little too loudly. "No, baby, I don't think that. Not at all. What I think is that all the cards you've been handed in life make it a lot easier for that to happen." I take a deep breath as my eyes begin to burn. "And I'm scared that I'll lose you to it if I don't say anything."

Beau looks at me then, really looks at me, eyebrows scrunched and lips downturned in focus.

"You promise you don't think that?" he asks carefully.

"No, no, I promise I don't think that at all, Beau. I know you." This is it, the moment of truth. This is my chance to tell him exactly how I feel. The words feel like they're stuck in my chest, right above my heart, where they've lived all this time. "I—" They stay stuck.

We just sit there while I silently fight with myself to build up the courage to tell Beau I love him.

Because I do love him.

I love his smiles. I love his passion. I love his fears and doubts, and I love his flaws. I love all the little things that make up *Beau*.

He's talking, saying something, but I can't focus. All I can think of are those stuck words buried deep in my chest, until they're bubbling up my throat and I'm blurting them out.

"I love you."

Silence.

Beau isn't looking at me, but to be fair, my eyes are squeezed shut, so I guess I don't really know where he's looking.

"Milo?" His voice is so quiet, so unsure. I squeeze my eyes tighter until I feel his hand on my face. I peel my eyes open slowly and peek at him. His cheeks are flushed, and there's a dark curl falling in his face. He looks dreamy like this.

"Yeah?" I ask, wondering if I should just pretend I didn't say anything. Maybe he'll let me skirt right past this as if nothing has even happened. I think I could possibly get away with it.

"I—" he starts, and my breath gets caught in my chest. "I love you too."

And I smile. I smile so wide before tackling him, gently, to the couch and catching his mouth with mine. Our kiss feels electric.

I love him.

I love him.

I love him.

And he loves me.

Chapter 30

Beau

Milo and I are lying in bed together, his fingers running through my curls, my hand holding him to me.

I love him.

Fuck.

There's something about that moment. That moment when he told me that felt so surreal. Like I can't believe how lucky I am *and* like I'm scared out of my mind. I think he could tell then that I was feeling both, because he wasn't clinging to me too tightly, a fact I couldn't be more grateful for.

The morning silence is lulling, so much so that I could easily fall back to sleep. Maybe it's the silence, or maybe it's the man whose arms I'm in. I couldn't tell you. All I know is that I feel completely at ease in this exact moment. His arms are exactly where I want to be.

Our peace doesn't last, though. It can't. Because today is the first day I'm allowed back to the practice rink. Just to do light cardio, but still, better than being cooped up all day alone.

"Are you ready for it?" Milo asks, his voice a careful calm. Its gentle lilt is music to my ears.

"Ready for what?" I ask, as if I don't know exactly what he's asking about. As if my chest isn't thrumming with excitement. Because what else could he possibly be asking about?

He gives me a look like he's thinking exactly that.

"Practice, getting back to the rink. Do you think they'll let you skate at all?" His voice is a little excited at the prospect, and even though I know there's absolutely no chance that they will, I play along with his enthusiasm.

"Maybe, I don't know." I do my little half shrug still, since one arm has been entirely out of commission for far too long now. I barely know how to function with two anymore, even if it's only been a week.

"Do you think we have time before we have to get ready?" Milo asks, a sultry smile on his face. I groan, wanting nothing more than to sink into his warmth but knowing we have, at most, ten minutes before we need to get going. "Hand jobs?" I ask, and he growls. Like he really growls before he pounces on me.

We're rolling around in the bed, the sheets kicked off, and our dicks in each other's hands. It's a race against time as I thrust and thrust, desperate to come but even more desperate to see him lose it.

"Whoever comes first has to drive to practice." I laugh when Milo instantly slows his jerking of my cock. "C'mon, I'm not *that* bad of a driver." His eyebrows fly up his forehead. Okay, maybe I am that bad. By Texas standards, I'm a gold-star driver.

I start jerking Milo leisurely.

"At this rate, neither of us is going to come, and we'll be going to practice with our dicks hard." Milo laughs.

"That'll be pretty awkward to explain to the other guys, huh?" I shrug, because teasing him like this is just too fun.

"Fuck, baby," he groans when I give his cock a particularly heady squeeze. "Please let me come." He begs so prettily for me. "Please, baby."

My hand picks up speed, and I watch as his balls draw up.

"That's it, baby girl, come for me."

And he obeys.

We're holding hands the entire car ride to the rink, but our hands drop when we get there. It doesn't quite feel right to not be holding him in some way, but he's not ready to come out, and I'm going to respect his decision.

I feel like I could scream it from the rooftops, but until he's ready to whisper it to our team, I'm going to keep it under wraps. I know he talked to Coach, and we've talked to Miranda, but neither person is going to out us to the whole team. The team feels like a different step. A step that may be a little scary.

We are still walking next to each other when we push into the locker room. Everyone is chatting loudly, laughing and enjoying themselves. We move to get ready for practice.

I'm dressed for cardio, basketball shorts and a sweatshirt. The athletic trainer, Mia, meets me in the weight room, and we head over to the treadmill. She's short, has to only be five foot two, but she's terrifying as she threatens me within an inch of my life.

"And you're not going to *touch* the speed, do you understand?" she glowers at me, and I nod so damn hard it hurts my neck a little.

I start walking, music blasting in my ear, and watch out of the corner of my eye as she talks to the physical therapist.

Their heads are bent close together as they chatter, the gossips. I guess I'll know soon enough what they're saying.

I've always enjoyed cardio like this, just the peace of alone time.

Time ticks slowly by. Tick, tick, tick, and I'm walking, walking, walking with music blasting in my ear when suddenly my headphones die.

"Well, that blows," I say out loud to no one. And then I'm just there, walking, the whirring sound of the treadmill the only sound I hear. I leave my headphones in, not wanting to lose them, and just listen to the silence.

When you have no music, your mind has time to wander, and the places it wanders are ... interesting. I wonder about treadmills. What was the first one like? I wonder about that weird dog treadmill that I've seen videos of on TikTok. Are those expensive? I wonder if it's just big dogs that use those treadmills or if anyone ever brings their corgis to use them. I wonder about dogs and if Milo has ever wanted one. I've always wanted one, but with our away schedule, it would be so hard.

Milo.

Fuck, I told him I love him.

It took me a year to tell Bianca that I loved her, and yet it's barely been three months. Is he my boyfriend? Do I want him to be my boyfriend?

I think I do.

I thought I was ready for the ultimate hoe phase. I was ready to sleep with all of Minneapolis when I got here, then this six-one, wide, princess-eyed, gorgeous man box jumped into my life.

We should probably talk about...

"Beau!"

I trip over myself, my hand slamming on the emergency stop.

Mia is glaring at me.

"I've been calling your name for, like, three minutes!" she crosses her arms in an adorable little pout. "Turn your music down next time."

I don't correct her, pulling out my earbuds and tossing the case in my bag.

We move through the gym with the physical therapist, working on passive shoulder movements and lower arm exercises. All the while, my mind stays stagnant.

Milo.

Milo.

Mia and the physical therapist, Terry, are getting irritated with me, I can tell. Because I'm barely paying attention to them and just thinking about my man on the ice.

I can't wait to be out there playing with him again.

"Beau!" Terry is calling to me, his dark eyes glaring a hole into the side of my head. "You have to be *here* right now if you ever want to get back on that ice. I need your mind present."

And I do want to get back onto that ice, more than anything, so I buckle down and we work out this fucking shoulder.

I'm already in the locker room and showered clean when the guys get off the ice and start piling in. When Milo clambers through with all his heavy pads, my eyes find his instantly. Those grassy greens, like a field I want to lie out in and soak up the sun.

Paxton walks by me and elbows me, albeit carefully, but still.

"You're looking at him with heart eyes," he whispers to me, a tiny secret smile on his face. I turn back to my man, who's giving us a questioning look. Paxton smiles a little wider and shakes his head. "You two are so obvious."

Something flashes in Milo's eyes, something akin to recognition. He's looking at me like he's seeing our future.

I hope he likes what he sees.

Then, without warning, he's clapping his hands together, trying to get everyone's attention.

"Hey, everyone, hey, I have an announcement," he calls out to the other guys in various states of undress.

What is he doing?

I look at him, my many questions obvious in my pinched brow.

Once he's apparently gotten everyone's attention, he looks at me as if gathering his strength. I try to give him moral support with just a look.

Is he..?

"I'm gay."

Oh, wow.

He doesn't say that we're dating or that we're in love, because that would mean outing me and we absolutely have not talked about this. But why can't I come out to my team? I no longer have an overbearing agent demanding I keep both feet planted firmly in the closet.

I walk over to him with purpose and grab him. I hear movement behind me, like maybe they think I'm going to punch him or have some other horrible response to the love of my life coming out to our team.

But no.

I kiss him.

I grab his handsome face and kiss him like this is the end of the line and we have nothing left to lose.

We come up for air, and the locker room is silent. I wouldn't have expected thunderous applause, but the air feels somber.

Brennan has this look in his eyes like he's missing exactly what we have. Oskar is staring at his feet, shuffling them a little. Kirill's face is set in a hard line, not happy but not really unhappy, just kind of neutral. He meets my eyes before looking down at his skates. Paxton's face is flushed, and his eyes are wide. I definitely don't think he expected that.

What did we just do?

Chapter 31

Milo

I t's been a few months since we've come out to the team, and everyone really seems to have gotten on board. At the very least, they're not giving us uncomfortable side-eyes anymore. Paxton must have talked to them at some point. I so appreciate that man and his awesome captaining skills.

Home life has been incredible. Beau has been trying—like, genuinely trying—with his sobriety. Neither of us subscribes to the twelve-step program, and the research we've done together talks about sobriety not being a linear journey. We've looked into support groups, but for now, I'm just supporting him as best I can.

We still haven't actually labeled what we are, which I find incredibly frustrating, but I'm too embarrassed to ask him. Are we boyfriends? Partners? Lovers?

Ew. That sounds so gross.

In all honesty, though, I don't need a label, as long as I have Beau.

Though, one would be nice.

My face breaks out into the dopiest smile thinking about my man. Thinking about his dark eyes and wild curls. The man in question is curled up next to me on the couch, his head on my lap, my fingers running through said curls.

His body is tense, and I know he's thinking about the game tomorrow.

We're flying out tonight to play in Dallas. It's his first game back. It's also the first playoff game that Minnesota has been a part of in years. I can tell he's feeling so much pressure about everything.

"I really want a drink," he mutters. I start petting his head because I know he loves it, but also because I don't really have anything to say to that. The first few times I responded with something, Beau told me that my words came off as judgmental. That's the last thing I want.

I really want to be there for him in every way possible. It's just hard when he's also on this difficult journey. A journey that I've never experienced myself and that I've already come off as judgmental about. How can I be supportive if I don't know what to say?

So I've decided I'm going to start seeing someone. A therapist. Not all the time, just enough so I know how to respond in moments like right now. So I know how to support him without sounding like I'm judging him.

Because, in all honesty, I'm so proud of him, of everything he's done so far this year. How far he's come just since being injured. How far he's come with his sobriety. I'm so, so proud of him.

But in moments like this, quiet moments where he's scared and unsure of himself, when he wants to fall back into old patterns, I'm just not sure how I can best support him. I want to be the best boyfriend, partner, lover, whatever he could ever ask for. I want to be the best *person* for him.

I wonder sometimes if maybe my parents did something of a number on me. Part of me doesn't trust that any of this is really real. That I have a man who loves me. I've spent nights so convinced that I'm going to wake up and none of it will have been real, or that the love we've professed to each other will be treated like nothing more than a passing fancy.

But maybe that's because for years I've been told by my parents that what I believe is a lie.

But I'm starting to see now.

They are the liars.

They said that if I came out, my career would be over. That my life would be over. They told me to hide that part of myself and never let it out, because if anyone ever saw that side of me, they would be disgusted with me.

They were wrong.

Looking back, it was blatant homophobia disguised as parental concern.

That seems so much more obvious now. Like I should have been able to see it if I didn't have the blinders of my own fear on.

It's hard not to immediately blame myself for trusting them all those years, as if they weren't the only source of truth I knew growing up.

But Beau has helped me navigate that in his own weird way. It feels like for every instance they told me I would be nothing, he's made me feel like I am everything.

But that's a lot of weight to put on one person, especially someone who's going through their own mental health issues. So, yeah. Therapist.

I think I'm going to give it a go and see if I can encourage Beau to go, for his sobriety and just all the bullshit with his parents. I bet he would. I don't feel nervous telling him I'm going myself, but the thought of suggesting he go... Sometimes people can be sensitive about their mental health.

I'm not going to be a dick about it or anything. I just think it may help. I'm not going to be one of those assholes who gives him an ultimatum. I'm going to support him, whatever he chooses.

He pushes himself to sit up and looks at me, really looks at me, like he's trying to see my soul through my eyes. I wonder exactly what it is he's looking for.

He must find it, because he sidles up next to me, rubbing his shoulder against mine and starting his suggestive little dance. One thing I will never complain about is Beau's chosen method of distraction from needing a drink: sex.

I stand, laughing, and pull him to his feet. When he's standing, he decides to show off a little by pulling me into his arms and sweeping my legs up around his waist. I'm still laughing as he carries us into the kitchen and has his way with me.

I hate the atmosphere in other teams' arenas. I hate the boos and the jeers. I hate the animosity stifling the air. But I absolutely love knowing the Zambonis are going to be cleaning their blood off the ice later.

Oh fuck.

That was kind of intense.

I shake the ugliness from my head and focus on the warmups, my teammates smashing puck after puck in my direction. I feel like I'm going to be on fire tonight.

Another puck thuds against my heavy padding when I notice Dallas's side looking over at us. It may just be my ego, but it feels like they're looking at me. They better not try the same shit, not when Beau is still healing. Not when he shouldn't be getting into any kind of fights.

Speaking of, he skates over to me, grabbing my water bottle from on top of the pipes.

"Does something seem kind of off tonight?" he asks as he aims and squirts water past my mask and into my mouth. The move feels kind of slutty, and I will my cock to calm down. I nod, eyeing the ice to make sure no one is going to blast either of us with a lightning-fast puck.

He's looking toward the other end of the rink, and I follow his gaze. Erickson, the player who crowded the crease that one game, is glaring our way. Beau, the antagonistic little shit that he is, blows him a kiss. I'm sure if he wasn't wearing giant gloves, he'd be flipping us off.

I smack Beau's shoulder, the better of the two, and he laughs. His smile is wide and his eyes crinkle a little at the sides. I love when he laughs, when it's a real, full, genuine laugh like this.

"I love you," I say earnestly, albeit quietly. And I do. And I have to say it right now, because the smile on his face could destroy me, and I simply have to let him know.

His smile becomes a small, secret thing, just between us, and I match it.

"I love you too. Now, let's kick some ass."

The game gets underway, and there's no time for settling in. Dallas puts me right to work with a dump-and-chase, obviously trying to unsettle me. Their defense crashes the crease early. It's as if they're trying to make the crease entirely unlivable. There are several warning whistles but no penalties as my stick gets kicked, my pads get hacked, and I'm snowed on.

It's an all-out war against me. They're not trying to simply beat me. They want me to flinch.

Rebound after rebound is shoved back toward me. Kirill and Oskar are scrambling. It feels like the ice is absolute chaos.

Suddenly, Dallas—Erickson specifically—bowls into me. No call, no whistle, nothing. I push him off me as I force myself to stand. Beau is flying toward us.

"Here comes your boyfriend, you fag." He spits at my skates. "Can't wait to get him ejected from the game again."

But the body that slams into Erickson isn't my Beau. I see the number thirty-two. It's Oskar, who's thrown his gloves and is smashing his fist into Erickson's face.

Beau slides to a stop next to me, checking me over before looking down at the heap of punches and flailing skates on the ice.

When the refs finally break it up, it's not just Oskar who gets a penalty. He skates past us and smiles.

"Nobody goes after my goalie," he says with a jaunty wink. "We've got your back." And off he skates to the sin bin.

Beau and I look at each other. Maybe we're not so alone.

Chapter 32

Beau

Nerves flutter in my belly, a million tiny butterflies moshing and going wild. Tonight, I'm going to do it. I'm going to ask Milo to be my boyfriend.

Sweat is pooling under my arms and down my chest, and I'm soaking through another undershirt. I need some extra-strength shit to get this under control or I'm not going to be able to actually make it out the door.

Milo looked so cute and excited when I told him I wanted to take him out tonight. His face lit up, and a blush spread across his cheeks, those lovely freckles standing out against the flush.

He's standing in the room, *our* room. I don't bother with the guest room. I haven't in a long time. Why would I want to sleep anywhere but in his arms? Why would I want to be anywhere but with him?

Fuck, he looks good.

He's standing in front of the full-length mirror, doing up a deep green button-down. His slacks hug his delicious ass and the curve of his thighs. I want to fall to my knees and worship it. To pull down those tight slacks and bite his bubble butt.

Oh, he's saying something.

"What was that?" I ask. He smirks because he knows I was distracted by his ass. Of course I was. It's the perfect ass.

"I said, if you would pay attention…" I roll my eyes at him, and he laughs. "What are you wearing to this place? Where are we going again?"

"Okay, okay." I throw my hands up in mock surrender because that was way more than one question. "You look great in that, perfect even. I just can't find the shirt I was going to wear."

I walk out of the room and to my bag in the guest room because, okay, so I'm not sleeping in there, but moving my stuff into his room feels like such a huge step. We already passed so many steps by living together before we even started seeing each other. I'm scared to pass any more.

I rifle through the closet before finding the black shirt I'm looking for. I'm simple, classic. I want the focus to be on Milo and making him feel special. Because he is special. He's so special to me.

Speaking of, he pokes his head into the open doorway, looking around. There's a tiny frown on his face until he spots me, then it spreads into a big, beautiful smile.

"You look amazing." His words are so sweet, so demure. I walk over to him with purpose, and he stares up at me through thick lashes. My hand caresses his cheek, and he leans into the touch, before leaning in for a kiss.

The kiss is sweet, tender, nothing hurried or rushed about it, just enjoying the feeling of his lips pressed against mine. I long to taste him, but I know what that will turn into if I'm not careful, so I pull away from the kiss and just stare at him longingly.

We stand there for several moments, eyes locked, arms wrapped around each other, just lost in each other's eyes. I want to get lost in him for days.

His eyes, in this light, look like a wild field, grassy slopes I could lose myself in.

"Should we go, or..." he asks me, kind of shyly. I know what he's suggesting, and I want it too. I want it so bad, but I want tonight even more. I lean forward and kiss his forehead, his pretty blond curls getting in my way, before I pull him out the door.

We walk outside, and before I can pull out the keys to his BMW, he's already walking toward Buck.

"Sorry, baby." I chuckle. "You're driving. The roads are still a little icy." He rolls his eyes at me before catching the keys I toss to him. "We don't want another off-roading adventure." I laugh and wink at him. "I'm fresh out of lube packets in Buck."

He flushes the deepest red. It spreads down his neck, and I would bet anything that if I opened up that shirt, I'd find his chest a splotchy pink mess.

That time in the truck, lewd as it was, is one of my most fond memories. One of my most treasured memories with Milo.

It was when I felt my most connected with him, connected in every sense of the word.

Now I'm blushing.

The restaurant is nice, dark, secluded, really private for two closeted queer men to go on a date and hopefully not be recognized. I understand we're two incredible hockey players in the dead center of the land of hockey, but a man can dream.

We're seated in the very back of the restaurant. The lighting is dim, and the tables are well spaced. Maybe this will be a smooth evening. I reach across the table and grab Milo's hand, giving it a gentle squeeze. He smiles at me.

"I hope you two are having a… Oh! It's you!" a voice I don't recognize exclaims, albeit, somewhat quietly. I groan and drop my face into my hands with a thud.

"Oh, Jamie, hi." Milo's voice is low.

My head springs up, and I glare at the man standing by our table. Eyes narrowed into angry slits, lips downturned, I turn my frustration on *Jamie*.

"What are you doing here? Don't you work at McFolley's?" I ask, a little venom in my voice.

"Shockingly, not all of us are on multi-million-dollar hockey contracts and can just afford to live in such a big city without stretching things a little thin." Jamie raises a brow at me and cocks his hip.

Oh.

Okay. Well, that is fair.

I'm so embarrassed by my outburst that I don't recognize that he's clocked us.

"I didn't realize you were spoken for. I wouldn't have flirted so much." Jamie is looking at Milo, a sly smile on those plush lips.

Milo's blushing. I'm blushing. The only one not blushing is Jamie. Why would he be embarrassed? He's clearly secure in his sexuality.

I mean…

I am too. I just…

Fuck, it shouldn't be this hard to be with the man I love. To take him out to dinner, to show him how much I appreciate him. This should be easy.

My hands clench by my side, and I suddenly feel simultaneously so embarrassed and so envious. Embarrassed for my outburst, and envious that Jamie is able to be exactly who he is without hesitation.

Jamie smiles at me and winks. I flinch. Not for any dumb homophobic reason, just because I feel like I can't have what he has. But I want it.

Jamie takes our drink orders, sparkling water for me because I desperately need a drink and the bubbles ease my anxiety, and walks off to grab them for us. Milo looks at me with a cocked head and an even more cocked brow.

"I don't know what that was," I lie, then I shake my head. "No, I know exactly what that was. That was jealousy rearing its ugly head again. All I could think about was how he flirted with you at the bar, and my jealousy just shot through the roof."

Milo is nodding slowly as I speak, letting me get out all the words I have to say. He's so good like that, such an excellent listener.

"I think you should consider apologizing to Jamie," he says finally, and I flush harder, because he's right. I know he's right. All Jamie did was see an assumedly single and incredibly sexy man and act. Did he know that I had called metaphorical dibs? No. So can I really hold that against him? Again, no.

Jamie comes back with our waters. He's all smiles and charm and ease, like I wasn't just an ass to him. He sets them down in front of us and grabs his notepad from his little apron, pulling out a pen and staring at us expectantly.

"Well, what can I getcha?" His voice is bubbly and sweet and every bit the professional who was not just seethed at.

I unclench my fists and place them on the table, palms tilted up in a kind of surrender.

"I'm sorry I came for your neck there." My hand flies up to rub the back of my neck. "Earlier, you know. And at McFolley's." I meet his eyes and square my shoulders. "I was jealous. I still kind of am, if I'm going to be honest." My hands clasp together and I wring them nervously. "Jealous of you flirting with Milo, obviously, but I think I'm also jealous of you getting to be out." I let out a sigh, glad to have finally said it.

Milo rubs my knee under the table, smiling his secret smile.

Jamie smiles at me as well, placing a friendly hand on my shoulder.

"I get it. Being in the closet fucking sucks. I will tell you, though, for me, the closet door was glass, so it made coming out a lot more insistent." He pats my shoulder and smiles, kind of a sad smile. "Look, I'll forgive you, but only if you give me the number of one of your other teammates, preferably someone else who's actually queer," he says with a jaunty wink. "Now, seriously, what can I get you?"

"Seriously, we haven't even looked at the menu." Milo laughs, and I smile at him.

When Jamie walks away, I take Milo's hand from across the table.

"I wanted to bring you here for a few reasons," I start, suddenly nervous again. "One, I really just wanted to take you on a proper date. I've fucked you every which way in every room of the house, but we haven't gone out together. We haven't fought over the bill, but I've licked your asshole." Milo is blushing furiously and shaking his head, his lips pursed so I know he's fighting a smile.

"And two," I continue, "I wanted to ask you something." I take a deep breath, and Milo gasps.

"You're not about to do anything stupid, are you?"

"Define stupid?" I respond, taking a sip of my water.

"Like marriage kind of stupid." He balks, and I spit water all over the table. Coughing and spluttering, I knock the air back into my lungs and gulp a few deep breaths.

When I finally get my breathing back under control, I continue.

"Um, no, not that." I smile at him brightly. "Skipping a few steps there, bud." He laughs.

"Nothing about our relationship is normal." He laughs, gesturing widely to our general surroundings. "Case in point..." I laugh with him.

I look at him and just smile. He looks so beautiful tonight, his hair down and wild, blond curls floating around his face.

My love for him overwhelms me.

"I want you to be my boyfriend," I finally blurt out.

Silence.

Milo is staring at me, eyes wide.

"Beau," he starts, his voice low. When he continues, he speaks a little slowly. Not in an insulting way, but in a confused way. "We've been dating for months."

"No, I know that," I say hurriedly, waving him off. "But no one's asked the question, so I'm asking."

"So you're asking." He smiles, a soft, sweet kind of smile.

He pulls out his wallet and places a couple of twenties on the table.

"We haven't ordered yet."

"If you think I'm going to be able to stay here and eat when all I can think about is how much I want you to ravage me…" He leans in like he's telling me a secret, and fuck, he's undressing me with his eyes.

I push myself to a stand and grab his hand, pulling him behind me. We've gotta go.

Chapter 33

Milo

I can feel him everywhere, his hands rubbing all over my body. Touching me in places I didn't think could possibly be sensual, yet here he is, making shivers run up and down my spine just by caressing my clavicle.

I've known, obviously, that Beau has magical hands. He just does; that's a fact. The way those twisted fingers work their way inside me, ugh... It undoes me completely. But here, with just the two of us exploring each other's bodies, I feel captivated.

"You're so beautiful," he whispers in my ear, so low I have to strain to hear him. Maybe that's part of the appeal. That he's forcing me, in some sense. He knows I love a little strength tossed around, but who doesn't love a few mental hurdles?

He lazily kisses my body, my shoulders, my chest, my neck. Soft lips pressing against my warm skin.

"So, so beautiful," he whispers, kissing my earlobe before sucking it into his mouth and nibbling it a bit.

His tongue licks a stripe down the column of my neck, and I let out a tiny gasp, as if that's all the noise I'm capable of making. He chuckles at the sound, licking small circles at the juncture of my neck and shoulder before biting down. I howl. My straining erection seeks any kind of friction, but he has my arms pinned above my head, no binding necessary, my legs spread wide.

I'm entirely at his mercy.

A fact I think he is all too happy about right now as he teasingly runs his fingers down my arms, reminding me that I'm his. That I could move, but I'm choosing to obey him.

He pulls away and looks down at me, admiring the squirming mess I am.

I whine at the loss of contact until he takes pity on me, ducking down and biting one of my nipples harshly. I cry out, but he knows I love it, the pain mixed with pleasure.

While he tongues one nipple, his hand toys with the other, and my cock is left entirely abandoned. I'm humping the air like a rutting animal, desperate for contact.

"Please, Beau," I beg, trying desperately to catch his thigh, his hip, anything, as my pelvis humps fruitlessly.

Chuckling, he takes mercy on me and wraps a steady hand around my weeping cock.

"We're going to play a little game." He looks down at me, his smile wicked. "You're going to tell me when you're about to come, and I'll stop touching you." I whine, and he presses a finger to my lips.

"I promise, if you play along, you'll get the most incredible orgasm."

"I know the concept of edging, thank you," I snap at him, immediately not liking where this is going. "What happens if I don't tell you?"

"Then you will have a boring, ordinary orgasm." He shrugs, then looks at me with narrowed eyes. "Is that really what you want tonight? To be boring?"

The fucker's got me there. After all this build up and the dinner tonight, I want extraordinary. I let out a sassy puff of air and shake my head, bracing myself for his torture.

He gives my cock a little squeeze, causing the precome to bead up at the top and I suck in a sharp breath.

Reaching over my body to grab the lube, his own erection brushes mine and my hips jump.

"Naughty boy." He tsks, squirting a generous amount into his hands before wrapping his fingers delicately back around my aching dick.

"Beau, please," I beg again, but he just smiles down at me.

"Let's play, baby."

And we do.

I am howling, my body bowing toward the ceiling, unable to control the fervent yowls as Beau leaves me dangling on the edge *again*.

I've been brought to the brink a grand total of seven times and have yet to come. My body feels like it's on fire. My balls are heavy, drawn up tight, desperate to explode.

"Beau, Beau, Beau!" I cry out his name as he jerks and jerks my cock, fingers teasing my hole. It feels like I'm being zapped by lightning in the best possible way, my body tingling with desire and unshed need. I need to come so badly I feel like I might burst from my skin.

Just when I think he might *finally* let me find release, he stops, and I scream. Tears stream down my cheeks, my face and chest burning hot. I need, need, need to come.

"What, princess?" he coos, leaning in close and kissing my forehead. He licks at my tear-soaked cheeks. "Mmm." He hums in approval, clearly enjoying my lack of restraint.

"Are you ready to come, baby girl?" he asks, faux pity in his eyes.

He's teasing me.

More tears spill over, and he gently wipes them away.

"Don't cry, princess. I'll let you come." He presses a tender kiss to my lips, and I sob into his embrace, my aching cock twitching, so desperate for release. My body trembling with need. His thumb swipes beneath the head, and my back bows, chasing the sensation.

Please, please, please, I beg, unsure if I'm even speaking anymore. Unsure if I'm even able to.

All I know is lust.

All I know is want.

All I know is need.

My eyes must be shut, because I don't see him move. I don't feel him move. Honestly, I can barely feel anything besides my heart beating in my cock, making it twitch violently.

He's suddenly straddling my face, his cock bobbing in front of me. I take him into my mouth like I'm starving, ravishing him with my tongue and swallowing around him. He groans his approval before diving down on my dick. I'm fully enveloped in the warm heat of his mouth, and it takes everything in me not to thrust blindly and fervently.

My hips pump shallowly, pushing between his plush lips as I chase my release.

It's right there, within my grasp.

His tongue runs circles around the head before sliding down the shaft, and my eyes roll back into my head. One of his hands tugs on my balls, and I see stars.

"Beau! Beau, I'm gonna…"

I lose all ability to speak as I come, rope after creamy rope spilling into Beau's mouth. It overflows, dripping from the corner of his lips.

His tongue peeks out to clean up the mess I've made. His eyes meet mine, and he smiles.

Fuck, he drives me wild.

I dive back onto his cock, sucking and licking, desperate for his come. He's moaning, groaning, encouraging my ministrations.

"Yes, baby," he coos, reaching back to awkwardly run his fingers through my hair. "Fuck, fuck, fuck," he curses, and I swallow around him as he bursts down my throat.

I continue to suck on his spent cock until he's whining and pulling free from my mouth, a little lingering revenge for the delicious edging.

We lie there, side by side, completely worn out.

Beau curls around me, my arms still bound above my head, my legs still spread wide. He makes me feel so safe.

"I love you," I whisper into his hair.

I can feel him smile against my chest.

"I love you too."

Somehow, after all of that, I'm able to just make us dinner, like my mind wasn't just blown out of the water. Like my life didn't fully leave my body for a few minutes there when I finally came.

Beau is sitting at the table in only a pair of sweats, arms crossed over his chest, watching me.

The burger patties are sizzling on the stove, the smell filling the air around me. I flip one patty and then the other when muscled arms wrap around my waist. He plops his chin on my shoulder, kissing my skin there, then up my neck to my cheek.

"You look so beautiful, your skin flushed, your muscles still taut," he whispers against my skin, pressing a kiss where his words land. "Was that as incredible for you as it was for me, my love?"

I lean against him, letting him hold me close.

"Every moment with you feels wonderful," I whisper, feeling my face blush. "But yes, that was something incredible."

He turns me to face him, kissing my flushed cheeks, before sauntering back to the table. I glance at the patties once more before following him.

Beau leans back in his chair, arms behind his head, just relaxing. We're deep into the night after our failed attempt at the restaurant and our sexathon, the moon high in the cloudy sky.

A thought occurs to me, and I sit up straight.

"Should we talk about coming out? Like, what that would look like?"

Beau startles a little.

"Do you think we need to?" he asks, leaning toward me, his arms crossing on the table.

"I don't think it'll hurt anything," I say, letting my body relax again. "What's holding us back from coming out? Our coach supports us, our agent supports us, and our team supports us. So is there anything holding us back anymore?"

He gets a pensive look on his face as he thinks about it, his brows scrunched and his lips downturned.

"Yeah, I guess Miranda has a better outlook than Grady ever had." He chuckles awkwardly. Something about this is making him uncomfortable. His hand busies itself, fidgeting with a loose thread on the centerpiece.

"What's wrong?" I ask, reaching across the table and taking his hand in mine. He stares at where my hand holds his. His knee starts bouncing, nervous energy pouring off him. "You know, we don't have to come out together if you're not ready," I say gently.

He looks up at me, brows still pinched together.

"But you're ready." He says it matter-of-factly.

I nod slowly, a smile loading.

"We may be boyfriends, but we're still two separate people. If you're not ready, then you're not ready." I let go of his hand and sit back, letting out a huff of breath. "I don't even know if I'm ready yet, in all honesty."

Those pinched brows lift in question.

"Then why do you want to talk about it?"

I shrug, feigning nonchalance when all I feel is anything but.

"I thought it would be nice to gauge where we both are."

A part of me had been hoping we were both ready. It would be nice to have some big coming-out moment together. But the last thing I want is to make him feel bad for not being sure yet.

I'll wait for him.

I would wait forever for him.

Chapter 34

Beau

I wake from a night of fitful sleep for the first time in a long time. The sound of birds singing fills the air. Rolling over, I run into a wall of muscle and inhale deeply before I wrap my arm around him

Citrus.

Citrus and rain.

His scent is my safe space. It envelopes me like an embrace, and I'm ready to face the day. I wish I could bottle it up and wear it around my neck so I could keep him with me at all hours.

The sun shines through the curtains, illuminating my boyfriend's sleeping body.

My *boyfriend*.

I can't believe I'm saying—thinking—those words. I can't believe they're real. It feels surreal and crazy, but so right.

I feel Milo breathe out and fold into my embrace, his deep sigh music to my ears. I want to just lie here with him for the rest of the day, but I know we have morning skate soon.

Our game tonight is against Detroit, and the Avalanche won't know what hit them.

"Are you awake?"

Milo's voice is full of sleep, crusted and gunky, but somehow still very him. I rub my nose into his back as my answer before flipping him onto his back and straddling him. We kiss lazily, slow strokes of our tongues against each other.

Our erections are straining against each other, and who are we to ignore our desires?

He must read my mind, because Milo looks up at me with a wicked glint in his eyes.

I push down my briefs, freeing my cock and Milo does the same. I hold my hand to Milos mouth, and he spits like the good boy he is.

I wrap my fist around our aching cocks, and we simultaneously groan at the relief of the pressure.

I begin lazily stroking us together when Milo decides to pipe in.

"We have five minutes before we absolutely need to get ready, so you better come quick."

Challenge accepted.

We end our game in victory after a brutal shootout. The locker room is a raucous celebration, people clapping my shoulders, congratulating me on the absolutely beautiful shot that won us the game.

I find Milo's eyes in the crowd and feel like I'm home. Things have been great since coming out to the team—so great, actually. We're happy where we are, so why rock the boat?

I want to rock the boat.

I'm not afraid of capsizing.

I love him. Obviously I love him, but I just feel stranded. We're stuck together in a boat in the middle of the ocean, and I know there are resources to help us. We just have to ask for them.

I'm ready to ask.

I want to be out. Like, officially out.

I move through the locker room, dressed in only my base layers, and make my way to Coach's office.

I knock on the door, listening for him to grant entry before letting myself in.

"Bennett." Coach's voice is gruff, but he's a good man. "That was a hell of a shot. What can I do for you?" He's not looking at me, but I need him to be.

I clear my throat, and he looks up.

"I want to come out," I tell him, not really taking the time this probably deserves, dammit.

He blinks at me a few times before smiling and nodding.

"Okay, have you talked with your agent about this?" His voice is steady, calm, not at all surprised. I guess I already came out to the team. How surprised can he be?

"No, but I want to come out, like, now," I say, a rush in my voice. This feels urgent. This feels like something I should do right now, something I *need* to do right now.

"Well..." Waldor is drawing this out way too much. I'm a man of action, and the time is *now* to move.

Christian Grady, the asshole, is no longer my agent. I'm a free man. I can come out to the world if I want to. Nothing is holding me back.

Not anymore.

Oh fuck, fuck me.

I should probably tell Milo. He'll want to know.

Fuck, did he want to come out first?

"Can I grab Milo?" I ask Coach. He nods, and I just lean my head out the door. "Milo, come 'ere." I feel about a mile high right now.

Milo looks up from his lap with a start, meeting my eyes before standing. He makes his way to me slowly.

Once he's in the office, I shut the door and encourage him to sit down.

"Your boyfriend would like to come out. I need your help to convince him to wait until I can get ahold of Miranda." He's typing away on his phone.

Milo sighs and looks at me with exasperation.

"Baby," he says wistfully, "I'm proud of you for wanting to take that step. It's such a big one. But realistically, we should talk to Miranda first."

"We?" I ask, eyes wide.

"We," he says definitively, nodding. "We're in this together, you and I." He pauses and taps his foot in thought. "I definitely can't imagine coming out to the locker room press. I would imagine doing an exclusive piece would be more lucrative for us."

Coach Waldor nods and places his phone in the middle of his desk. It's on speakerphone. Miranda Mason's voice blares through the speakers.

"Beau Bennet, you better not come out to a bunch of sweaty locker room reporters," she scolds loudly. "I can have several prominent magazines and blogs lining up and foaming at the mouth for the chance to tell your coming-out story."

Milo leans into me, and I wrap an arm around him, looking into his eyes. Everyone is quiet for a moment.

"What if we came out together?" he says, his voice low. But because she has super hearing, Miranda hears and latches onto it.

"Okay, you two give me the green light, and I'll start putting out feelers. We'll do this right." I can hear the clacking of her computer keyboard as she makes her plans for us.

I've taken a few relatively deep breaths at this point and calmed down from whatever possessed me earlier. They're right. They're all right. I need to do this strategically. Right now, I'm happy. I have my man, my team knows, and I'm okay with the world finding out. Why shouldn't I get a brand deal out of my coming-out story?

I laugh a little at the thought.

Miranda has jumped into action. She's chattering away with Coach, and I sit here with Milo, just letting the world kind of fall away from us. He smiles at me, no longer small or secret. It lights up his whole face.

I smile back at him, suddenly feeling a thousand pounds lighter.

"You know, I've wanted to come out since my rookie season," I say, grabbing Milo's hand and holding it in my own. "I've known I was bi for a long time, and I've never been ashamed of it. I've just never had such a positive support system before. I've never had so many people believe in me or be there to lift me up."

Milo squeezes my hand in his grip. "I'm sorry you didn't have the people to support you before, but selfishly, I'm glad you waited for me."

"I fucking knew it." Miranda is laughing. "You two are not slick at all. I knew you were a couple the moment I met you, Beau." She cackles, and Waldor laughs too.

"You didn't tell your agent you were in a relationship?" he asks incredulously.

"We weren't even ready to tell each other," Milo says, exasperated.

I chuckle because, looking back, it feels so obvious how in it we both were. How infatuated we were with each other. How obsessed we were with each other.

"Alright, Miranda," I say, grabbing Milo's hand and pulling it into my lap, "what do we do?"

"Okay guys, just a few more shots on the ice before we can move to the locker room."

Milo and I are standing at center ice, dressed in our best game-day suits, and both of us have a little makeup on. The makeup artist tried to cover Milo's freckles, and I just about walked out.

"Can you try to be serious this time?" Milo asks me, but I don't know if I can. He's dressed in my favorite of his suits, this gorgeous burgundy number. Not only does he look beautiful in the color, but the way it hugs his body is almost obscene.

I swear his ass somehow defies gravity.

The way we're posed, I'm able to slide my hand down his back to pinch his butt, and he jumps.

"Fuck, Beau!" he cries out. I laugh, and the camera person sighs loudly.

"Maybe we should take shots separately and edit them together after?" one of the PAs suggests. I frown. Because, yes, they'd get the shots done in a timely manner, but that definitely would be no fun.

They walk over and pose us, moving my hand from Milo's butt and shoving them into my pockets. With my all-black suit, the pose makes me look so much more serious than I really am.

Miranda is off to the side, watching everything like a hawk. She gave them a list of approved questions already and shot down the underwear shoot, though I wasn't opposed. Milo had blushed so deeply when they suggested it that I wanted to capture the expression in a bottle and keep it always.

"Okay, so if you can keep your expression more…" I try to make my face as lifeless and devoid of emotion as possible. "Yes, just like that, perfect." They snap the picture of me before doing the same to Milo.

"We've got it. Let's go to the locker room and finish up there," the art director, Ferris, says, eyeing me. "And we're not going to have any funny business, right?"

I roll my eyes but nod. They've put up with enough of my shit today. I guess I can be easygoing for the rest of the shoot.

In the locker room, the poses are kind of ridiculous. Me leaning against the stall, staring at Milo, who sits on the bench next to me. They pose us draped all over each other, sitting on each other, leaning on each other. There's no way they're using most of these. I think Ferris just wanted a little laugh at our expense, and I can't blame them. Now that I've had time to calm down, I was being a bit of an ass on the ice.

The interview itself goes by quickly, asking about what it was like in the closet, when we *knew* we were queer, the challenges of self-acceptance, et cetera.

"What is the most rewarding part of living openly?" the interviewer asks, and I smile at Milo.

"Him," I say with confidence. "Being able to be myself with my boyfriend is the best part of living openly."

He smiles broadly, all toothy, and it makes his eyes crinkle a little at the corners. I want to pepper kisses over every little wrinkle, to hold his face in my hands and simply adore him.

The interviewer side-eyes Miranda, then makes eye contact with me. They're about to go off script.

"What's one thing you wish people understood about addiction or recovery?" they ask quickly. Miranda looks ready to swoop in, but I put my hand up.

"No, I'll answer this." I kind of expected this direction. "It looks different for everyone. Everyone has their own reason for doing it, but what's most important is that you have a support system. I can't imagine doing this alone, without Milo by my side." I look at him, and he takes my hand. "Can we maybe include the Suicide and Crisis Lifeline at the end of the interview?"

The interviewer nods fervently.

We wrap up the interview, and Milo and I flop down on the bench in the locker room. He leans his head against my shoulder, and I wrap my arm around him, pulling him close.

"We did it," he says, his voice low. "We came out."

Neither of us says anything for a moment.

"Kind of anti-climactic, don't you think?" he asks, raising a brow as he looks up at me. I chuckle. He's right, this isn't all the wild excitement I thought it would be.

"You know," I ponder aloud, "now that I've checked that off my bucket list, there is something else I've always wanted to try."

Chapter 35

Milo

"Fuck, Beau." My voice is hoarse and echoey in the empty locker room. The interview was a success, an opportunity for both of us to step out into the light and shine as our true selves. To shine together. I look at him now, his eyes bright and full of hope. I feel like I'm finally seeing the real Beau.

To say I'm proud of him is an understatement.

I run my hands up and down his body, desperate to show him just how proud I really am. His skin is so fucking warm where it's exposed, and I long to touch more. To run my tongue over every inch of him and map out his different tastes.

My hands slide under his shirt, feeling every divot of his abs and the supple curve of his pecs. I reach up and pinch his nipples, teasing them to make him let out the prettiest sounds. He practically purrs as my fingers pluck and tug, finding a perfect rhythm.

One of my hands slides up to his neck, gripping and guiding him to look at me. His eyes pop open, and his mouth slackens like he wants to let loose the prettiest moan.

"Who's making you feel good, Beau?" I ask, my voice more gravelly than I thought it could be. "Who's making your tight little nipples so perky?" I push his shirt up and lean down, not waiting for an answer before I take one of those pierced nipples between my teeth and tug. He moans for me, and god, it's such a lovely sound. It garbles under my hand, still firmly wrapped around his throat, keeping his head pointed straight ahead. "Who's making this cock rock hard and desperate?"

My other hand palms his gorgeous cock through his slacks. He whines for me.

"You are," he finally says on a gasp. His words are stuttered as I hum my approval.

I lick and lap and suck at his pretty little nipples, pulling them taut in my mouth, my dick getting harder and harder as we press against each other. The cold metal lockers press into his back, my calf biting into the bench.

I growl as I push against his body, wanting to feel every inch of him. I yank at his shirt, trying to signal for him to pull it over his head so I can lick a line from his chest up his neck to that sensitive spot behind his ear. He obeys so beautifully.

My hand slides down the front of his body, unbuttoning his slacks, reaching into his pants and fisting his throbbing cock.

"Is this for me, baby?" I ask playfully, whispering my naughty words into his ear. He shivers and nods carefully, his bottom lip tucked between his teeth. I pull his cock from his pants and look down to admire it.

It is *weeping* for me, angry and red, and *aching*. He whines as I slide my thumb over the tip, collecting the precome and giving it a rough jerk. His balls are drawn up tight, and he looks like he is ready to tip over the edge.

"Oh, *baby*." I croon for him, reaching down and giving his balls a little tug. "These look ready to burst."

Something about watching Beau fall apart at my fingers is bringing out a side of me I didn't know I possessed.

I snake my hand up and around the back of his neck, keeping his eyes on his cock.

"Look how ready you are. So wet for me."

I maneuver his gaze back to mine. His pupils are blown with lust. I pull him in for a heated kiss. All lips and tongue and teeth, biting and caressing and simply loving. The kiss turns sweet for a moment as I think about this man, *my* man, here in my arms. I rise onto my toes and kiss his forehead, allowing one tender moment before I dive back down and devour his ass.

My hands run down his body and grab his hips, fingers digging into his flesh. I use the moment to flip him around, his chest banging into the cubby panel. He throws his head back and groans. My man likes a little pain?

I drop to my knees and drag his pants down the rest of the way over his delicious ass. Taking a cheek in each hand, I spread him open and admire his tight little asshole. It winks at me as he whimpers and pushes back toward my face. I guess someone enjoyed the treatment he got last night.

"Patience, patience," I chastise him, shaking my head. I let my nose brush the skin of his ass with each pass, and he shudders. I can see it travel down his spine, and I know it shoots straight to his cock.

After a few long seconds of his groans and moans and ass seeking pleasure, I finally cave and give myself what I desire.

Leaning in, I give his crack a long, languid lick, circling his hole with my tongue. He *whines*, and I groan, my tongue vibrating with the sound. His back is arched, and his sexy little back dimples pop. I break away from his hole for a second to lick each dimple. The way his body twists and scrunches, ugh. It's so beautiful.

My fingers dig into his hips, holding him steady so I can go back to just tongue-fucking his ass.

Fuck, he's so delicious. I moan against him again, appreciating every movement he makes. His pretty little hole flutters, and I press a kiss to it.

My tongue begins to press into his ass, forcing its way past the ring of muscle. He whimpers his appreciation, and I moan into him. I just want my man to feel good, so, so good.

I finally pull back, admiring the work my tongue put into relaxing his hole. He looks fucking breedable right now.

I pull out the little foil packet of lube, squeeze some onto my finger, and begin circling his hole.

"Remember, you can say stop at any time. Do you understand?" He nods, but I grip his chin and halt the motion. "I need words, beautiful." He whines, eyes pinching shut, cheeks flushing.

"I understand." His voice is shaky but sure.

"Good." I slowly push my finger into him, and he immediately clamps down with a low whine. "Come on, my good boy, relax." I kiss the back of his neck, my breath whispering lightly against the hairs. After some sweet convincing, he begins to relax and allow me to push in further. Just a few more centimeters and I'll find...

He howls.

Ah, there it is.

I chuckle low and give his prostate a generous rub. His cock is leaking everywhere, dripping into a wasted puddle on the floor.

I start to push a second finger in, and he hisses. I like the burn of the stretch personally, but it's not for everyone.

"That's it, baby." I try to keep my voice low and steady, but the excitement in me is ramping up. "Relax, sweetheart." He shudders out a sigh, and I can feel his hole fluttering around my fingers.

Fuck, he feels incredible. I can't wait to sink my cock into him.

I bite his ass cheek, my teeth sinking into the supple flesh. The gasp that leaves him is heaven to my ears.

"You like that, baby?" I whisper against his skin as I slide the third finger into his sloppy hole. He accepts me eagerly, sucking me in and fluttering around my fingers.

His hole is so pretty stretched out like this, pink and begging for me. He whines as I continue my assault with my fingers, filling and fucking into him.

I pull my fingers free and groan as his sloppy hole winks at me. I give it a wet kiss, sticking my tongue in as far as it will go. His answering whine is so pathetic-sounding I cannot help but smile against his skin.

I stand back up, sliding up his body, my hands running over his curves, squeezing his pecs.

"Are you ready, my love?"

I love the imbalance, me fully dressed while he has his pants around his ankles, but I want to feel his skin against mine as I fuck into him.

He turns around to watch me as I undress, his gaze following through his lashes, my button-down sliding over my shoulders. His hands grab at my pants and pull me into a kiss.

This kiss is soft, tender, sweet. Full of love.

Fuck, I love him. I smile into his kiss, and he smiles back. We stay there for a moment, smiling at each other and kissing into our shared joy.

He kisses all over my face next, whispering *I love you* into every kiss.

I unzip my jeans, pulling out my throbbing cock. My hand pulls his against mine, and I stand there for a moment, holding our lengths together and giving them a languid tug. We both groan in tandem. The pressure is just too amazing.

But it's still not the pressure I'm after.

I maneuver him around again, slamming him against the wall and letting my pants fall from my waist.

I grip my weeping cock, a drop of precome gathering at the tip before I slather it in lube, slicking it up. We're really doing this. I let out a shaky sigh as I push the tip against his entrance.

"You're sure you're okay for us to go without a condom?" I ask for probably the billionth time, based on how loudly Beau groans.

"Please, I need it so bad," Beau begs, his voice barely above a whisper. "I need *you*."

I push into him painfully slowly. I want every second of this to feel good for him, but fuck, I didn't realize how overpowering the need to just plow into him would be.

Inch by aching inch, I push into him, and he just whines and whines and whines for me.

His words are incoherent. *More*, and *yes*, and *please*. And I don't want to deny him.

I push and push until finally I'm fully seated, my balls slapping against his, my hips pressed against the bouncy curve of his ass.

My fingers reach around and grope at his meaty pecs, toying with his nipples. I pinch and pull at them, and his ass jiggles as he tries to get away from my eager fingers.

I kiss his nape, licking and sucking the skin there while I rock into Beau's body. I look down to where our bodies are joined and moan. Fuck, the sight of my cock buried in Beau's ass is a fucking dream. It's enough to bring me right to the edge immediately. I slow my hips, but I'm still right there.

"Fuck, baby," I tell him, so desperate to just stay here and enjoy fucking my boyfriend with nothing between us. But I can feel him clench, and I know he's just as desperate as I am.

"I'm gonna—I need to..." He can't finish his sentence before I'm there. I'm there and I'm coming. I'm coming, and I'm filling him. His hole is clenching around me, milking me.

"Yes, baby, yes. Take every fucking drop I give you." I grip the base of my dick and give tiny pumps of my hips, feeding him my come. He's whining and moaning and tipping his head back to meet me.

I capture his lips in a punishing kiss, biting and nibbling on his lips in my appreciation of him, in my appreciation of the way his ass is still clinging to my softening cock.

"Fuck, baby, you were amazing." I press my face against his back, just enjoying the sweat-slick cling of my body to his.

I'm kissing along his back when I suddenly hear the click of a door.

"Are you guys done? I really need to go home." Brennan's voice calls out, echoing through the empty locker room.

Fuck.

THE END

Acknowledgements

ow, I did that. I wrote a book.

I've wanted to write a book my entire life, but who would have thought that all it would take is a queer hockey show and a *very specific* scene in Episode Three to finally get the courage to finish one.

Okay, okay, that wasn't what pushed me over the edge. Yes, it inspired the story, but finishing it was a feat that could only have come from two very special people. That blame would be entirely on the incredible support team I have.

I have my wife, Madee, who dealt with so much bull-shit as I pushed to finish this book. Who kept texting me "ten-day push" every time I wanted to give up. Who read raunchy queer sex between two penis-having men when she is very much a gold star-lesbian. Who encouraged me and continues to encourage me as I start the next story.

And then I have my dear friend Nova, who saw me writing a story and made me ask, "Why can't I just finish it?" Who encouraged me and loved my characters with me. Who saw me fall apart when I got edits back because I'm *very* sensitive, and who used her feminine rage to put me back together and keep me pushing. She helped me realize that this was a story that needed to exist because I needed to tell it. She's also was a big help with the artistic direction of this book. She helped me pick my artist, helped with the cover and back cover layout, helped make my marketing material actually look good. Basically I would have flopped without her support.

Speaking of edits, I was very lucky that I came across Nina. She was incredibly thorough in her edits and listened to me when I asked her to cater to my sensitivity. She is an editor, but more than that, she is supportive, always looking to lift you up.

Because I'm horrible at time management, I did have to hire a second editor in a pinch. Miracle Smith swooped in to do copy-edits for me and literally saved the day. I am eternally grateful for her contribution to making my book shine

If you follow me on Instagram/Threads, you have seen my character art because I have not, nor will I eve,r shut up about it. I got so lucky when I sought out an artist on reddit and came across Pan. She did the majority of my character art and also did my cover, and I'm absolutely obsessed. If you have liked any of her art that I've shared, you should check her out. Gabriela is another artist I actually happened upon on Threads. She was sharing Heated Rivalry art and I was obsessed. Both artists are tagged in my posts sharing their art.

My beta readers and sensitivity readers: Mariah, Miracle, Laurynn, Myrtle, and Taylor. Y'all were instrumental in the final edits of this book. You made *Goalie Oriented* ebb and flow exactly how it needs to, and I'm eternally grateful to you. Thank you for your notes and suggestions and for pointing out the hundreds of spelling errors. Seriously, I appreciate y'all so much.

And finally, to you, my reader. Thank you for taking a chance on this first-time indie author. Thank you for taking a chance on Milo and Beau. Thank you.

* 9 7 9 8 9 9 9 4 9 1 2 9 0 4 *